Also by Charlaine Harris from Gollancz:

SOOKIE STACKHOUSE

Dead Until Dark
Living Dead in Dallas
Club Dead
Dead to the World
Dead as a Doornail
Definitely Dead
All Together Dead
From Dead to Worse
Dead and Gone
A Touch of Dead
Dead in the Family
True Blood Omnibus
True Blood Omnibus II

HEATHER CONNELLY

Grave Sight
Grave Surprise
An Ice Cold Grave
Grave Secret

The First Aurora Teagarden Omnibus
The Lily Bard Mysteries Omnibus

GRAVE SECRET

Charlaine Harris

First published in Great Britain in 2010 by
Gollancz
An imprint of the Orion Publishing Group
Orion House, 5 Upper St Martin's Lane,
London WC2H 9EA
An Hachette UK Company

This edition published in Great Britain in 2010 by
Gollancz

1 3 5 7 9 10 8 6 4 2

A CIP catalogue record for this book
is available from the British Library

Printed and bound in the UK by
CPI Mackays, Chatham ME5 8TD

www.charlaineharris.com
www.orionbooks.co.uk

To my son Patrick, simply because I think he's great.

ACKNOWLEDGMENTS

My thanks to Ivan Van Laningham, Kerry Hammond, Ashley McConnell, Mary Fitzsimons, Gina and her anonymous friend, Beth Groundwater, my assistant and friend Paula Woldan, Nancy Hayes (my Gun Angel), and Dr. Ed Uthman, a college crony, for their assistance in getting the details right. Any mistakes are my own, as much as I would love to blame someone else.

one

"ALL right," said the straw-haired woman in the denim jacket. "Do your thing." Her accent made the words sound more like "Dew yore thang." Her hawklike face was eager, the anticipatory look of someone who is ready to taste an unknown food.

We were standing on a windswept field some miles south of the interstate that runs between Texarkana and Dallas. A car zoomed by on the narrow two-lane blacktop. It was the only other car I'd seen since I'd followed Lizzie Joyce's gleaming black Chevy Kodiak pickup out to the Pioneer Rest Cemetery, which lay outside the tiny town of Clear Creek.

When our little handful of people fell silent, the whistle of the wind scouring the rolling hill was the only sound in the landscape.

There wasn't a fence around the little cemetery. It had been cleared, but not recently. This was an old cemetery, as Texas cemeteries go, established when the live oak in the middle of the graveyard had been only a small tree. A flock of birds was cackling in the oak's branches. Since we were in north Texas, there was grass, but in February it wasn't green. Though the temperature was in the fifties today, the wind was colder than I'd counted on. I zipped up my jacket. I noticed that Lizzie Joyce wasn't wearing one.

The people who lived hereabouts were tough and pragmatic, including the thirtyish blonde who'd invited me here. She was lean and muscular, and she must have tugged up her jeans by greasing her legs. I couldn't imagine how she mounted a horse. But her boots were well-worn, and so was her hat, and if I'd read her belt buckle correctly, she was the previous year's countywide barrel-riding champion. Lizzie Joyce was the real deal.

She also had more money in her bank account than I would ever earn in my life. The diamonds on her hand flashed in the bright sunlight as she waved toward the piece of ground dedicated to the dead. Ms. Joyce wanted me to get the show on the road.

I prepared to dew mah thang. Since Lizzie was paying me big bucks for this, she wanted to get the most out of it. She'd invited her little entourage, which consisted of her boyfriend, her younger sister, and her brother, who looked as though he'd rather be anywhere else but in Pioneer Rest Cemetery.

My brother was leaning against our car, and he wasn't going to stir. Until I'd done my job, Tolliver wouldn't pay attention to anything but me.

I still thought of him as my brother, though I was trying to catch myself when I called him that out loud. We had a much different relationship, now.

We'd met the Joyces that morning for the first time. We'd driven down the long, winding driveway leading between wide, fenced-in fields, following the excellent directions Lizzie had sent to our laptop.

The house at the end of the driveway was very large and very beautiful, but it wasn't pretentious. It was a house for people who worked hard. The Latina who'd answered the door had been wearing nice pants and a blouse, not any kind of uniform, and she'd referred to her boss as "Lizzie," not "Ms. Joyce." Since every day on a ranch or farm is a working day, I hadn't been surprised to see that the big house felt pretty empty, and the only glimpses I caught of other people had been distant ones. As the housekeeper led us through the house, I'd seen a Jeep coming up one of the tracks that ran between the huge fields at the rear of the house.

Lizzie Joyce and her sister, Kate, had been waiting in the gun room. I was sure they called it the den or the family room, or something else to indicate it was where they gathered to watch television and play board games, or whatever really rich people did with their evenings when they lived way the hell out in the sticks. But to me, it was the gun room. There were weapons and animal heads all over, and the décor was supposed to imply this was a rustic hunting lodge. Since the house had been built by the Joyce grandfather, it reflected his taste, I guessed, but they could have changed it if they'd objected. He'd been dead for a while.

Lizzie Joyce looked like the pictures I'd seen of her, but the impression was strictly practical. She was a working woman. Her sister, Kate, called Katie, was a scaled-down version of her big sister: shorter, younger, less seasoned. But she seemed just as confident and hard. Maybe being brought up with gobs of money did that to you.

The gun room had a wall of French doors leading out onto a wide brick porch. There were urns that would be filled with flowers in the spring, but it wasn't time yet. The temperatures still dipped below freezing sometimes at night. I noticed that the Joyces had left their rocking chairs outside during the winter, and I wondered what it would be like to sit out on the roofed brick porch in the morning in the summer, drinking coffee and looking out over all that land.

The Jeep came to a stop at the foot of the gentle slope leading up to the back porch, and two men climbed out and came in.

"Harper, this is the manager of RJ Ranch, Chip Moseley. And this is our brother, Drexell."

Tolliver and I shook hands with the men.

The manager was rugged, weathered, and skeptical, green eyed and brown haired, and he was as ready to leave as the brother. Both of them were only here because Lizzie wanted them to be. Chip Moseley gave Lizzie a casual kiss on the cheek, and I realized he was her man as well as her manager. That might be awkward.

The brother, Drexell, was the youngest of the Joyces and the most anonymous looking. Lizzie and Katie both had a certain hawk-nosed flamboyance, but Drexell's round face was still a bit babyish. He didn't meet my eyes as his sisters had.

I had a niggling feeling that I'd seen both men somewhere before. Since the huge Joyce ranch wasn't too far from Texarkana, and I'd grown up there, it wasn't beyond the realm of possibility that I'd met Chip and Drexell—but the last thing I wanted to do was bring up my previous life. I hadn't always been the mysterious woman who could find bodies because she'd been fried by lightning.

"I'm so glad you could find time to come here," Lizzie said.

"My sister likes to collect the unusual," Katie told Tolliver. She definitely had her eye on him.

"Harper is one of a kind," he said, and he glanced at me. He looked a little amused.

"Well, you better give Lizzie a good show for her money," Chip said, his weathered, handsome face giving me a big dose of warning. I looked at him more closely. I didn't want to be seen showing interest in someone else's honey, but there was something for me in Chip Moseley, something that spoke to my special talent. He was moving and breathing, which normally meant disqualification.

My business is with the dead.

Since Lizzie Joyce had found a website that followed my travels, she apparently hadn't been able to rest until she thought of a job for me to do. She'd finally decided she wanted to know what had killed her grandfather, who'd been found far away from the main ranch house, collapsed by the side of his Jeep. Rich Joyce had a skull injury, and the presumption was that he'd slipped and fallen when he was getting into or out of his ride; or maybe the Jeep had hit a rock and tossed him sideways, cracking his skull against the Jeep's frame, though no evidence of such an impact had been found. Anyhow, the Jeep's ignition had been switched off, and Rich Joyce had been dead, and no one else was within miles; so his death had been attributed to heart failure, and he'd been put in the ground years ago. Since Rich's only son and his son's wife had died in a car accident some years before, his three grandchildren had inherited, though not equally. Lizzie was legally in charge of the family's fortunes now, Tolliver's research had indicated, but the other two had shares that were slightly less than a third apiece; just enough to keep Lizzie in the driver's seat. Easy to tell who Rich Joyce had trusted.

I wondered if Rich Joyce had ever known his granddaughter had a streak of mysticism, or maybe simply a love of the unusual. That was why Lizzie had led us to Pioneer Rest Cemetery, and why I was standing waiting for her to give me the go-ahead.

Hardheaded Lizzie wanted value for her money, so she wasn't going to lead me directly to the grave that was her grandfather's. She hadn't even told me the purpose of my search until I'd gotten out of my car thirty minutes before. Of course, I could wander around to read all the headstones until I found one with appropriate dates. There weren't that many Joyces under the dirt and rocks. But I'd spin this out, give her some freebies, because she hadn't flinched at my fee.

I'd taken off my shoes for the reading, though I had to watch where I put my feet. There are thorns hidden in the grass in Texas, no matter how pretty it looks. I cast a final glance across the panorama of rolling ground and trees and emptiness. This little cemetery might as well have been on the moon, the landscape was such a contrast from the thickly clustering housing developments and settled communities we'd seen as we drove to our last job in North Carolina. We'd ended up in a small town, but it hadn't had the isolated feel that I got from the landscape here. There'd always been the awareness that another settlement was within a few minutes' drive.

At least it wasn't as cold here, and at least we could be almost certain there wouldn't be any snow. My feet stung in the chilly air, but nowhere near as much as my whole body had ached in freezing, wet North Carolina.

The Joyces were buried close to the live oak. I could see a large boulder that had been chiseled smooth on one side, and the name JOYCE was carved in it in huge letters. It would have looked willfully naïve to have ignored that clue. I stopped at the first grave I reached in that plot, though it was clearly not the one I'd come to read. But what the hell, I had to start sometime. The tombstone read, *Sarah, Beloved Wife of Paul Joyce.* I took a deep breath, and I stepped on top of it. The connection with the bones beneath my feet was electric and immediate. Sarah was waiting, like all of them, the longtime dead and the recently dead, those buried neatly in graves and those tossed aside like debris. I sent that extra sense I had down into the ground. Connected. Learned.

"Woman in her sixties, aneurysm," I said. I opened my eyes and stepped to the next grave. This was an older one, much older. "Hiram Joyce," I said. I stood there, trying to get a firm fix on the few remaining bones in the ground under my feet. "Blood poisoning," I said finally. I walked to the next one, rested for a moment until the buzzing impelled me: that was the call of the bones, the remains. They wanted me to know about them, what had killed them, what their final moments had been like. I looked at the headstone. No point in reinventing the wheel.

This was not a Joyce, though the burial was within the family plot. The date was eight years and a few months before. The carved name was *Mariah Parish.* Though I sensed the two men, waiting under the scanty shade of a twisted tree, were standing much straighter, I was too intent on the connection to wonder about that.

"Oh," I said, softly. The wind whooshed past, lifting my short dark hair and teasing it. "Oh, poor thing."

"What?" asked Lizzie, her harsh voice sounding simply confused. "That's my grandfather's caregiver. She had a burst appendix or something."

"She had a hemorrhage, bled out after childbirth," I said. I put two and two together and glanced over at the two men. Drexell had actually taken a step closer. Chip Moseley was stunned; he was also furious, whether because the information was a shock to him, or because I'd said it out loud, I couldn't say. But whatever they were feeling, it was too late for Mariah. I looked away and stepped over to the right grave, the one I'd been brought to read. It was the biggest headstone in the plot, a double one. Richard Joyce's wife had predeceased him by ten years. Her name had been Cindilynn, and I discovered she'd died of breast cancer. I said so out loud, and I glimpsed Kate and Lizzie look at each other and nod. I stepped to the ground just adjacent, Rich Joyce's side of the headstone. Rich had died eight years ago, not long after his caregiver. I cocked my head as I listened to Richard's bones.

He'd seen something that startled him. I got that, but it took me a few seconds to understand that he'd stopped the Jeep and gotten out because he'd seen someone he knew.

I didn't have a picture of that person in my head. It's not like I'm watching a movie. It's like being inside the person for a moment or two, thinking the person's thoughts, feeling his emotions, in the last seconds of the person's life. So I understood from Rich Joyce that he'd stopped because he'd seen someone. I didn't go through the process of recognizing that person and reasoning that I should stop because he was standing there. As Rich Joyce, I turned off the Jeep, stepped out, and then the snake came flying through the air, the rattlesnake, giving me (Rich Joyce) such a shock that my (his) heart stopped working properly. *So hot no water can't reach phone oh my God to end like this* and then it had all gone black. With my eyes closed to see that scene more clearly, that scene visible only to me, I related what was happening.

When I opened my eyes, the four people in the Joyce party were staring at me as if I'd developed stigmata. Sometimes it grabs people that way, even when they've asked me there to do exactly what I just did.

I creep people out or I fascinate them (not always in a healthy way) . . . or both. However, the fascination thing wasn't going to be a problem today. The boyfriend was looking at me as if I were wearing a straitjacket, and the three Joyces were gaping. Everyone was silent.

"So now you know," I said briskly.

"You could've made that up," Lizzie said. "There was someone there? How'd that happen? No one has said they were there. Are you telling me someone threw a rattlesnake at Granddaddy? And that gave him a heart attack, and then that someone just left him? And you're saying Mariah had a baby? I didn't hire you to tell me lies!"

Okay, that pissed me off. I took a deep breath. From the corner of my eye, I noticed Tolliver had started over to me, the beginnings of alarm evident on his face. Behind them all, Chip Moseley had retreated to the Jeep and was standing with one hand braced on it, doubled over. I realized he was in pain, and I knew he wouldn't thank me if I drew attention to him.

"You brought me here to do this," I said. I spread my hands. "There is nothing you can verify, even if you dug your grandfather up. I warned you that might be the case. Of course, you can find out about Mariah Parish, if you really are concerned. There should be a birth record, or some paper trail."

"That's true," Lizzie said. Her face was more thoughtful than repulsed now. "But aside from the issue of what happened to Mariah's baby, if she really had one, it makes me sick that someone would do that to Granddaddy. If you're telling us the truth."

"Believe me; don't believe me. That's up to you. Did you know about his heart condition?"

"No, he wasn't one for doctors. But he'd had a stroke already. And the last time he went in for a checkup, he came back looking worried." She'd thought about this many times since her grandfather's death, it was obvious.

"He had a cell phone in his Jeep, right?" I said.

"Yeah," she said. "He did."

"He was trying to reach it." Some last moments are more informative than others.

I glanced quickly in Tolliver's direction, and then away. The tension was leaving his shoulders. I thought we were going to be okay.

"You believe this stuff?" Chip asked the sisters incredulously. He'd recovered from whatever had ailed him, and he was standing at Lizzie's side. He looked at her as if he'd never seen her before, when I knew from our research that he'd been her escort for the past six years.

Lizzie was too confident to be hurried. She appeared to be thinking hard as she got out a cigarette and lit it. Finally, she tilted her face up to him. "Yes, I believe it."

"Shi-it," Kate Joyce said and pulled off her cowboy hat. She slapped it against her lean thigh. "You'll be wanting to bring in that John Edward next."

Lizzie shot her sister a look that was not fond. Drexell said, "I think she made all of this up, you ask me."

We had gotten a deposit from Lizzie. We were coming to Texas anyway, but we sure wouldn't have stopped if we hadn't gotten the up-front money. Clients this rich, oddly enough, often change their mind. Poorer people don't. So, though we'd already deposited the first check from RJ Ranch, the balance was due, and a blind man could tell the whole Joyce party was dubious about what I'd accomplished. Before I could get a good start on worrying about it, Lizzie pulled a folded and creased check from her hip pocket and handed it to Tolliver, who'd gotten close enough to slide his arm around me. I was a little shaky. This hadn't been as hard as some readings, because Rich Joyce'd only had a second's surge of fear before he passed over, but direct contact with the dead is draining.

"Need candy?" he asked.

I nodded. He got a Werther's Original out of his pocket and unwrapped it. I opened my mouth and he popped it in. Golden buttery goodness.

"I thought he was your brother," Kate Joyce said, inclining her head toward Tolliver. Though I knew she had to be in her late twenties, there were more years of experience than that in the way she walked and spoke. I wondered if this was the result of being brought up rich but practical in Texas, or if life in the Joyce household had had other sources of stress.

"He is," I said.

"Looks more like your boyfriend." Drexell sniggered.

"I'm her stepbrother and her boyfriend, Drex," Tolliver said pleasantly. "We'll be on the road. Thanks for asking us to help you with your problem." He nodded at them all. He's less than six feet, but not by much, and he's thin, but he has a set of shoulders on him.

I love him more than anything.

THE sound of the shower woke me up. We see the inside of so many motel rooms that sometimes I have to spend a second or two recalling where the particular motel room is located. This was one of those mornings.

Texas. After we'd left the Joyces, we had driven most of the previous afternoon to reach this motel off the interstate in Garland, outside of Dallas. This wasn't a business trip; it was personal.

I had that consciousness when I opened my eyes, that grim awareness that I was thinking too much about the old, bad times. Whenever we visit my aunt and her husband outside of Dallas, the bad memories resurface.

It's not the fault of the state.

When I'm close to my little sisters, I start remembering the broken trailer in Texarkana, the one where Tolliver and I lived with his father, my mother, his brother, my sister, and our two mutual sibs, who were practically babies at the time that household dissolved.

The delicately balanced deception we older kids had maintained for several years had collapsed when my older sister, Cameron, vanished. Our unpleasant home life had been exposed to public view, and our little sisters had been taken away. Tolliver had gone to live with his brother, Mark, and I'd gone to a foster home.

The two little girls didn't even remember Cameron. I'd asked them the last time we saw them. The girls live with Aunt Iona and Uncle Hank, who don't like us to visit. We do, though; Mariella and Grace (called Gracie) are our sisters, and we want them to remember they have family.

I propped up on one elbow to watch Tolliver drying himself off. He'd left the bathroom door open while he showered, because otherwise the mirror became too foggy for him to use while he shaved.

We don't look unalike; we're both thin and dark haired. Our hair's even about the same length. His eyes are brown; mine are dark gray. But Tolliver's complexion is pitted and scarred from acne, because his dad didn't think of sending him to a dermatologist. His face is narrower, and he often has a mustache. He hates wearing anything besides jeans and shirts, but I like to dress up a bit more, and since I'm the "talent," it's more or less expected. Tolliver is my manager, my consultant, my main support, my companion, and for the past few weeks he's been my lover.

He turned to look at me, saw I was watching. He smiled and dropped the towel.

"Come here," I said.

He was quick to oblige.

"WANT to go for a run?" I asked in the afternoon. "You can take another shower afterward, with me. So you won't waste water."

We had our running clothes on in no time, and we took off after we'd stretched. Tolliver's faster than I am. Most often, he pulls away for the last half mile or so, and today was no exception.

We were pleased to find a good place to run. Our motel was on the access road right off the interstate. It was flanked by other hotels and motels, restaurants and gas stations, the usual assortment of services for road warriors. But to the rear of the motel, we found one of those "business parks": two curving streets with careful, still-small plantings in the flower beds in front of the one-story buildings, each with a parking area. A median ran down the middle of these two streets, wide enough to support a planting of crepe myrtles. There were sidewalks, too, to give the place an inviting and friendly look. Since it was late Friday afternoon, the traffic was minimal among the rows of rectangular buildings chopped up into characterless entities like Great Systems, Inc. and Genesis Distributors, which might conduct business of any sort. Each block was marked off by a driveway running between the buildings, a narrow thing that must lead to a parking lot in back for the employees. There were almost no cars parked in front; customers were gone, the last employees were leaving for the weekend.

In such a place, the last thing I expected to encounter was a dead man. I was thinking of the ache in my right leg, which has flared up from time to time ever since the lightning ran down that side, so I didn't hear his bones calling me at first.

They're everywhere, of course, dead people. I don't hear only the modern dead. I feel the ancient dead, too; even, very rarely, the faint, faint echo of a trace of people who walked the earth before there was writing. But this guy I was connecting with here in the Dallas suburbs was *very* fresh. I ran in place for a moment.

I couldn't be sure unless I got closer to the body, but I was thinking this one felt like a suicide by gun. I pinpointed his location—he was in the back part of an office called Designated Engineering. I shook off his overwhelming misery. I've had practice. Pity him? He'd gotten to choose. If I pitied everyone I met who'd crossed over, I'd be weeping continuously.

No, I wasn't spending my time on emotion. I was trying to decide what to do. I could leave him where he was, and that was my initial impulse. The first person to come into Designated Engineering the next workday would get a rude shock, if the guy's family didn't send the police to check his office tonight when he didn't come home.

It seemed harsh, leaving him there. However, I didn't want to get involved in a long explanation to the police.

Running in place was getting old. I had to make up my mind.

Though I can't agonize over every dead person I find, I don't want to lose my humanity, either.

I looked around for inspiration. I found it in the rocks bordering the ho-hum flower bed at the entrance door. I pulled out the largest rock I could handle and hefted it. After a little experimentation, I decided I could throw it one-handed. I glanced up and down the street; no cars in sight, and no one on foot. Standing a safe distance back, I took a balanced stance and let the rock fly. I had to retrieve the rock and repeat this action twice more before the glass shattered and an alarm began to go off. I took off running. I had to take a metaphorical hat off to the police. I had barely reached the motel parking lot when I saw the patrol car turning off the access road and speeding by the motel to cruise into the business park.

An hour later, I was telling Tolliver what had happened while I put on my makeup. I'd had a long shower, and sure enough, he'd jumped in again to "help you wash your hair."

I was leaning my clean self over the sink to peer into the mirror to apply my eyeliner. Though I was only twenty-four, I had to get closer to the mirror now, and I just knew the next time I had an exam, my eye doctor was going to tell me I needed glasses. I'd never considered myself vain, but every time I pictured myself wearing glasses, I felt a pang. Maybe contact lenses? But the thought of sticking anything in my eyes made me shudder.

Every time I thought about this, I worried about the money correcting my vision might cost. We were saving every cent we could to make the down payment on the house we were hoping to buy here in the Dallas area. St. Louis was more centrally located from a business point of view, but we could see our sisters more often if Dallas was our home base. Probably Iona and Hank wouldn't care for that, and they might throw a lot of obstacles in our way. They'd formally adopted the girls. But maybe we could persuade them that the girls would benefit from seeing us as much as we would from seeing them.

Tolliver came into the bathroom and paused to kiss my shoulder. I smiled as my eyes met his in the mirror.

"Police activity down the street," he said. "You know anything about that?"

"As a matter of fact, I do," I said, feeling guilty. I hadn't taken the time to explain to Tolliver before I'd gotten in the shower, and he'd distracted me after that. Now I told Tolliver about the dead man, and I explained about the rock and the window.

"The cops have found him by now, so you did the right thing. I have to say, I wish you'd just left him," Tolliver said.

Pretty much what I'd expected him to say; he was always cautious about being pulled into any situation that we hadn't been paid to deal with. Since I was watching him in the mirror, I saw the subtle changes in his stance that said he was going to switch the subject, and he was going to talk about something serious.

"Do you ever think maybe we should just let go?" Tolliver said.

"Let go?" I finished my right eye and held my mascara wand to the lashes of my left eye. "Let go of what?"

"Mariella and Gracie."

I turned to face him. "I don't understand what you're asking," I told him, though I was very much afraid that I did.

"Maybe we should only visit once a year. Just send Christmas presents and birthday presents the rest of the time."

I was shocked. "Why would we do that?" Wasn't that the whole purpose of saving every cent we could—so we could become a bigger part of their lives, not smaller?

"We're confusing them." Tolliver stepped a little closer and put his hand on my shoulder. "The girls may have their problems, but they're doing better with Iona than they would with us. We can't take care of them. We travel too much. Iona and Hank are responsible people, and they don't use alcohol or drugs. They take the girls to church; they make sure they're in school."

"Are you serious?" I said, though I'd never known Tolliver to be facetious about family topics. I felt blindsided. "You know I've never thought we should take the girls away, even if we could legally manage it. You seriously think we should keep even our visits to a minimum? See them even less?"

"I do," he said.

"Explain."

"When we show up—well, to start with, we come here so . . . irregularly, and we never stay long. We take them out, we try to show them things they don't get to see, we try to interest them in things that're not part of their daily life—and then we vanish, leaving their, well, their 'parents,' to deal with the result."

"The result? What result? We're the bad fairies or something?" I was trying very hard not to get angry.

"Iona told me last time—you remember, you took them to the movies—that it usually took her and Hank a week to get the girls back into their routine after one of our visits."

"But . . ." I didn't know where to start. I shook my head, as if that would arrange my thoughts in order. "We're supposed to do things for Iona's convenience? We're the girls' brother and sister. We love them. They need to know the whole world isn't like Iona and Hank." My voice rose.

Tolliver sat down on the bathtub's side. "Harper, Iona and Hank are raising them. They didn't have to take them in; the state would have taken them if Iona and Hank hadn't volunteered. I can almost guarantee that the court would have kept Mariella and Gracie in a foster home rather than giving them to us. We're lucky Iona and Hank were willing to give it a shot. They're older than most parents of kids that age. They're strict because they're scared the girls will turn out like your mom, or my dad. But they adopted the girls. They're the parents."

I opened my mouth, closed it. It was like a dam had broken in Tolliver's head, and I was hearing thoughts I'd never heard before, pouring straight out of his mouth.

"Sure, they're limited in their thinking," he said. "But they're the ones who have to cope with Gracie and Mariella, day after day. They go to the teacher conferences; they go to the meetings with the principal; they take the girls to get their shots; and they take them to the doctor when they're sick. They enforce the bedtimes and the study times. They buy the clothes. They'll get the braces." He shrugged. "All that stuff. We can't do that."

"So what do you think we ought to do? Instead of what we're doing?" I stepped out of the bathroom and sat down on the edge of the unmade bed. He followed and sat beside me. I braced my hands on my knees. I tried not to cry. "You think we should abandon our sisters? Almost the only family we've got?" I didn't count Tolliver's father, who'd been in the wind for months.

Tolliver squatted in front of me. "I think maybe we should come for Thanksgiving and Christmas, or Easter, or the girls' birthdays . . .

expected times. Arranged way in advance. At the most, twice a year. I think we should be more careful about what we say in front of the girls. Gracie told Iona that you said she was too rigid. Except Gracie said 'frigid.'"

I tried not to smile, but I couldn't help it. "Okay, you're right about that. Bad-mouthing the people who take care of the girls, that's not cool. I thought I was being so careful."

"You try," he said, and he smiled just a little. "It's the expression on your face rather than your words . . . most of the time."

"Okay, I get your point. But I thought we would become closer to them if we moved here. Maybe break down some walls between Iona and Hank and us. We'd see the girls more often, and the situation would get more relaxed. Maybe the girls could spend the weekend with us sometimes. Surely Iona and Hank want to be by themselves from time to time."

Tolliver countered this scenario with his own issue. "Do you really think Iona will be able to accept *us*? Now that we're together?"

I fell silent. The fact that we'd become a couple would shock my aunt and her husband, and that was putting it mildly. I could understand that point of view, even. After all, Tolliver and I had grown up together in our teen years. We'd lived in the same house. My mother had been married to his father. I'd been introducing him as my brother for years. Sometimes I still referred to him as my brother, because it was the habit of years and because we'd shared an upbringing. Though we weren't blood relations at all, there was a certain ick factor in our sexual relationship, to an outsider's point of view. We'd be fools not to recognize that.

"I don't know," I said, simply to be argumentative. "They might just accept it." I was lying.

"You're lying," Tolliver said. "You know both Hank and Iona are going to go ballistic."

When Iona went ballistic, God got mad. If Iona thought something was morally questionable, God thought so, too. And God, as channeled through Iona, ruled that household.

"But we can't conceal from them what we are to each other," I said helplessly.

"We shouldn't, and we won't. We'll just have to see what happens."

I tried to change the subject, because I had to think over everything we'd just said. "When will we see Mark?" Mark Lang was Tolliver's older brother.

"We're supposed to meet him at the Texas Roadhouse tomorrow night."

"Oh, good." I managed a smile, though I'm sure it was a weak one. I'd always liked Mark, though I'd never been as close to him as I'd been to Tolliver. He'd protected all of us as much as he was able. We didn't manage to see Mark every visit to Texas, so I was glad he'd found the time to have supper with us. "So this evening we're invited to Iona's for a brief visit? And we'll just see what happens. We have no plan?"

"We have no plan," Tolliver confirmed, and we smiled at each other.

I tried to keep hold of the smile when we got into the car to drive over to the small house in Garland where our sisters lived. Though the weather was clear and bright, I wasn't seeing blue skies ahead.

Iona Gorham (nee Howe) had based her character on being anti-Laurel. Laurel Howe Connelly Lang, my mother, had been Iona's only sibling, and older than Iona by almost ten years. In my mother's teen years and through her twenties, before her drug addiction, she had been fairly attractive, popular, and party loving. She had also made great grades, and she'd gone to law school. She'd married a man she met there, my dad, Cliff Connelly. My mother had been a little wild—well, more than a little—but she'd also been a high achiever.

To compete and contrast, Iona had gone the sweet-and-religious route.

Looking at Iona's face when she answered the door, I wondered when the sweetness had turned sour. Iona had always looked disappointed. Yet today, she seemed a little less sour than usual, and I wondered why. Usually, the arrival of Tolliver and me would make her look like she'd sucked a lemon. I tried to remember how old Iona was, and decided that she must be a little less than forty.

"Well, come on in," my aunt said, and stepped back into her living room.

I always felt like we were invited to enter only grudgingly, that Iona would have loved to shut the door in our faces. I'm five foot seven, and my aunt is shorter than I am. Iona is pleasantly rounded, and her hair is graying in a pretty way, as though her light brown hair was simply fading a little. Her eyes are dark gray, like mine.

"How are you?" Tolliver asked pleasantly.

"I'm feeling wonderful," Iona said, and our mouths fell open at the same moment. We'd never heard Iona say anything remotely like that. "Hank's arthritis is acting up," she continued, oblivious to our reaction, "but he can get up and go to work, thank God." Iona worked at Sam's Club part-time, and Hank was the manager of the meat department at a Wal-Mart Supercenter.

"How have the girls been doing in school?" I asked, my standard fallback question. I was still trying not to look at Tolliver, because I knew he was just as floored as I was. Iona was preceding us into the kitchen, where we usually had our conversations. Iona saved the living room for real company.

"Mariella's been doing pretty good. She's a middle-of-the-road-type student," Iona said. "Gracie, they always say she's a little behind where she ought to be. You two want some coffee? I've got the pot on."

"That would be great," I said. "I take it black."

"I remember," she said with a sharp edge to her voice, as if I'd accused her of being a bad hostess. That sounded more like the Iona I knew, and I felt a little more comfortable.

"And I take mine with some sugar," Tolliver said. While her back was to us, he looked at me and raised his eyebrows. Something was up with Iona.

In short order, a mug was in front of him, and a sugar bowl and a spoon and a napkin. I was served second, and I got the plain mug. Iona poured herself some coffee, too, and settled herself in the chair closest to the coffeepot in a way that indicated she was really, really tired. For a minute or two, she didn't speak. She seemed to be thinking hard about something. The table was round, and there was a pile of mail in the middle. I automatically scanned it: phone bill, cable bill, a handwritten letter protruding from its envelope. The handwriting looked sort of familiar in an unpleasant way.

"I'm wore out," Iona said. "I been on my feet at work for six hours straight." Iona was wearing a T-shirt and khakis and sneakers. Clothes had never been a priority for her the way they had been for my mother, until she'd stopped caring about anything at all but the drugs and where they'd come from next. I felt an unexpected flash of sympathy for Iona.

"That's hard on the body," I said, but she wasn't listening.

"Here come the girls," she said, and then my ears caught what hers had already registered: the sound of footsteps outside the garage door.

Our sisters burst into the room and tossed their backpacks against the wall right under a coatrack. They hung their jackets on the coatrack and took their shoes off to park beside the backpacks. I wondered how long it had taken Iona to establish those habits.

The next second, I was taken up with examining my sisters. They've always changed when I see them. It takes me a minute to absorb it. Mariella is twelve years old now, and Gracie is just over three years younger.

The girls were surprised to see us, but not startled. I didn't know if Iona had even warned them we were stopping by to see them. Mariella and Gracie hugged us dutifully, but without enthusiasm. I wasn't surprised at that, given how Iona had tried hard to get the girls to regard us as unnecessary and maybe even bad. And since they didn't remember Cameron, I knew their memories of the trailer had to be faint or nonexistent.

For their sakes, I hoped so.

Mariella was starting to look more like a girl and less like a sack of flour. She had brown hair and eyes, and was square-built like her father. Gracie had always been small for her age, and she'd always been moodier than Mariella. She kissed me voluntarily, which was a first.

It's always hard to get comfortable with our sisters. It's uphill work, reestablishing a bond that has always been tenuous. They sat at the table with us and the woman who'd been a mother to them, and they answered questions, and they acted pleased with their little presents. We always got them a book apiece to encourage them to read, a pastime that wasn't the norm in the Gorham household. But we generally got them something else, too, something cute to wear in their hair or little trinkets, something frivolous. It was hard not to light up like a Christmas tree when Mariella said, "Oh, I read the other two books this lady wrote! Thanks!" I kept my "You're welcome" down to a pleased smile.

Gracie didn't speak, but she smiled at us. That was the more significant because she's not a smiley girl. She doesn't look a thing like Mariella; but then, my sister and I hadn't looked alike, either. Gracie looks like a little elf: she has greenish eyes, long wispy pale hair, an aggressive little nose, and a cupid's bow mouth.

Maybe I'm not a kid person. I find Gracie more interesting than Mariella, though this confession sounds simply cold. For all I know, real mothers have secret favorites, too. I'm pretty sure I don't show this partiality. I'm waiting for Mariella to do something that interests me, and I was delighted that she was happy about the book. If Mariella turned out to be a reader, I'd find a way to connect with her. Gracie had been so sick, at the same time I'd been sick. It had been the unstable taking care of the weak; I'd been laid low by being struck by lightning, and Gracie had had chronic chest and breathing problems.

"Are you a bad woman, Aunt Harper?" Gracie asked. The question came completely out of the blue.

This "aunt" business had originated with Iona, who'd thought we were so much older than our sisters that they ought to address us with respect. But that wasn't why I was so dumbfounded. "I try not to be bad," I said, to buy some time until I found out what had prompted that question.

Iona made herself mighty busy with her coffee, stirring it with a spoon over and over. I could feel my mouth clamp down in anger, and I was trying to keep the bitter words inside. After a moment, it became clear Iona was going to act like she wasn't involved in the conversation, so I went on. "I try to be honest with the people I work for," I said. "I believe in God." (Not the same God Iona worshipped, apparently.) "I work hard and I pay my taxes. I'm the best person I can be." And this was all true.

"Because if you take money from people and you can't really do what you say you can do, that's bad, right?" Gracie said.

"It sure is," Tolliver said. "That's called fraud. And it's something Harper and I would never, never do." His dark eyes drilled holes in Iona. Gracie looked at her adoptive mother, too. I was sure they were seeing two different people.

Iona was still not meeting our eyes, still stirring the damn coffee.

Hank came in the garage door then, which was good timing. Hank was a big man, with a broad, high-complexioned face and thinning blond hair. He'd been very handsome when he was younger, and he was a good-looking man still, now that he'd reached forty. His waist was barely thicker than it had been when he and Iona had married.

"Harper, Tolliver! Good to see you! We don't see you-all enough."

Liar.

He kissed the top of Gracie's head and chucked Mariella under the chin. "Hey, you two!" he said to the girls. "Mariella, how was that spelling test today?"

Mariella said, "Hey, Daddy! I got eight out of ten right."

"That's my girl," Hank said. He was pouring some Coca-Cola out of a two-liter bottle. He chunked a few ice cubes into the glass and pulled up a folding chair that stood beside the refrigerator. "Gracie, did you have a good time in chorus today?"

"We sang good," she said. She seemed relieved to be on familiar conversational ground.

If Hank had noticed the tense atmosphere in the tiny kitchen, he didn't comment on it.

"How are you two doing?" he asked me. "Find any good bodies lately?" Hank had always talked about our livelihood as if it were a big joke.

I smiled back faintly. "A few," I said. Evidently, Hank didn't read the newspapers or watch the news on television. I'd been mentioned more often than I wanted to be in the past month.

"Where you traveled to?" Hank also thought it was amusing that Tolliver and I were always on the road, pursuing this strange living of ours. Hank had been out of Texas when he was in the army, but that was the extent of his traveling experience.

"We were in the mountains of North Carolina," Tolliver said. He paused to see if either Iona or Hank would pick up on the reference to our last, most notorious, case.

Nope.

"Then we went to another job between here and Texarkana, in Clear Creek. Now here we are in Garland to see you-all."

"Any big news in the corpse-finding business?" Again with the teasing smile.

"We have other news," Tolliver said, irritated by Hank's facetiousness. This happened every time. Every damn time. I looked at Tolliver, saw the intent way his eyes were focused on Hank.

Uh-oh, I thought.

"You found you a girlfriend and you're going to settle down!" Hank said jocularly, since Tolliver's lack of a steady girlfriend had long been the subject of many pointed jokes from both Iona and her husband.

"As a matter of fact, I have," Tolliver said, and the smile on his face made me close my eyes. It was bright and hard.

"Well, listen to that, girls! Your uncle Tolliver has got himself a girl! Who is she, Tol?"

My brother hated it when someone abbreviated his name.

"Harper," Tolliver said. He reached across the table and took my hand. And we waited.

"Your . . ." Iona almost said "sister," but recalled the word in time. "But . . . you two?" She looked from me to Tolliver. "That's just not right," she said hesitantly. "You two . . ."

"Are not related," I said, smiling brightly at my aunt.

The girls were looking from one adult to another, confused.

"You're my sister," Mariella said suddenly.

"Yep," I said, smiling at her.

"Tolliver is my brother," she said clearly.

"Also true. But we're not related to each other. You understand that, right? I had a different mom and dad from Tolliver."

"So," said Gracie, "you gonna get married?" She looked pleased. Confused, but pleased.

Tolliver looked across the table at me. His smile gentled. "I hope so," he said.

"Oh, boy! Can I be in the wedding?" Mariella said. "My friend Brianna was in her sister's wedding. Can I wear a long dress? Can I get my hair done? Brianna's mom let her wear lipstick. Can I wear lipstick, Mom?"

"Mariella, we may not have a big wedding," I said, since I could guarantee that wasn't going to happen. "We may just go to a justice of the peace. So it might not be in a church, and I wouldn't wear a long white dress."

"But whatever we do, you can be there, and you can wear whatever you want," Tolliver said.

"Oh, for goodness' sake!" Iona said, sounding thoroughly disgusted. "You two got no business getting married! And if you do, which God forbid, Mariella and Gracie sure wouldn't be there!"

"Why not?" Tolliver asked, in that dangerous voice. "They're our family."

"It just ain't right," Hank said, his face serious, giving us the correct and final verdict on our relationship. "You two was raised too close for comfort."

"We're not related by blood," I said, "and we'll get married when we want to." Then I realized I'd been sucked into the argument much further than I'd counted on. Tolliver was grinning at me. I closed my eyes.

Apparently Tolliver had just proposed and I had just accepted.

"Well," said Iona, her lips pursed in the old Iona way, "we got us some news, too."

"Oh, what is it?" I was willing to be interested. I was willing to dispel the angry atmosphere that had made my sisters so unhappy. I made myself smile at my aunt to show a decent anticipation.

"Hank and I are gonna have a baby," Iona said. "The girls will have a little brother or sister."

After a long moment of intense struggle not to blurt out, "After all these years?" I managed to say, "Oh, what great news! Girls, aren't you excited?"

Tolliver's hand found mine under the table and gripped it hard.

We'd never considered that Iona and Hank might have a baby of their own, and, speaking for myself, I'd never been curious about why they didn't have any. In fact, I'd just regarded the two as inconvenient irritants who got in our way when we wanted to see our sisters. However, they were mighty convenient when it came to doing the day-to-day care for those two little girls, who were no walk in the park to deal with.

In a flash of clarity, I realized all this, and I knew we couldn't possibly interfere with Iona and Hank's relationship with the girls now. I looked into Mariella's face and saw the uncertainty there. Neither she nor Gracie needed any other problems to handle at the moment. The girls were trying to feel happy about the baby, but they'd been thrown for a serious loop.

I could sympathize.

two

AT the Texas Roadhouse the next night, we'd already put our name on the list for a table when Mark arrived. Mark looks like he's Tolliver's brother, all right; they have the same cheekbones, the same chin, the same brown eyes. But Mark is shorter, thicker, and (an observation I have kept to myself) not nearly as smart as Tolliver.

I had so many great memories of Mark, though, that I knew I'd always be fond of him. Mark had done his best to protect all of us from our parents. Not that our parents had always intended to hurt us . . . but they were addicts. Addicts forget to be parents. They forget to be married. They're only addicted.

Mark had suffered a lot because he had more memories of his dad when his dad was a real person than Tolliver did. Mark remembered a father who'd taken him fishing and hunting, a father who'd gone to teacher conferences and football games and helped him with his arithmetic. Tolliver had told me that he remembered that passage in his own life a little, but the last few years in the trailer had overlaid most of that memory until the hurt had extinguished the flame that kept it alive.

Mark had recently become a manager at JCPenney, and he was wearing navy slacks, a striped shirt, and a pinned-on name tag. When I spotted him entering the restaurant, he looked tired, but his face lit up when he noticed us. Mark had clipped his hair very short and shaved off his mustache, and the cleaner look made him seem older and more confident, somehow.

Tolliver and his brother went through the guy greeting ritual, thumping each other on the back, saying "Hey, man!" a number of times. I got a more restrained hug. Just at the right moment, we got a buzz to tell us we could be seated. When we were in a booth and supplied with menus, I asked Mark how his job was going.

"We didn't do as well as we should this Christmas," he said seriously. I noticed how white and even his teeth were, and I felt a stab of resentment on his brother's behalf. Mark had been old enough to get his teeth aligned, unlike Tolliver. By the time Tolliver should have been getting his middle-class-American-teen complement of braces and acne medicine, our parents had started their downward spiral together. I shook off that unworthy twinge of resentment. Mark had just been lucky, on that count. "Our sales weren't as high as they should've been, and we're going to have to scramble this spring," he said.

"So what do you think happened?" Tolliver asked, as if he gave a rat's ass why the store wasn't performing as well as it ought to have.

Mark rambled on about the store and his responsibilities, and I tried to show a decent interest. This was a better job than his previous position managing a restaurant; at least, the hours were better. Mark had put himself through two years of junior college, and he'd taken night classes since then. Eventually, he'd earn a degree. I had to admire that dedication. Neither Tolliver nor I had done that much.

The truth was that though I made sure I looked like I was listening, and I truly was fond of Mark, I was bored silly. I found myself remembering a day Mark had knocked down one of my mom's visitors, a tough guy in his thirties who'd made a blatant pass at Cameron. Mark hadn't known if the guy was armed (many of our parents' buddies were), and yet Mark hadn't hesitated a second in his defense of my sister. This memory made it easy for me to pretend I was hanging on Mark's every word.

Tolliver was asking relevant questions. Maybe he was more into this than I'd thought. I wondered, for the hundredth time, if Tolliver would have enjoyed having a regular life, instead of the one we led.

But I figured he'd pretty much set that fear to rest the day before.

We'd left Iona and Hank's in a very subdued state. We'd been stunned equally by Iona's news. Though we'd tried to congratulate her and Hank with enthusiasm, maybe we hadn't sounded excited enough. We'd been a little shaken by their reaction to our relationship, and it had been hard to be delighted for their good news since they'd been so aghast at ours.

Of course the girls had picked up on all the stress and anger. In the course of a few minutes, they'd gone from being happy for us to being confused and resentful about all the emotions swirling around. Hank had retreated to his tiny "office" to call his pastor and consult with this unknown man about our relationship, which had made something tiny in my head explode. He'd taken Tolliver with him, and Tolliver had emerged looking indignant and amused.

Since we'd left Hank and Iona's, we hadn't said another word to each other about the marriage issue, which had popped up like a jack-in-the-box.

Oddly, not talking about it felt . . . okay. We'd gone to the workout room for some treadmill time and then watched a *Law and Order* rerun. We'd been comfortable with each other and relieved to be by ourselves. While we'd been walking on the treadmills, I'd realized that every time we visited our sisters, it was the same emotional wringer. After a short time in that cramped house, we needed to retreat, regroup, and refresh ourselves.

I worried about the bad feelings between my aunt and myself until I reflected that all was well between Tolliver and me, and that was the only relationship I really cared about . . . well, other than the one I was trying to form with my little sisters.

Still, at odd moments during the past evening, I admit that the uncomfortable situation occupied my thoughts. I know it was naïve of me, but I was shocked every time I thought about Iona's pregnancy. I'd lived through my mother's two pregnancies with my sisters, and it still seemed amazing to me that Gracie had been born with all the correct physical attributes and no apparent mental or neurological problems, considering my mother's extensive drug use. She'd had enough will left to restrain herself somewhat during the time she was carrying Mariella, but with Gracie . . . Gracie had been awfully sick when she was born, and many times after that.

I was thinking about those bad days after our treadmill workout the night before. After I'd had a break, I'd taken our hand vacuum out to the car to give the trunk a once-over. I'd taken a shopping bag with me for the trash. When you're in your car as much as we are, it tends to get pretty junky in a short time. While I tossed old receipts and empty cups into the bag, and got all the corners with the vacuum, I worried about my aunt. Iona was healthy, as far as I knew, and she never drank or used drugs. But she was definitely on the older side to be experiencing a first venture into motherhood.

While part of my brain had been trying to remember if I'd seen an oil-change place down the access road, the other part tried to pooh-pooh my own fears. I told myself that lots of women were waiting until later in their lives to start their families. And more power to them, waiting for financial security or a good relationship to form a foundation for child rearing. The problem was, I knew from personal experience how exhausting caring for an infant was. Maybe Iona would be able to quit work.

While I pretended to listen to Mark and sipped the drink our waitress had brought me, I was reliving our little sit-down at Iona's kitchen table. Something I'd seen had troubled me, something I hadn't been able to recall after the hubbub over our family revelations.

As Mark and Tolliver spent way too long discussing retail, I mentally examined every person who'd been sitting around the table. Then I reviewed my memory of the objects on the table. Finally, I succeeded in tracking down the source of my unease. I waited until the brothers fell silent before I obliquely introduced the subject.

"Mark, do you go over to see the girls very often?" I asked.

"No," he said, ducking his head in a guilty way. "It's a long drive from my house, and I work horrible hours. Plus, Iona always makes me feel bad about something." He shrugged. "To be honest, the girls just aren't that interested in me."

Mark had left the trailer and started living on his own as soon as he could, which we'd all agreed was the best thing for him to do. He came by when our parents weren't there—or when they were out cold—and he'd (God bless him) brought us supplies whenever he could. But that meant he hadn't been present like we had when the girls were babies, and he hadn't had as much opportunity to bond with them. Cameron and Tolliver and I had taken care of Mariella and Gracie. On the nights when bad memories woke me up and wouldn't let me sleep, I got scared all over again when I thought of what might have happened to the girls if we hadn't been there. That wasn't the girls' concern, though—and it shouldn't be.

"So you haven't talked to Iona lately." I had to think in the here and now.

"No." Mark looked at me, a question on his face.

"You know that Iona's heard from your dad?" It was my stepfather's handwriting I'd seen on the letter protruding from the stack of mail.

Mark would never be a successful poker player, because he didn't look anything but guilty. I had to smile at his obvious relief when the waitress picked that moment to take our orders.

But that smile didn't sit on my lips for long. I was scared to look sideways at Tolliver.

When the waitress had bustled off, I opened my hands to Mark, indicating it was time for him to come clean.

"Well, yeah, I was gonna tell you about that," he said, looking down at his silverware.

"What were you going to tell us, brother?" Tolliver asked, his voice even and pleasant and forced.

"I got a letter from Dad a couple weeks ago," Mark said. No, he *confessed* it. Then he waited for Tolliver to give him absolution—but Tolliver wasn't about to. We both knew Mark had responded to the letter, or he wouldn't be so hangdog.

"Dad's alive, then," Tolliver said, and anyone but me would have called his voice neutral.

"Yeah, he's got a job. He's clean and sober, Tol."

Mark had always had a tender heart for his father. And he'd always been incredibly gullible where his dad was concerned.

"Matthew's been out of jail how long?" I asked, since Tolliver wasn't responding to Mark's assertion. I'd never been able to call Matthew Lang "Father."

"Um, a month," Mark said. He folded the little paper ring that had circled his silverware and napkin. He unfolded it and folded it again. This time he compressed it into a smaller rectangle. "He got early release for good behavior. After I wrote back, he called me. He wants to reconnect with his family, he says."

I was sure that (entirely coincidentally) Matthew also wanted money and maybe a place to stay. I wondered if Mark truly believed his father, if he could really be that foolish.

Tolliver didn't say a word.

"Has he been in touch with your uncle Paul or your aunt Miriam?" I asked, struggling to fill the silence.

Mark shrugged. "I don't know. I never call them."

While it wasn't technically true that Tolliver and I were each other's only adult family, with the exception of Mark it might as well have been. Matthew Lang's siblings had been hurt and disgusted too often by Matthew to want to maintain any relationship with him, and unfortunately that exclusion had spread outward to include Matthew's kids. Mark and Tolliver could have used help—could have used a *lot* of help—but that would have entailed dealing with Matthew, who had been too difficult and frightening for his more conventional siblings. As a result, Tolliver had cousins he barely knew.

I wasn't sure exactly how he felt about Paul's and Miriam's self-preserving decisions, but he'd never made any attempt to contact them in recent years, when Matthew had been safely behind bars. I guess that spoke for itself.

"What's Dad doing?" Tolliver said. His voice was ominously quiet, but he was holding together.

"He's working at a McDonald's. The drive-through, I think. Or maybe he's cooking."

I was sure Matthew Lang wasn't the first disbarred lawyer to work the drive-through window at a McDonald's. But given the fact that while I'd lived in the same trailer with the man, I'd never seen him cook beyond popping something in the microwave, and I'd never seen him wash a single dish, that was kind of ironic. Not enough that I'd bust out laughing, though.

"What happened to *your* dad, Harper?" Mark asked. "Cliff, was that his name?" Mark felt it was time to point out that Matthew wasn't the only bad dad around.

"Last I heard, he was in the prison hospital," I said. "I don't think he knows anyone anymore." I shrugged.

Mark looked shocked. His hands moved involuntarily across the table. "You don't go see him?" He actually sounded amazed at my heartlessness, which I found almost incredible.

"What?" I said. "Why would I? He never took care of me. I'm not going to take care of him."

"Wasn't it okay before he started using drugs? Didn't he give you a good home?"

I understood this wasn't about my father at all, but it was still really irritating. "Yes," I agreed. "He and my mother gave us a nice home. But after they started using, they never thought twice about us." There were lots of kids who'd had it worse, who hadn't even had a trailer with a hole in the bathroom floor. Hadn't even had siblings who were willing to watch their back. But it had been bad enough. And later, awful things had happened when my mother and Tolliver's father had had their crappy "friends" over. I remembered one night when all of us kids had slept under the trailer, because we were so scared of what was happening inside.

I shook myself. *No pity.*

"How'd you know to bring up Dad, anyway?" Mark asked. He looked sullen. Mark had always been a transparent sort of guy. It was clear I wasn't his favorite person at the moment.

"I saw a letter from him on Iona's table. It took me a while to remember where I'd seen the handwriting. I wonder why he wrote her. Do you reckon he's trying to get Iona to let him see the girls? Why would he be doing that?"

"Maybe he thinks he ought to see *his daughters,*" Mark said, and he flushed, a sure sign he was angry.

Tolliver and I looked at our brother, and neither of us said a word.

"Okay, okay," Mark said, rubbing his face with his hands. "He doesn't deserve to see them. I don't know what he's asking Iona for. When I saw him, he told me he wants to see Tolliver. He doesn't have an address to send Tolliver a letter."

"There's a reason for that," Tolliver said.

"He'd seen some website that tracks her," Mark said, nodding toward me as if I were sitting far away. "He said you-all's website had an email address, but he didn't want to contact you through her website. Like he was a stranger."

The waitress came up with our food then, and we took the little ritual of spreading napkins and using salt and pepper to regroup.

"Mark," Tolliver said, "is there any reason you can think of that I *ought* to make any effort to include that man in my life? In Harper's life?"

"He's our dad," Mark said doggedly. "He's all we've got left."

"No," Tolliver said. "Harper's sitting right here."

"But she's not *our* family." Mark looked at me, this time a little apologetically.

"She's *my* family," Tolliver said.

Mark froze. "Are you saying I shouldn't have left you-all in that trailer? That I should have stayed there with you? That I let you down?"

"No," Tolliver said, astonished. We exchanged a quick flicker of a glance. "I'm saying Harper and I are together."

"She's your stepsister," Mark said.

"And she's my girlfriend," Tolliver said, and I smiled down at my salad. It seemed such an inadequate term.

Mark's mouth hung open as he stared at us. "What? Is that legal? When did this happen?"

"Recently; yes, it is; and we're happy, thanks for asking."

"Then I'm glad for you," Mark said. "It's good that you have each other." But he still looked doubtful. "Isn't it kind of weird, though? I mean, we grew up in the same house."

"Like you and Cameron," I said.

"I never felt like that about Cameron," he said.

"Okay," I said. "But this is the way we feel. We didn't start out this way, but it's the way we ended up." And I smiled at Tolliver, suddenly feeling ridiculously happy.

He smiled back. Our circle closed.

"So what do you want me to tell Dad?" Mark said. There was a little desperation in his voice. I couldn't imagine how Mark had pictured this conversation going, but it had not turned out to his satisfaction, obviously.

"I thought I'd made myself clear. We don't want to see him," Tolliver said. "I don't want him to get in touch with me. If he emails us through the website, I won't answer. That last year . . . you were lucky you were out on your own, Mark. I'm glad you were old enough to leave, to start your life. I've never blamed you for leaving, if that's what you're thinking. Even if you'd been in the trailer, you couldn't have stopped anything that happened. And you brought us food and diapers and money when you could. We were glad one of us had made it out into the real world. My job at Taco Bell wouldn't have been enough."

"You don't think I was just running away?" Mark sawed on his steak, his eyes on his knife.

"No, I think you were saving your life." Tolliver put down his fork. His face was serious. "That's what I really believe. And that's what Harper believes."

Not that Mark was so concerned with my opinion, but I nodded. It had never crossed my mind to think any differently about it.

Mark tried to laugh, but it was a pretty pitiful attempt. He said, "I never intended this evening to get so intense."

"It's your dad reappearing. Not your fault." I smiled at him, trying to will him to lighten up.

But that seemed to be a lost cause. "You really haven't visited your dad?" he asked me. He was wrestling with my attitude.

"No," I said. "Why would I lie about that?"

"What is his illness?"

"I don't know."

"Has he heard your mom died?"

"I have no idea."

"He know about Cameron?"

I thought about that for a moment. "Yeah, because some of the newspeople tracked him down and talked to him when she went missing."

"He never came to see . . ."

"No. He was incarcerated. He wrote me a few letters. My foster parents gave 'em to me. But I didn't answer. I don't know what happened to him after that. More of the same, I expect. I never heard from him, or about him, until he got so sick. Then the prison chaplain wrote me."

"And you just . . . didn't answer?"

"I just didn't answer. Tolliver, can I have a bite of your sweet potato?"

"Sure," he said and slid his plate sideways toward me.

He always orders one when we're at a Texas Roadhouse, and I always have one bite. I swallowed it. It wasn't as good as it usually was, but I didn't think that was the staff's fault. I thought it was Mark's.

He was shaking his head, his eyes turned down to his plate. He looked up, meeting first Tolliver's eyes, then mine. "I don't know how you two do it," he said. "When Dad comes calling, I have to answer. He's my *dad*. If my mother was alive, it'd be the same way."

"I guess we're just not as good as you, Mark," I said. What else could I say? *He'll drain you and leech off of you. He'll break his word and your spirit.*

"I don't guess you've heard anything from the police since the last time I talked to you?" Mark said. "Or from that private eye?"

"You're determined to push all the buttons tonight, Mark," I said, and now it was a struggle to sound even civil.

"I have to ask. I keep thinking someday there'll be news."

I let my anger go, because I sometimes thought the same thing. "There's no news. Someday I'll find her." I'd said it for years, and it had never happened. But one day, when I least expected it—though on some level I always expected it—I'd feel her nearness, like I'd felt the proximity of so many dead people before. I would find Cameron, and I would know what had happened to her that day.

She'd been walking home alone after helping to decorate the high school gym for the prom. I had become the kind of girl who doesn't do things like that, by that time. The lightning had done its job on me. I was still settling into my new skin, terrified of my new and weird ability, recovering from the physical damage. I was still limping, and I tired easily. I'd gotten one of my terrible headaches that day.

It had been in the spring, and we'd had a cold snap. The night before, the temperature had dropped below forty. That afternoon, it was only in the sixties. Cameron had been wearing black tights and a black and white plaid skirt and a white turtleneck. She looked great. No one would have guessed she'd pieced the outfit together at the thrift store. Her blond hair was long and shiny. My sister Cameron had freckles. She hated them. She made all As.

While Mark and Tolliver made conversation, I tried to imagine what Cameron would look like now. Would she still be blond? Would she have gained weight? She'd been small, shorter than me, with thin arms and legs and a will of iron. She'd run track with some success, though when the paper had called her a "track star" after she'd vanished, we'd all looked at each other and rolled our eyes.

My sister hadn't been a saint. I'd known Cameron better than anyone else. She was proud. She could keep a secret till it screamed. She was smart. She studied hard. Sometimes she resented our situation, our fall from affluence, with such anger that she screamed out loud. She hated our mother, Laurel, hated her passionately, for dragging us down with her. But Cameron loved our mother, too.

She couldn't stand Matthew, who was Mother's second husband but her hundredth "boyfriend." Cameron had had this persistent delusion that our father would return to his pre-drug self, and that he would show up at the dismal trailer someday and take us off with him. We would go back to living in a clean house, and someone else would wash our clothes and cook our meals. Our father would show up at the school for PTA meetings, and he'd talk to us over the supper table about where we might want to go to college.

This was Cameron's fantasy, her happy one. She had some that were darker, much darker. She told me, one morning on our walk to school, that she also dreamed one of our mother's dealers would show up at the trailer while we were gone and kill our mother and stepfather. After they were dead, we'd be put in a nice foster home. Then, when we'd graduated from high school, we'd get jobs and rent an apartment and work our way through college.

That was as far as Cameron's dream had gone. I wondered what she'd imagined would happen after that. Would we each have found a good and prosperous man, and lived happily ever after? Or maybe instead we'd have continued living together (in our modest but clean apartment), wearing our new clothes (a very important part of Cameron's tale), and eating our good food that we'd learned how to cook.

"Honey?" Tolliver said. I turned to him, startled. He'd never called me that before.

"Do you want dessert?" he asked. I realized that the waitress was waiting, smiling in that pained way that said she was being so, so patient.

I almost never eat dessert. "No, thanks," I said. To my irritation, Mark ordered pie, and Tolliver got coffee to keep him company. I was ready to go; I wanted to get away from all this remembrance. I shifted a little to a more comfortable position, stifling a sigh.

When Tolliver and Mark resorted to talking about computers, I was once more free to think about other things.

But all I could think about was Cameron.

three

WHEN we were back in our room, we were both reluctant to start talking about Mark's perfidy in renewing contact with their dad. Tolliver booted up the laptop and went to a fan website that tracks my activities; he monitors it regularly because he's worried that I might acquire a crazy stalker. I never look at it, because there are posts from guys who want to do things with me and to me; and that's scary, not to say repellent. Now, I was worried that Matthew might be reading it at the same moment Tolliver was; he'd be looking for clues on how to find his son.

A nagging pain interrupted my worry session.

I rummaged through my medicine bag to unearth some Icy Hot to rub into my right leg. That's where I feel the long-term effects of getting struck by lightning most of all. I pulled off my shoes and jeans and sat on the bed, stretching out the aching muscles and joints. My right thigh is covered with a tracery of red lines—broken capillaries or something. It's been like that since I got hit, when I was fifteen. It's not pretty.

I worked the cream into my skin for a while in silence. I rubbed hard, trying to get the muscles to give up the discomfort. After a few minutes of massage, I felt some relief. I lay back on the pillows, telling each muscle group to relax in turn. I closed my eyes. "I'd rather be out in the snow finding a corpse than talking to Iona and Hank, just in general," I said. "And sometimes talking to Mark is just as hard."

"Last night at Iona's . . ." Tolliver said, then paused. When he resumed, he sounded cautious. "Hank pulled me aside while you were in the bathroom and asked me if I'd gotten you knocked up."

"He did *not*."

"Oh, yeah. He did. He was serious, too. He was like, 'You gotta marry her if you got her pregnant, boy. If you can't do the time, don't do the crime.'"

"Great perspective on marriage and fatherhood."

Tolliver laughed. "Well, this is the guy who calls Iona his 'ball and chain.'"

"Married, not married, I don't care," I said, before I realized this was a less than tactful way to put it. "I do care," I said hastily. "I mean, I love you and being with you is what I want. I don't care about the marriage part of it. Shit, that wasn't right either."

"We'll do what's right when the time comes," Tolliver said, in a voice heavy with elaborate unconcern.

Apparently he *did* want to get married. Why couldn't he just say so? I put my hands over my face, which felt strange because they were tingling from the Icy Hot.

Of course I would marry him, especially if it was a make-or-break issue of our relationship. I would do almost anything to get him to stay.

That wasn't a romantic realization. I lay there thinking, listening to Tolliver's fingers touch the keyboard. I thought, *If anything happens to him, I might as well die.* I wondered if that said a lot for Tolliver—or not much for me.

There was a knock at the door of our room. We looked at each other, puzzled. Tolliver shook his head; he wasn't expecting anyone, either.

He got up and pulled the curtain back a little. He let it drop back into position. "It's Lizzie Joyce," he said. "With her sister. Kate, right?"

"Right." I was as startled as he was. "Well," I said. "What the hell?" We gave each other little shrugs.

Tolliver, having decided they weren't armed and dangerous, let the Joyce sisters inside. I pulled my jeans back on and rose to greet them.

You'd think they'd never seen a middle-of-the-road motel before. Kate and Lizzie examined the room with nearly identical slow scans. The sisters looked a lot alike. Katie was a little shorter than Lizzie, and maybe two years younger. But she'd colored her hair the same blond as Lizzie's, and her brown eyes were narrow like Lizzie's, and her lean build was the same, too. They were both wearing jeans, boots, and jackets. Lizzie had slicked her hair back into a ponytail at the nape of her neck, while Katie's was loose and bouncy. Between necklaces, earrings, and rings, I figured they each were wearing a couple of thousand dollars' worth of jewelry. (After a subsequent trip to a mall store, I revised that figure upward.)

Katie's eyes were avid as she examined Tolliver. She wasn't so enthusiastic about our paraphernalia: our clothes, his crossword puzzle book, the open laptop, his shoes put neatly by his suitcase.

"Hello, Ms. Joyce," I said, trying to inject my voice with some warmth. "What can I do for you?"

"You can tell me again what you saw when you stood on Mariah Parish's grave."

It took me a second to recall. "Your father's caregiver," I said. "The one who had the childbirth problems. The infection."

"Yeah, why'd you say that? She had complications after her appendectomy," Lizzie said. She was issuing a very low-level challenge.

Oh, for goodness' sake. This was hardly my fight. "If that's what you're calling it, okay," I said. It made no difference to me. Mariah Parish wasn't the one I'd been paid to read, anyway.

"That's what *happened,*" Katie said.

I shrugged. "All right."

"What the hell do you mean, 'all right'? She either did or she didn't." The Joyce sisters were not going to let go of this bone.

"Believe what you want to believe. I already told you what she died of."

"She was a good woman. Why would you make that up?"

"Exactly. Why *would* I make that up?" And what was wrong with a woman having gone through childbirth?

"So who was the father?" Lizzie asked, as abruptly as she'd asked about the death.

"I have no idea."

"Then . . ." Lizzie floundered to a halt. She was a woman who wasn't used to floundering. She didn't like it. "Why'd you say it?"

I really had to restrain myself from rolling my eyes. "I said it because I saw it, and you wanted me to find your grandfather's grave myself," I said, with fabulous diction. "To give you your money's worth, I went from grave to grave, as you obviously wanted me to."

"Everything else you said was right," Katie said.

"I know." Had they expected me to be surprised at my own accuracy?

"So why'd you make up that one?"

If they hadn't been so agitated, this would have been boring. My leg hurt, and I wanted to sit down. But I didn't want to invite them to, so I felt obliged to remain standing. "I didn't. Believe me or not. I don't give a damn."

"But where's the baby?"

"How should I know?" I'd reached the end of my patience.

"Ladies," Tolliver said, just in the nick of time, "my sister finds the dead. The baby was not in the grave she scanned. Either the baby is alive or it's buried somewhere else. Or it might have been miscarried."

"But if the baby was my granddad's, that baby inherits some of what he left," Lizzie said, and suddenly their agitation became understandable.

To hell with them. I sank down on the bed, stretching out my aching leg. "Please have a seat," I said. "Do you want a Coke or a 7-Up?"

Tollilver sat by me so the sisters could have the two room chairs. They accepted a drink apiece, and though Katie kept looking at the laptop to see what Tolliver had been up to, they both seemed calmer and less accusatory, which was a relief to me.

"Neither of us had any idea Mariah was pregnant," Lizzie said. "That's why we're so shocked. And we didn't realize she was dating anyone. She and my grandfather were pretty good friends, and we're imagining that maybe that became something else. Maybe not. We need to know. Aside from the legal and financial considerations, we owe any child who might be a member of the Joyce family . . . We want to meet that kid. Can I smoke?"

"No, sorry," Tolliver said.

"The baby must be alive somewhere; there must be some record of its birth," I said. "Even if it was born dead, there should still be hospital records. It's knowing who to ask and where to ask. Maybe you can hire a private investigator, someone who can get through the records easily. I only contact the dead, myself."

"That's a good idea," Katie said. "Do you know any?"

"Since you're already here in Garland," Tolliver said, "there's a woman a little farther into Dallas who's good. Her name's Victoria Flores. She used to be a cop in Texarkana. And I know there's at least one ex-military guy even closer to your ranch; I think he's based in Longview. His name's Ray Phyfe."

"There are dozens of big agencies in Dallas, too," I said, as if that would have been hard for them to figure out.

"We don't want a big agency," Lizzie said. "We just want this to be very, very private."

That was the response I'd been waiting to hear; I'd been curious about their asking us, of all people, for a recommendation. The Joyce empire, of which RJ Ranch was only a part, surely had employed private detectives in the past. Under normal circumstances, I was sure the Joyces would go to an agency they'd used before, where they'd get the deluxe treatment they were used to.

At the moment, I didn't care what they wanted or how they went about it. I wanted to take a lot of Advil and crawl into the bed.

Lizze was talking to Tolliver about Victoria Flores, and he was giving her Victoria's phone number. That name brought back some memories.

"You really saw that?" Katie asked me directly. "You're not just making this up to jerk us around? No one paid you to play a joke on us?"

"I don't play jokes, in case you missed that about me. I don't take money to make fake pronouncements. Of course I really saw that. It's not a likely thing to make up."

Lizzie had appropriated our little pad of paper by the telephone and the cheap motel pen to write down Victoria Flores's information.

"She switched locations recently," Tolliver said. "This is the right number, though." I looked down, not wanting my face to reveal how surprised I was.

After more reassurance and more repetition of the things we'd already said, the Joyce sisters were out our door and back on the road. I wondered if they'd spend the night in Dallas or try to make it back to their ranch, which would be quite a drive. They'd stay in some place more palatial if they were lingering in the area, I was sure. Probably had a Dallas apartment.

"So," I said, when the door had closed behind them and Tolliver had reseated himself at the table to finish his computer work, "Victoria Flores."

I didn't need to say anything else.

"I call her from time to time," Tolliver said. "Every now and then she hears something new. Every now and then she runs something down. She sends me a bill. I pay her."

"And you didn't tell me this—because?"

"You get so upset," he said. "I just couldn't see what purpose it served. When I used to tell you, every time she called, you'd get all upset. Every time, it would come to nothing. She doesn't call much now, maybe twice a year, and I just couldn't do that to you anymore."

I took a deep breath. My impulse was to launch into him. It was my business how I reacted to possible news of my sister. It was my right to suffer for her.

Then I had a second thought. On the other hand—Tolliver's hand—did it serve any purpose? Hadn't I been okay, not knowing? Hadn't I been calmer and happier, just waiting to locate Cameron in my own way? Was it not okay to have something done for you, some pain spared you, even if it meant you were ignorant about something that you considered your personal business?

Could that idea have gotten more convoluted?

But I knew what I meant, and I knew what Tolliver meant. And I thought maybe he was right. Or at least, it was okay that he had done that.

I nodded finally. He seemed relieved, because his shoulders relaxed and he blew out a breath. He sat on the bed to pull off his socks, then tossed them into our laundry bag, which reminded me that we were low on detergent.

I had ten little thoughts like this while I got ready for bed. I'd been reading through the novels of Charlie Huston and Duane Swierczynski, but it was like getting a jolt of caffeine if I read either one before bedtime; I definitely didn't need that tonight. Instead, I opened a crossword puzzle book. I crawled into bed in my soft sleep pants and my T, and I lay on my stomach, absorbed in the crossword. Tolliver was better at them than I was, and it was hard not to ask him questions.

Another exciting night in the life of corpse-reader Harper Connelly, I thought. And I was happy that this was so.

Four

WE were scheduled to take Gracie and Mariella skating that next afternoon, Sunday, but not until two p.m. On Saturday mornings they had to pick up their rooms and do chores before they could go anywhere, and on Sundays they had church and lunch as a family. These were ironclad rules of Iona's. And not bad ones, I thought. I'd run and showered and was about to dress when Tolliver's cell phone rang. He'd been lazy and was still in bed, so I answered it.

"Hey, this must be Harper."

I recognized the voice. "Yeah, Tolliver's not up yet, Victoria. How's it going?"

Victoria's great-grandparents had been the immigrants. Victoria, born and bred in Texas, didn't have a trace of an accent. "It's good to talk to you," she said. "Listen, nothing new on your sister, I'm sorry to say. I'm calling about the clients you-all referred to me. The Joyces."

"They already got in touch?"

"Honey, they already been here in my office and wrote me a check."

"Oh, good. But I can't take any credit for the referral. Tolliver was the one who told them your name and gave them your phone number."

"That's what Lizzie said. That woman, she's Texas all the way through, huh? And the sister, Kate? I think she's interested in your brother."

"He's not my brother," I said automatically, though I called him that myself about half the time. I took a deep breath. "In fact, we're engaged," I said.

Tolliver rolled over and fixed me with a sharp eye.

"Oh . . . well, that's just . . . great. Congratulations to the two of you." Victoria didn't sound thoroughly delighted. Had she been interested in Tolliver herself?

"Let me know the date of the wedding and where you're registered, okay?" Victoria said, more brightly.

"We haven't planned that far ahead," I said, thrown off balance and scrambling to get my conversational feet back under me. "You need to have a word with Tolliver? He's right here." Tolliver was shaking his head no, but he took the phone from me with a dour look when Victoria told me she'd like to talk to him.

"Victoria, hey. No, I was awake. Yeah, we're together. We haven't set any dates, though. We'll pick a date soon. No hurry." And he gave me a significant nod, looking right into my eyes.

Okay, got it, Tolliver. No pressure from you. Except who'd told Iona we were getting married in the first place? I turned my back on him and bent to rummage in my suitcase for clothes.

After a second, I felt a finger stroking in a very interesting place. I froze. Stealth-attack sex. This was something new. My body decided that I liked this, and didn't pull away and slap Tolliver's hand. The stroking grew more aggressive, more rhythmic. Oh, oh, oh. I wiggled. Then I felt the warmth of him behind me. Though he was still talking to Victoria, he was sounding more than a little distracted.

"Yeah, I'll call you back," he said. "I've got another call coming in."

The phone snapped shut. Something more substantial replaced the fingers.

"Are you ready?" he asked, his voice hoarse.

"Yeah," I said, and reached out to brace my palms against the wall. And then the sharp upward curve of his penis pushed into me, and we rocked together.

Tolliver was all about keeping things fresh.

I hadn't been very experienced when we admitted we were interested in each other. But I was learning a lot from him, and the adventure of it was giving me a whole new light on his nature. I'd thought I'd known him so well that he couldn't surprise me. I'd been wrong.

I gave a sharp cry, a sound I was startled to hear coming from my own throat, and he echoed it a second later.

"Why do you think Victoria called?" I asked, when I could talk. We'd collapsed on the bed after disengaging, and we were wrapped around each other in a very happy way. "It seems a little off base that she'd just call to say thank you. An email or a text would have been more in line." I kissed his throat.

"She was always fascinated by you," Tolliver said, and that was completely unexpected.

"Ah . . . that way?"

"No, I don't think she's gay or bi. I think she just finds your ability, and the whole thing with the lightning, really interesting. Maybe even fascinating. Over the past few years, Victoria must have asked me a hundred questions about how you do what you do, what it feels like, what the physical effects are."

"She's never asked me anything."

"She told me once that if she asked you questions, you might think she thought you were a freak or had some kind of disability."

"Like I was in a wheelchair or had a big birthmark on my face? Something I might feel self-conscious about?"

"I think she was showing sensitivity about hurting your feelings or making you feel different. I think Victoria kind of holds you in awe." Tolliver sounded a little chiding, which maybe I deserved. After all, if Victoria had been trying to spare my feelings, I shouldn't disparage her efforts.

"It just seems strange she wouldn't want to come right to the source." By which I was hinting that I thought Victoria had wanted reasons to talk to Tolliver, rather than that she was genuinely interested in my little problem.

"Maybe she had both things in mind," Tolliver said, admitting and giving due credence to my suspicion. "But I don't think she's ever been very interested in me. It was you. I think Victoria has a kind of mystical streak. I think your ability feeds into that."

"Like seeing the Virgin Mary on a piece of toast, or something?"

"Something."

"Hah." I turned that over in my head. "Then she should come to a cemetery with us, if she's so interested. See firsthand. She's been a lot of help to us over the years. I wouldn't mind."

It was Tolliver's turn to be surprised. "Okay, I'll tell her. I'm sure she'd really get into that."

He rubbed his chin against the top of my head. I stroked my thumb across one of his flat nipples. He made a little noise of pleasure. I told myself I should get up to shower, since we had to go soon to meet the girls, but I put it off for a few more minutes. We had time. I tried to imagine taking Victoria Flores with us when we went to a cemetery. It would have to be when we didn't have a job set up, when I was visiting to . . . okay, I know this sounds very strange, but if I haven't had a job in a while, I go to a cemetery to keep in shape. With my strange ability.

Having Victoria there would feel funny, but I didn't think her presence would bother me. "So, she has computer skills, I guess, since most private eyes have to these days," I said.

"We still talking about Victoria? Yeah, I think so," Tolliver said. "She's mentioned a tech guy who works with her part-time."

I lay there thinking, while Tolliver got up and showered and dressed.

Victoria Flores had suddenly become a lot more interesting to me.

I wondered if she'd find the missing baby, the baby we weren't even sure existed. Whether or not Mariah Parish had borne a living child shouldn't make a bit of difference to me, but I found myself rooting for the Joyces to track down the baby. I suspected that child might not be their grandfather's offspring. On second thought, if the girls had been so ready to believe Richard Joyce had fathered a child with his caregiver, maybe the baby had been his. But Lizzie and Katie hadn't been looking in the direction I'd been looking when I told them what had killed Mariah Parish. I'd been looking at their brother and Lizzie's boyfriend, and they'd looked mighty damn worried. About what, I didn't know, and I might never find out. But I hoped Victoria would.

Maybe they'd both had sex with Rich's caregiver. Maybe one of them had impregnated her. Or maybe they were guilty of helping to bury the baby or put the baby up for adoption.

Whatever the brother—Drexell, his name was—had done, I realized it was no concern of mine, and that the search for the whereabouts of baby Parish was not up to me and not in my area of expertise . . . unless the baby was dead. I thought of proposing I help Victoria look for a dead child. But infants were the hardest. They had so little voice. They registered more strongly when they were buried with their parents.

I abandoned thought of the possible child, possibly dead, in the scramble to get ready to pick up the living children that we were kin to. Both girls ran out to our car when we pulled into the Gorham driveway. They seemed happy, looking forward to the afternoon.

"I got an A on my spelling test last week," Gracie said. Tolliver told her how good that was, and I smiled. But as I looked into the backseat at her, I noticed Mariella was silent and looked a little dampened.

"What's up, Mariella?" I asked.

"Nothing," she said, which was obviously untrue.

Gracie said, "Mariella has to stay after school and do extra work tomorrow."

"Why, Mariella?" I made my voice matter-of-fact.

"The principal said I caused trouble in class." Mariella wasn't looking at me.

"Did you?"

"It was that Lindsay."

"Lindsay is a bully," Gracie said. "We're not supposed to let people bully us, right? That's bad." Gracie looked self-consciously righteous.

I wanted Gracie to butt out. "We'll talk about it later," I said, and I thought Mariella relaxed a little bit. I wasn't used to problems like this; I wasn't used to children. But I recalled that at Mariella's age, this would have been an all-consuming issue.

When we got to the skating rink, Tolliver gave me a questioning look, and I inclined my head toward Gracie. "Come on, Gracie, let's go get our skates," he said, and she hopped out happily and held his hand as they walked to the door.

Mariella got out, too, and we walked more slowly behind them.

"So, tell me," I prompted.

As I'd expected, it wasn't a huge thing. Lindsay had said something ugly to Mariella about being adopted because her dad was in jail. Mariella had punched Lindsay in the stomach, which from my point of view was the correct and proper response. From the school's perspective, apparently Mariella should have begun crying and gone to her teacher to complain. I liked Mariella's reaction better. This led me to a dilemma. Did I go with my gut, or support the school's position? If I'd been a real parent, I might have known the right answer. As it was, I took a deep breath and began to fumble my way through.

"That was really ugly of Lindsay," I said. "You can't help what your birth dad did."

Mariella nodded, her jaw set in a very familiar way. The image of Matthew, I couldn't help but notice.

"That's what I said to the principal," Mariella told me. "That's what Mom told me to say. I guess that's what I should have said to Lindsay. She just made me feel so bad."

I thought the better of Iona for preparing Mariella for the cruelty of other children. "I probably would have hit Lindsay, too, in your situation," I said. "On the other hand, every time you hit someone you're going to get into trouble."

"So hitting is wrong?"

"It's not the best way to solve a problem," I hedged. "What could you have done instead?" That seemed appropriately touchy-feely.

"I could have told the teacher," Mariella said. "But then I'd have to talk to her about my birth dad, and she'd get that funny look on her face."

"True." Hmmm.

"I could have walked away, but then Lindsay would have done it again."

"Also true." Mariella was more insightful than I'd ever imagined. And she was really enjoying talking to someone who didn't tell her God would solve her problems.

"I could have . . . I can't think of anything else." My sister waited for my reaction.

"Neither can I. I guess you had an impulse, and you acted on it, and it didn't turn out well for you. What happened to Lindsay?"

"She lost four recesses," Mariella said. "For being a bully."

"So that was good, right?"

"Yeah. But it would have been better if she'd kept her mouth shut in the first place."

Whoa. Little warrior woman. "You're right about that. It's not your fault that your birth dad used drugs. You know that. But there are some kids who don't understand what it's like to have parents who do bad things. Those kids are lucky, but they can't seem to get that it's nothing you want to talk about. They just know it'll make you feel bad. So when they want you to feel bad, that's the first thing they're going to throw at you." I took a deep breath. "We went through that, too, Mariella. Tolliver and me. When you were really little. Everyone at the school knew how crappy our parents were."

"Even the teachers?"

"Maybe not the teachers. I don't know how much they guessed. But the other kids, they all knew. Some of them bought drugs at our trailer."

"So they said mean stuff to you?"

"Yeah, some of them. Others thought we were doing the same bad stuff your mom and dad were. Drugs and stuff."

"Sex stuff?"

"That, too. But the kids who thought we were the same as our folks? Those were the kids that didn't really know us. We had friends who knew better." Not too many, but a few.

"So, did you date?"

Whoa! She wasn't even having periods yet. Right? I almost panicked. "Yes, I dated. And I never went out with a boy who thought I was going to have sex with him right away. The more careful you are, the more reputation you get for being the other way, being very . . ."

"Holding out," Mariella said knowledgeably.

"Not even that," I said. "Because if you say 'holding out,' that means you're going to give it up someday, that you're just waiting for some boy to say the right thing to unlock your legs. You can't even let that be a *possibility*." I knew Iona would explode if she could hear this conversation. But that was why my sister was having it with me, not Iona.

"But then no one will date you."

This was simply awful. "Then to heck with them," I said, recalling just in time to rein in my language. "You don't need to go out with a guy who's sure you're going to give him sex if he goes out with you long enough."

"Why are they gonna go out with you, then?" she said, looking baffled.

That was nothing compared to the way I felt. "A boy should go out with you because he likes your company," I said. "Because you laugh at the same things, or you're interested in the same things." At least, that was the theory. Was it ever that way in practice? And it shouldn't even be arising at Mariella's age, which was what? Twelve?

"So he should be your friend."

"Yes. He should be your friend."

"Is Tolliver your friend?"

"Yes, he's my best friend."

"But you're, you know . . ."

She couldn't quite bring herself to say the words, and I could only be thankful for that.

"That's kind of our business," I said. "When it's the real thing, it means so much you don't want to talk about it with other people."

"Oh." Mariella looked thoughtful. I hoped she was. I hoped I hadn't just committed a colossal blunder. I'd told her not to have sex with the boys she was going to date. Then I hadn't contradicted her assumption that Tolliver and I were doing that very thing. I felt totally inadequate.

I was so glad to see Tolliver and Gracie waiting for us, I found myself hurrying toward them. Tolliver gave me a funny look, but Gracie was simply impatient.

"Let's get our skates!" she said. "I want to skate!"

After we'd all put on our skates and Tolliver and I'd helped the girls out onto the rink floor, then seen that they were okay when they stuck to the wall railing, we skated off to do a round by ourselves. We held hands and went slowly at first, because it had been a good eight years since either of us had skated. There'd been a rink within walking distance of the trailer, and since it hadn't cost too much at the time, we'd spent hours there.

We enjoyed a few rounds together, and then we went back to our sisters, who were already arguing about who was doing the best. Tolliver took Mariella and I took Gracie, and we got them away from the wall and went around with them, slowly and carefully. I couldn't stop Gracie from falling once, and another time she took me down with her, but she was improving by the time we called it quits. Mariella, who'd played basketball at one of the after-school clubs for kids, had fared a lot better, and she was inclined to brag about it until Tolliver cut her short.

We were coming off the floor, laughing, when I realized someone was watching us: a gray-haired man about five foot eleven, pumped up and muscular. My eyes passed over him once, and then came back to his face. I knew him. I looked right into his dark eyes.

"Hello, Dad," Tolliver said.

Five

OUR sisters shrunk closer to us, their eyes fixed on their biological father with—at least on Gracie's part—a mixture of loathing and longing. Mariella seemed more hostile. Her little hands had clenched into fists.

He wasn't *my* father. My feelings were relatively unmixed. "Matthew," I said. "What are you doing here?"

He'd been looking at Tolliver and Mariella, his eyes avid. He glanced at me briefly, without affection. Gracie shrunk behind me. "I wanted to see my kids," he said. "All of them."

There was a long moment of silence. I digested the fact that his voice was clear: no slurring, coherent. Maybe he wasn't using, as he'd told Mark; though I knew it was only a matter of time before he reverted to his old ways.

"But we don't want to see you," Tolliver said, keeping his voice carefully hushed. We drew aside, to get out of the way of other skaters. "We didn't answer the feelers you put out through Mark. I didn't answer your letters. I'm willing to bet Iona hasn't given you permission to see the girls, and she's their legal mom now. Hank's their legal dad."

"But I'm their real father," Matthew said.

"You gave them up," I reminded him, giving each word a lot of weight.

"There was a lot of pressure." He reached out as if he wanted to stroke Mariella's hair, but she flinched back, still gripping her brother's hand as if she would lose him if she let go.

The rink wasn't really crowded, but people had begun to cast sideways glances at our tense little group. I didn't give a damn about the spectators, but the last thing I wanted was any confrontation, physical or verbal, in front of the girls.

"You need to leave," I said. "We're taking the girls back to their home right now. You've ruined our good time. Don't make it any worse."

"I want to see my children," he said again.

"You're looking at 'em. You've seen them. Now go."

"I'm only leaving because of the little ones," he said, nodding toward Mariella and Gracie, who were confused and miserable. "I'll see you again soon, Tolliver." And he turned on his heel and left the rink.

"He followed us," I said stupidly.

"I guess he was waiting somewhere around Iona's house," Tolliver said. We stared at each other, silently postponing more discussion. Simultaneously, we took deep breaths. It would have been funny if we hadn't been so jangled.

"Well," I said to my sisters, trying to sound brisk and upbeat, "I'm glad that's over. We'll talk to your mom about this, okay, tell her all about it? It won't happen again. We had a good time until this happened, right?" I sounded like an idiot, but at least the girls began stirring, removing their skates. They stopped looking quite so much like deer in headlights.

Our sisters were subdued on the ride back to their house—no big surprise there—and they scrambled out of our car and into the door under the carport as if they were afraid of snipers. Tolliver and I followed more slowly, not eager to relate what had happened to Iona and Hank—though it was no fault of ours.

We weren't too surprised to find our aunt and uncle standing in the kitchen waiting for us.

"What happened?" Iona asked. To my astonishment, she didn't seem angry, only worried.

"My dad showed up at the rink," Tolliver said, plunging right in. "I don't know how long he was watching before we knew he was there." He shrugged. "He wasn't high; he wasn't hostile. But the girls were shaken up."

"We were having a good time until we saw him," I said, realizing that sounded weak. But it was a point I felt obliged to make.

"We got a letter from him last week," Hank said. "We didn't answer him. I never thought he'd do this."

So they were shouldering their own share of guilt, for not warning us they knew Matthew was out of jail.

Though I was reluctant to lose the advantage, I said, "He's been out of jail for a while. When we had dinner with Mark, he told us that much. But he didn't say any more than that Matthew had a job and was straight."

"Oh, Mark's in contact with his dad?" Iona frowned and sat

heavily in one of the kitchen chairs. Cautiously, we sat down, too. We were surprised that the Gorhams weren't throwing us out and blaming us for the whole incident. "That Mark, he's too tender-hearted where his dad's concerned," Iona said.

I secretly agreed. Or maybe not so secretly—Tolliver gave me a look. He could read me almost too easily.

"Could you tell what he wanted?" Iona asked me suddenly.

"What do you mean?"

"With your whatever sense?" Iona waved a hand in front of her like she was waving off a gnat.

"I'm not psychic, Iona, or I'd be glad to uncover what Matthew wants. I wish I knew myself. All I can do is find corpses." Too late, I saw Mariella over Iona's shoulder. She'd come in from the hall to the bedrooms. Her eyes were open wide. But this couldn't be too big a shock to her, right? What on earth had Iona and Hank been telling her? She spun and ran out of the kitchen.

Well, that just made the day perfect.

"Well, what is that sense telling you?" Iona was nothing if not persistent.

"Nothing helpful, right at the moment," I said. "There's not a dead person around here, if that's what you're asking. The nearest corpse is so old it probably predates statehood, and it's way under the soil of your neighbor's front yard. Indian, probably. I'd have to get closer to be sure."

I had finally shut them up. My aunt and uncle simply gaped at me. This was not moving us forward in our discussion. "But that doesn't have anything to do with Matthew showing up at the rink today," I reminded them. "Should you get a court order against him? I mean, he doesn't have any legal rights over the girls anymore, am I right?"

"That's correct," Hank said, recovering much more quickly than his wife. "We've adopted them. He gave up his rights."

"And I don't want to call the police," Iona said. "We've talked to the police enough to last us the rest of our lives."

"So you want him to show back up again? Scare the girls again?"

"No! But we had enough to do with the police when your sister was taken! We don't want them coming around here again."

I understood what it felt like to want to glide below the police radar, though most of the law-enforcement people I'd met had simply been human beings trying to do a tough job with less money than they needed. But I also understood that, aside from Iona and Hank's revulsion at the prospect of having police cars parked in front of the house again, my sisters were seriously upset. Maybe seeing the police arrive would make the girls fear they were in more danger than Matthew actually represented. After all, he had no reason to harm Mariella and Gracie. Maybe Iona and Hank were right, though for the wrong reason.

"Then there's nothing else we can do," Tolliver said, having reached the same conclusion I had. "We'll be on our way."

"How long are you going to be in town?" Iona said, sounding a little desperate. "Do you have another job to go to?"

She'd never been anxious for us to stick around before. In fact, she couldn't get us to leave fast enough, every other time we'd visited.

"We could be here a few more days," I said, after a glance at Tolliver. As a matter of fact, we didn't have anything on our schedule now, though that could change tomorrow.

"Okay," she said, nodding as if we had a bargain. "So we'll call you if he shows up again."

What were we supposed to do? I opened my mouth to protest, but Tolliver said, "All right. We'll talk to you again tomorrow, anyway."

"I'm going to talk to the school principal," Iona said. "I hate for them to talk about us, but at least the girls' teachers need to know that Matthew's around."

That was a relief. I noticed that my aunt was sitting as though she were exhausted, and that Hank was looking worried. I remembered she was pregnant. Hank caught my eye and jerked his head toward the door. I tried not to be exasperated that he thought we didn't have enough intelligence to leave when we needed to.

Tolliver said, "Talk to you tomorrow, then. 'Bye, girls!" he called down the hall. After a second, I saw the girls peeking out of Mariella's room, and I waved at them. They waved back, a little hesitantly. They were not smiling.

We got into our car in silence. I didn't know what to say.

"We've got to stay a little while, to make sure he's not bothering them," Tolliver said after we'd gone a block.

"So what's to stop him from waiting a couple of days after we leave and then showing up again?"

Tolliver shook his head as if a bee was buzzing around it. "Nothing will keep him away if he wants to follow them around. I don't know what to do."

"He can outwait us, and he will. Besides, what are we, a private army? Why are we suddenly so much protection?"

"I guess they see us as—worldly and much tougher than they are," Tolliver said, after some thought.

"Well, they're right about that. But that's not saying a whole hell of a lot, huh?"

"He's my dad. I feel like I have to do something."

"I can see that you feel that way," I said, which was as tactfully as I could put it. "And I can see you want to stay a couple more days, and that's fine with me. But we can't stay here forever, camping outside their house, waiting for your dad to approach the girls again. Unless he gets arrested again—and let's face it, he probably will be, because he'll start using again—there's nothing to do about him trying to see them, unless Iona and Hank will go to the police. Even then, the police can't watch the girls all the time."

"I know."

Tolliver's tone was abrupt. I snapped my mouth shut on any more words I might have uttered. Neither of us said anything else, all the way back to our motel.

If there's anything that makes me nervous and scattered, it's dissension with my brother. I reminded myself again to stop thinking of Tolliver as my brother, because that was just creepy, but it was a hard habit to break.

When we were in the room, I couldn't settle on an occupation. I didn't want to read, and television is a wasteland on Sunday evening unless you like sports. I couldn't focus on my crossword puzzle. I gathered up our laundry bags. "I'm going to find a Laundromat," I said and left the room. If Tolliver said anything, I was out of there too fast to hear it. We needed a break from each other.

I inquired at the motel desk, and the clerk gave me really good directions to a large and clean place about a mile away. We always keep a stock of quarters, and we carry detergent and dryer sheets in the trunk. I was good to go.

There was an attendant in the Laundromat, an older woman with crisp white hair and a comfortable body. She was sitting at a little table, reading, and she glanced up when I came in to give me a nod of acknowledgment. Since it was the weekend, the place was busy, but after a little searching I spotted two empty machines side by side. I found a plastic chair and dragged it over, and after I'd loaded the machines and gotten them started, I sat down and pulled my book out of my purse.

I could read, now that I was away from Tolliver's brooding presence. I don't know why that was so. But it was kind of nice to have bustle and people around me, and it was reassuring to have the achievement of clean clothes.

I was at peace. There weren't any bodies around. For a blissful period, I couldn't hear any buzz at all in my head.

From time to time I looked around me to make sure I wasn't in anyone's way, and I saw a woman about my own age looking at me when I raised my head when the spin cycle was almost over.

"Are you that woman?" she asked. "Are you the psychic woman who finds bodies?"

"No," I said instantly. "I've heard that before, but I work at the mall."

That's what I always said when I was in an urban area. It had always worked before. There was always a mall, and it provided a reasonable explanation for the questioner to have seen me before.

"Which mall?" the woman asked. She was pretty, even wearing her weekend sloppy clothes, and she was persistent.

"I'm sorry," I said, with an appropriate smile, "I don't know you." I shrugged, which was supposed to mean, *I'm sure you're okay, but I don't want to discuss my personal information with you anymore.*

This gal just didn't pick up on the cue. "You look just like her," she said, smiling at me as if that ought to make me happy.

"Okay," I said, and began pulling clothes out of the washers. I had already appropriated one of the rolling carts.

"If you were her, your brother would be somewhere around," the woman said. "I'd sure like to meet him; he looks hot."

"But I'm not her." I rolled my cart away with everything else thrown in it along with the wet clothes. I had to stay long enough to dry them. I couldn't leave now. If there was anything in the world I didn't want to do, it was talk to this woman about my life, my activities, and my Tolliver.

The woman watched me the rest of the time I was in the Laundromat, though she didn't approach me again, thank God. I pretended to read while our clothes tumbled, I pretended to be absorbed in folding them when they were dry, and I made up my mind that as far as I was concerned, she simply wasn't there. This technique had worked for me in the past.

By the time I was ready to load the clothes into the car, I figured I'd gotten clean away. But no—here she came, following me out into the parking lot.

"Don't talk to me again," I said, shaken and at the end of my rope.

"You are her," she said with a smug nod of her head.

"Leave me alone," I said, and got in the car and locked the door. I waited to drive away until after she'd reentered the Laundromat. I hoped that someone had stolen her clothes while she'd come out to look at me some more.

At least now I knew she couldn't follow me. But I did look into the rearview mirror a few times, just to be sure, which was how I noticed the car that actually *was* following me. It was hard to be sure, since it was dark by now, but since the area was so urban and well lighted, I was sure I was seeing the same gray Miata in my rearview mirror. I pressed the speed dial number for Tolliver.

"Hey," he said.

"Someone's following me."

"Then come straight back here. I'll go outside and wait."

So I did go straight to the motel, and he was standing in an empty spot right outside our room, to make sure it stayed empty. I parked, leaped from the car, and sped into the room while he waited outside.

After a minute, Tolliver called my name. I checked through the peephole. He wasn't alone.

"It's okay," he said, but he didn't sound happy.

So I opened the door, and he came in with his father in tow.

Crap.

Tolliver turned to face his dad, standing side by side with me.

"What do you want?" he asked Matthew. "Why'd you follow Harper here?"

"I just want to talk to you, son." Matthew glanced at me, tried to look apologetic. "Alone? This is family stuff, Harper."

He wanted me to leave my own motel room.

"Not possible," Tolliver said. He put his arm around me. "This is my family."

Matthew's eyes flicked from Tolliver to me, then back again. "I understand," he said. "Listen, I got to apologize to you. I was a terrible father. I let you down, and I let down Laurel's kids, too. And worst of all, I let down our children that we had together."

Tolliver and I stood together silently, our sides touching. I didn't even need to look up at my brother, because I knew how he felt. Matthew didn't need to tell us who he'd let down. We knew all about it.

And yet, he was obviously waiting for our reaction.

"None of this is news to us," Tolliver said.

"Laurel and I were addicted," Matthew said. "That's not an excuse for our negligence, but a . . . confession, I guess. We did bad things. I'm asking for your forgiveness."

I wondered if this was something Matthew was obliged to do as a step in some rehabilitation program. If so, he'd gone about it the wrong way entirely. Stalking his children, following me to get to Tolliver, this was not the way to express contrition.

After another moment of silence, I said, "Do you remember the night Mariella got so sick, and we tried to sneak out of the trailer to take her to the doctor, and you blocked the door and wouldn't let us leave because you didn't want the hospital to call social services? We were willing that night to be separated, if we could just get help for her."

"She got better!"

"Because we stayed up all night putting her in a cool bath and giving her baby Tylenol!"

Matthew looked blank.

"You don't remember anything about it," Tolliver said. "You don't remember the night we had to sleep under the trailer because it was full of your friends. You don't remember when Harper got hit by lightning and you wouldn't call an ambulance."

"I do remember that." Matthew looked straight at Tolliver. "You saved her life that day. You did CPR."

"And you did nothing," I said.

"I loved your mother," he said to me.

"Yeah, I'm really glad you were there for her at the end," I said. "When she died alone, and you were in another jail."

"Were you there?" he said, swift as a striking snake.

"I didn't claim to love her."

"Did you go to the funeral?"

If he thought he was heaping coals on my head, he could think again. "No. I don't go to funerals. For obvious reasons."

Matthew still didn't get it. He'd fried a few of his own brain cells over the course of the past years. He narrowed his eyes at me, asking a question.

"Presence of the dead. It's a real issue for me."

"Oh, *bullshit*. You don't have to pretend. This is me, here. I know you. You can fool other people, evidently, but not me." Matthew made a face that was meant to let me know that we were all in a big conspiracy together.

"Leave," Tolliver said.

"Oh, come on," Matthew said, incredulous. "Son, you're not claiming this corpse-finding thing is real. I mean, you can pretend in front of other people, but your sister is anything but some kind of occult witch."

"She's not my sister, at least not by blood," Tolliver said. "We're a couple."

Matthew's face reddened. He looked like he was going to throw up. "You make me sick," he said, and instantly regretted it.

Now nearly everyone we had told had had that reaction, to a greater or lesser degree. If I'd cared about how they felt, I might have been worried about our relationship just about now.

Fortunately, I didn't give a shit.

"Time to go, Matthew," I said, easing away from Tolliver. "For a reformed junkie and alcoholic, you're not very tolerant of other people's little differences." I held open the room door.

Matthew looked from me to his son, waiting for Tolliver to cancel my suggestion. Tolliver jerked his head toward the open door. "I think you better go before I get any madder than I am," he said, in a voice with no emotional weight whatsoever.

Matthew gave me a furious look as he walked by me on his way out the door.

I closed it and locked it behind him. I took a step over to Tolliver, hugged him, and looked up at his locked-down face. "You'd think somebody would be happy for us," I said, to break the silence. I didn't know what Tolliver was feeling. Was he having second thoughts?

It was now completely dark outside, and the blank window seemed like a big eye looking into the room, especially since we were on the ground floor. Tolliver gave me a little hug and stepped to the window to draw the curtains. I'd feel better when the night was blocked out and Tolliver and I were alone together.

Tolliver was standing in the center of the window, his arms extended to bring the curtains together. I was standing a little to the side and behind him, just about to sit on the bed to unlace my shoes. And then a hundred things happened in tiny layers of seconds. There was a huge noise; my face and chest stung; I was sprinkled with wetness. A gust of cold air blew across my face as Tolliver staggered backward, knocking me down on the bed. He landed on top of me and then slithered to the floor in a boneless way.

I catapulted back to my feet so fast I wobbled, aware that cold air was pouring in the window, inexplicably. I looked down at my cold chest. It was wet—not with rain, but with red spots. My T-shirt was ruined. I don't know why I cared. But I think I screamed, because I already understood on a subterranean level that Tolliver had been shot, that I was cut with glass and covered with blood, and that our world had completely changed in the space of a second.

six

I must have unlocked the door in answer to the pounding, because Matthew was in the room, and I was not being any help to Tolliver because I was standing there looking down at him, my hands held out in front of me because I'd touched my face and my hands were covered with blood. Since my hands were dirty I didn't want to touch Tolliver.

Matthew was on his knees beside his son. I pulled my phone out of my pocket and hit 911, though it required more concentration than anything I'd ever done. I gasped out the motel and its location, and I think I said we needed an ambulance immediately, and I said "sniper," because I was thinking of the word.

In a thought that went by so quickly I couldn't catch its trailing ends, I was sorry I'd mentioned a sniper because maybe the ambulance wouldn't come because the driver was scared, and then I tossed that idea overboard and joined Matthew on the carpet, facing him over Tolliver's body.

I'd been shot at through a window before, and it had been frightening. I'd had glass all over me then, too. But this was so much worse, terrible, it was the worst thing that had ever happened to me, because it had happened to Tolliver. That was all I could think of, the eeriness of such a thing happening twice, but I tried to yank myself out of the horror and I tried to help. Matthew was pulling off his shirt and folding it, and he pressed it to the bloodiest spot.

"Hold this, you idiot," he said, and I put my hands on the pad formed by the shirt. It was soaking through with blood under my fingers.

If he hadn't rushed back to the door so quickly, I would have accused him of doing this to Tolliver, but I just didn't think. It was an idea I definitely would have adopted if it had even occurred to me.

Tolliver's eyes opened. He was pale, bewildered.

"What happened?" he said. "What happened? Honey, are you okay?"

"Yes, okay," I said, pressing down with all my might. "Listen, they're coming, baby." I couldn't remember ever calling Tolliver "baby" in all the years we'd known each other. "They're coming, and they'll fix you up. You're not hurt bad, you're going to be okay."

"Was there a bomb?" he said. "Was there an explosion?" His voice faltered. "Dad, what happened? Harper's hurt."

"Don't you worry about Harper," Matthew said. "She's *fine.* She's going to be okay." He was examining Tolliver's wounds with his fingers, pulling Tolliver's shirt up to examine the skin.

Then Tolliver's eyes rolled up and his face went slack.

"Oh, *Jesus*!" I almost moved my hands, but even in the panic of the moment I knew I mustn't. I'd held on for what felt like hours. It was no time to let go.

"He's not dead," Matthew yelled. "He's not dead."

But he looked dead to me.

"No," I said. "He's not dead. He's not. He can't be. It's his right shoulder, and that's not the heart. He can't die from this." I knew what a fool I was being, but there was no shame in it right at that moment.

"No, he won't die," his father said.

I opened my mouth to scream at Matthew, though I don't know what I would have said, and then I clamped my lips together because I heard an ambulance.

There were people crowding in the door to the room, and they were talking and exclaiming, and I heard some of them shouting at the ambulance driver *Come over here, come over here,* and if I turned my head to my left, I could look out the window and see the flashing lights. More than anything else I'd ever wanted, I wanted someone who knew what the hell they were doing to come into this room and take the hell over, someone who could fix my brother and stop this bleeding.

There was more yelling outside, as the police got there right along with the ambulance and began urging everyone to move back, move back, and then the ambulance guys were there inside the room and Matthew and I had to get out of the narrow space so they could work.

The police took me outside, and I could not remember a single face after that night. "Someone shot him through the window," I said, to the first face that seemed to be asking me a question. "I was standing behind him and someone shot him through the window."

"What relation?" asked the face.

"I'm his sister," I said automatically. "This is his dad. Not my dad, but his." I don't know why I made the distinction, except I'd been making it clear to people for years that I had no kinship to Matthew Lang.

"You need to go to the hospital, too," said the face. "You need to get that glass pulled out."

"What glass?" I said. "Tolliver got shot."

"You have glass in your face," the man said. I could see now that he was a man, that he was an older man in his fifties. I could see that he had brown eyes and deep creases radiating from their corners, and a big mouth and crooked teeth. "You gotta get that pulled out and cleaned."

I needed to start wearing safety goggles if I was going to keep on getting glass in my face.

Then I was at the hospital, sitting in a cubicle, and someone had taken my wallet from my purse to get the insurance information. About a hundred people were asking me questions, but I couldn't talk. I was waiting for someone to come to tell me how Tolliver was doing, and there was no point in talking until I knew what had happened to him. The doctor who was removing the glass seemed a little scared of me. She tried to keep talking, maybe thinking I'd relax if her voice kept going.

"You need to look down while I get this piece out," she said finally, and when I looked down I could feel the tension go out of her body. I must have been staring. I was wishing that I could let go of my body and float down the hall to see what was happening to my brother. If I promised to give him up if he lived, would that help? The bargains you make when you are frightened are probably a true measure of your character. Or maybe just an accurate measure of your primitive nature, what you would be like if you'd never been to a mall or gotten a paycheck or relied on someone else to provide your food.

A woman in a pink smock asked me if there was anyone else she could call for me, anyone who would like to stay with me, and I knew I would start screaming if I saw Iona or Hank, so I said no.

They let his dad go in with him. Not me! I had to get the glass out! I was so angry I thought the top of my head was going to come off when my brain exploded. But I didn't scream. I kept it inside me. When the doctor and the nurse had finished with me, and they'd given me a couple of pills because they thought I'd have an uncomfortable time of it for a while, I nodded to them and went in search of Tolliver. I found Matthew sitting in a waiting room, talking to a policeman.

He looked at me when I came in, and I could see the caution in his face.

"This is Tolliver's stepsister. She was in the room with him, standing behind him," Matthew said, as if he were the master of ceremonies introducing the lineup.

The policeman was a detective, I guess, since he was in slacks and a shirt and a Windbreaker. He was very tall, and he looked to me like a former football star, which in fact turned out to be the case. Parker Powers had been a famous high school football player from Longview, Texas, who'd gotten injured two years into his contract with the Dallas Cowboys. That made him very nearly a star, certainly a notable. I got all that within ten minutes of meeting him, thanks to Matthew Lang.

Detective Powers was a medium shade of brown and had light blue eyes. His hair was dusty brown and curly and clipped close. He wore a wide wedding ring.

"Who do you think shot at you?" he asked me, which was more direct than I'd expected.

"I can't imagine," I said. "I would have said it was Matthew, here, if he hadn't gotten back in the room so quickly."

"Why his dad?"

"Because who else cares?" I said, realizing that wasn't the most coherent way to make my point. "Granted, some people don't like what we do, but we're honest and we don't make enemies. At least, not any that I knew of. Obviously, we made at least one." I don't know how the police made any sense of this, but presumably at some point I had explained what Tolliver and I did. I don't remember.

Detective Powers went through the whole question-and-answer routine about how we made our living, how long we'd been doing it, how much money we made, what our last case had been. I actually had to think for a minute about that, but then I remembered the Joyces' visit and I told him about it. He didn't seem too happy to discover that we were on speaking terms with a wealthy and powerful family.

A doctor came in, an older man with a fringe of hair and a worn-out face. I was on my feet in an instant.

"Mr. Lang's family?" He looked from me to Matthew. I could not speak; I was waiting. Matthew nodded.

"I'm Dr. Spradling, and I'm an orthopedic surgeon. I've just operated on Mr. Lang. Well, good news, on the whole. Mr. Lang was shot by a small-caliber bullet, probably from a .22 rifle or a handgun. It went through his clavicle, his collarbone."

I gasped. I couldn't help it. I was acting like a fool.

"So I've pinned the clavicle. There was no major damage to nerves or blood vessels from the bullet, so he was a lucky man—if you can call anyone who gets shot lucky. He made it through the surgery just fine," the doctor said. "And I think he's going to recover without many hitches. As far as what's going to happen next, he'll have to stay in the hospital for two or three days. If everything continues to go well, if no complications come up, he can be released. But he'll probably have to have IV antibiotics for a week after that. We can arrange for a visiting nurse to help with that, but you'll have to remain in the area, and I understand you don't have a residence here." He aimed his gaze more or less between us, as he waited to see what would develop.

I nodded frantically to assure him I understood. "Anything you say," I told Dr. Spradling.

"Where do you live, Miss Connelly? I understand he lives with you?"

I caught a glimpse of Matthew's face, and I thought maybe Matthew was about to try to take control of Tolliver's care. A huge fear bobbed to the top of all my other fears. Would they even let me in to see him if Matthew protested? I had to trump Matthew's fatherhood card. I opened my mouth and surprised myself by telling the doctor, totally out of the blue, "We're common-law married. What you call an informal marriage." Texas recognized an unmarried union, and I was pretty sure that was what they called it. Common-law wife might beat out stepsister. "We have an apartment in St. Louis. We've been together for six years."

The doctor couldn't have cared less. He just wanted to let me know what was going to be involved in taking care of Tolliver. He did, however, turn slightly so he was addressing me specifically. "It would be easier if you could find a place near to the hospital until he's stronger, when we release him. He's not out of the woods yet, but I really think he'll be all right."

"Okay." I ran all he'd said back through my mind, hoping I could remember it all. Broken clavicle, small-caliber bullet, no other major damage. Three days in the hospital. IV antibiotics a nurse would administer in the hotel. A closer hotel.

"They can stay with me and their brother if they need to," Matthew said, and the doctor nodded, clearly uninterested in the details. I could guarantee that wasn't going to happen, but this wasn't the time to settle it.

"As long as he can have someone responsible with him. He needs to be quiet and comfortable, get up and move around several times a day, take his meds on time, avoid alcohol, and eat good food," the doctor said. "And again, that's assuming he continues to do well. We'll know more tomorrow." Dr. Spradling wanted to be sure we were sufficiently warned.

I nodded vigorously, shaking with anxiety.

"I'll stay in his room here tonight," I said, and the doctor, who'd half turned away, made an effort to look sympathetic.

"Since he's just had surgery, he'll be checked on very frequently tonight," the doctor said. "And he won't be awake. You'd be much better off going home, cleaning up, and coming back in the morning. If you'll just leave a phone number, they'll contact you if there's any problem at all."

I looked down at myself. I had blood all over me, and it had dried. I looked . . . horrendous, and now I understood why everyone who walked by me glanced away. And I smelled like blood and fear. And I needed our car. So against my own inclinations, I asked Matthew to take me back to the motel.

The police had finished processing the ruins of our room by then. When I trudged into the lobby to talk to the woman at the front desk,

I was greeted by the manager, an African American woman in her fifties with clipped hair and a sympathetic manner. She was anxious to get me out of sight of any guests who might come in, and when we were in the little room in back of the check-in desk, she made me sit down and brought me a cup of coffee, which I didn't remember requesting. Her name tag read *Deneise.*

"Miss Connelly," she said, very earnestly and sincerely, "if you'll give your consent, I'll send Cynthia into the room to gather up your clothes and your personal items."

I wondered where this scene was leading. "All right, Deneise," I said. "That would be very helpful."

She took a deep breath and said, "We hope you'll accept our regret that this terrible incident occurred, and we want to make this time as stress free for you as we can. We know you have so many things to think about."

I finally got it. Deneise was wondering if we considered the motel to blame in the shooting, and she wanted to feel me out about my intentions. And I think she was genuinely shaken up and sorry the whole thing had happened.

After Cynthia had been dispatched to the ruined room to salvage what she could of our stuff—to my relief, Matthew offered to go with her—Deneise got down to terms. "You may not want to stay here another night, Miss Connelly, but if you do, we'd love to have you."

I felt that was less than sincere, but I also didn't blame the woman.

"If you do decide to stay, of course we'd be glad to supply you with a comparable room free of charge, to show our regret that you've been . . . inconvenienced."

I almost smiled. "That's an understatement," I said. "Yes, I'd like to have a room for the rest of the night, but I'll be checking out first thing in the morning. I have to find something closer to the hospital."

"How is Mr. Lang doing?" Deneise asked, and I told her he was going to be all right.

"Oh, that's good news!" She seemed relieved on several different levels, and I didn't blame her a bit.

Now that the motel situation was settled, I was anxious to get into a room and get clean. The manager called Cynthia on her cell phone and told her to take our luggage directly to room 203.

"I thought you might feel better if you weren't on the ground level," she explained as she hung up.

"You're right," I said. I thought of the black hole of the window, and I shuddered. My face and shoulders were hurting, I was covered with dried dots and smears of blood, and suddenly I began shivering, now that I had the luxury of time for myself. Now that I thought Tolliver would be all right.

Matthew appeared in the office doorway. "Your stuff's in your new room, and I don't think anything is missing. Everything seems to be in your purse."

I didn't like the idea of Matthew having access to my purse, but he had been a real help tonight, and I had to give the devil his due. I told Deneise I was grateful she'd been so thoughtful, and with my new key card in hand, I went out to the lobby with Matthew to get in the elevator.

"Thanks," I said, as it rumbled up to the open area with snack machines and the ice maker. A couple coming up the stairs glanced at us curiously, and when they'd absorbed my bloody state, they hurried away to their room.

"That's okay," Matthew said. "I heard the shot, and I heard you scream. I ran across that parking lot pretty damn fast." He laughed.

I hadn't even realized I'd screamed.

"You didn't see anyone in the parking lot?"

"Nope. And it makes me nuts, because the shooter had to have been really close to me."

I stowed that idea away to think over later. "Well, I guess I'll see you at the hospital tomorrow, if you can get off work," I said. Abruptly, I wanted to be alone more than anything.

"You want me to call Iona?" Matthew asked.

When I said, "No!" he laughed, a choky sort of laugh that made him sound like Tolliver for a moment.

"You don't mind me saying so, you're pretty dependent on my son," Matthew said, chiming in with my thoughts so neatly that I was instantly angry.

"Your son is my lover and my family," I said. "We've been together for years. While you were gone."

"But you need to be able to function on your own," Matthew said in the righteous tone of someone who's had counseling; and because he was trying to sound gentle, I was even angrier. I may not be your garden-variety person, but I am not as fragile as I seem. Or maybe I am, but that wasn't any of Matthew Lang's business.

"I don't believe you have the right to tell me how I ought to live, how I ought to be," I said. "You have no rights over me. You never did. You never will. I appreciate your help tonight. I'm glad you finally did something for your son, though it took him getting shot for you to do it. You need to go now, because I have to shower." I used the key card, and the door to the new room swung open. The lights were on, and the room was warm. Our suitcases sat on the floor beside the bed.

Matthew nodded to me and walked away without saying one other word, which was a very good thing. I looked at Tolliver's suitcase and began to cry, but I made myself go into the bathroom and shed my blood-speckled clothes. I took a very careful bath, mindful of my scores of cuts and nicks. I put on my pajamas.

I called the hospital again, and found Tolliver was still the same. I reminded them again to call me instantly if there was any change. I put the phone on the charger, and lay in bed, and listened for it to ring.

But it didn't. All night.

THE next morning as I went through a McDonald's drive-through, I realized I had to call Iona to tell her what had happened. Otherwise, she might read it in the papers. I didn't expect anything from her, and it was a strange feeling to realize that there was someone I should report to; Tolliver and I are used to being on our own. If we hadn't been in the same urban area, I would never have considered calling Iona about Tolliver's injury. I got to the hospital early, looked into his room to find Tolliver sleeping, and returned to the lobby to use my cell phone. The reception in the lobby wasn't good, so I stepped outside with the smokers. It was a cold, clear day, with a brilliant blue sky.

I checked my watch, felt there was a chance Iona hadn't left for work yet, and called the house. Iona wasn't best pleased to hear from me early in the morning, and she let me know it.

"Tolliver got shot last night," I said, and she was silent.

"Is he all right?" she asked, even now sounding grudging.

"Yes, he's going to make it," I said. "He's in a regular room at God's Mercy Hospital. He had some surgery on his shoulder. He'll be in the hospital for a couple more days, the doctor thinks."

"Well, I don't believe I need to tell the girls right now," Iona said. "Besides, Hank's already taken 'em to school. We'll talk about it when they come home today."

"Suit yourself," I said. "I've got to call Mark." I clicked the phone shut, angry and disappointed. It wasn't that I wanted my little sisters upset and worried, especially after the skating rink incident yesterday—it was that I knew my interaction with them would always be ruled and regulated by the troll squatting across the drawbridge that led to them. I was being pretty ungrateful to Iona with that comparison. I should be glad *every day* that she and Hank had had the nerve and grace to undertake the raising of two girls from such a damaging background.

But going through her was such an uphill battle.

For the first time, I thought Tolliver might be right. Maybe we should just butt out of our sisters' lives and send them Christmas presents and cards on their birthdays.

Then Mark answered his phone in a drowsy voice, and I had to chuck aside these bad thoughts and deal with the here and now. Mark had worked late the night before so he wasn't too coherent, but I made sure he got the gist of the story and knew the name of the hospital. He promised he'd come by when he could, probably later in the morning.

Then I had nothing else to do but return to the dreary room and watch Tolliver sleep. Of course I had a book in my purse, and I tried to read for a while, but I kept losing track of the narrative. Finally, I put the book away and simply looked at Tolliver.

Tolliver is seldom sick, and he'd never been hurt this seriously. The bandages and the IV and the gray tone of his skin made him seem almost a stranger, as if someone had crept in and usurped his body. I sat staring at him, willing him to sit up, willing the vigor to return to his body.

That worked as well as you'd expect.

I knew I had to be the strong one now. With my brother down, I had to take care of him, of us. It was good that we'd planned on spending a few days in Texas, because I knew we didn't have any other jobs booked that I should be rescheduling. However, I'd have to check the laptop for new messages. I'd have to take care of *everything.* I immediately began to worry that I wouldn't do a good job of it, that I'd forget something critical. But what could I forget that would matter so very much? As long as we didn't miss an engagement, as long as I kept gas in the car so we didn't run out, I would be doing a good job.

Finally, Dr. Spradling came in. Tolliver had been moving around a little, so I knew he was about to wake up. Dr. Spradling looked even more tired and old today. He gave me a glance and a nod before approaching Tolliver's bed. He said, "Mr. Lang?" in a penetrating voice. Tolliver's eyes flew open. He looked past the doctor, right at me, and relief relaxed the lines of his mouth.

"You okay, baby?" he said, trying to hold out a hand to me.

I stepped past the doctor, circled the bed to the other side. I took his left hand in both my own.

"How are you?" I asked.

Dr. Spradling was looking into Tolliver's eyes, reading his chart, and listening to our conversation.

"My shoulder hurts. What happened to you?" he asked. "The

window exploded. Someone throw a brick in? You have cuts on your face."

"Tolliver, you got shot," I said. I couldn't think of a tactful way to ease into the subject. "I only got hit by some of the glass from the window. It's nothing. You're going to be okay."

Tolliver looked confused. "I don't remember," he said. "I got shot?"

"His memory will clear up," Dr. Spradling said. I looked at him, blinking so I wouldn't cry.

"This is not uncommon," he told me, and I appreciated his trying to reassure us. "Mr. Lang, I'm going to look at your wound." A nurse came in, and the next few minutes were really unpleasant. Tolliver looked exhausted by the time he was rebandaged.

"Everything looks fine," Dr. Spradling said briskly. "Mr. Lang, you're coming along just like I'd hoped."

"I feel so bad," Tolliver said, not quite complaining, but as though he were worried.

"Being shot is a serious thing," Dr. Spradling said, glancing at me with a slight smile. "It's not like on television, Mr. Lang, when people hop right out of their hospital beds and go chase thieves."

I don't think Tolliver followed all that, because he was looking at the doctor with an uncertain expression. Spradling turned to me. "I expect he'll be here tomorrow, and we'll see the next day. He may have to have some physical therapy on that shoulder."

"But he'll have full use of his arm?" I said, suddenly realizing I hadn't even begun to worry as much as I had reason to.

"If everything continues to go well, that's probable."

"Oh," I said, flattened by the lack of certainty. "What can I do?"

Dr. Spradling looked as though he were as much at a loss as

Tolliver. The doctor clearly didn't think there would be much I could do for Tolliver except pay his bill. "It's up to him," Dr. Spradling said. "Your partner."

I don't think I would have liked any doctor that day, since a doctor couldn't give me a clear-cut answer. My mind knew Dr. Spradling was being logical and realistic, and my mind also told me I should appreciate that. But my mind was taking a backseat to my emotions.

I managed to keep myself under control, and Dr. Spradling departed with a cheery wave. Tolliver still looked a little confused, but he drifted back into a doze. His eyelids flickered when there was a sound in the hall, but they never quite opened. I couldn't figure out what to do next. I was standing by the bed, looking down at Tolliver and trying to make a plan, any plan, when Victoria Flores came in after a quick knock on the door.

Victoria was in her late thirties. A former police officer on the Texarkana force, she was both full figured and beautiful. I'd never seen Victoria wearing anything but a suit and heels. She had her own personal dress code. Victoria's dark, coarse hair was smoothed into a shoulder-length pageboy, and heavy gold earrings gave her some bling. Today the suit was a dull red, worn over a cream-colored blouse.

"How is he?" she said, nodding toward the silent figure on the bed. No hug, no handshake, no preliminaries. Victoria went straight to business.

"He's hurt pretty bad," I said. "He has a broken bone." I tapped my own collarbone by way of illustration. "But the doctor who was just in here, he said Tolliver would be okay if he did physical therapy. If nothing changes."

Victoria snorted. "So, what happened?"

I told her.

"What was your last case?" she asked me.

"The Joyces were."

"I'm meeting with them later this morning."

I didn't describe the reading I'd gotten at the cemetery, because the Joyces hadn't given me permission, but I did give Victoria an outline of the time we'd spent with them. And she knew they'd visited us at the motel.

"That has to be the most likely cause of the shooting," Victoria said. "What about the case before this one?"

"You remember the serial killer, the boys killed in North Carolina? All buried in the same place?"

"That was you—you found them?"

"Yeah. That was awful. Also, we did get a lot of publicity, most of it the wrong kind." I'd found that quiet word of mouth was better for getting actual paying jobs. Publicity might prompt a flare of interest, but that interest was mostly from people who wanted to explore the unexplained and lurid, not people who wanted to pay a lot of money to have it displayed in their neighborhood.

"So this shooting incident might be a fallout of the North Carolina case?"

"Now that I've said it out loud, that doesn't sound very likely." Tolliver needed a shave. I should do that, and then I had to comb his hair. I couldn't think of anything else I could do to help him.

He looked so helpless. He *was* so helpless. I was the only defense he had. I had to man up.

"The North Carolina murders really, really upset a lot of people," Victoria said, her voice thoughtful. She clearly believed Tolliver's shooting must be related to the only case of mass murder we'd ever discovered.

"But the bad guys got caught. Why would anyone want to shoot us because we helped to catch who did it?"

"You sure there weren't any more in on it? The two men were the only killers?"

"I'm sure, and what's more, the police are sure. Believe me, that was one thorough investigation. They haven't gone to trial yet, but the prosecutor's pretty damn sure they're going to get a conviction."

"Okay." Victoria looked down at Tolliver for a few seconds. "Then either you've got a stalker or it's something to do with the Joyces." She paused for a moment. "There hasn't been anything new about your sister for a long time. I am assuming the trail's too cold for Cameron's abduction to have any relation to what's happening to you now."

I nodded. "I agree. I think the Joyce case is the most likely. If they okay me talking to you, I'll be glad to tell you all about it. There's really not much to tell."

Victoria whipped out her cell phone and made a call, which I was pretty sure you weren't supposed to do in a hospital. She started talking. A few seconds later, she handed the phone to me.

"Hello," I said.

"This is Lizzie Joyce."

"Hi. Did you want me to talk to Victoria?"

"That's real ethical of you. You have my permission." Did she sound *amused*? I didn't think my morality was funny at all. "I'm sorry about your manager," Lizzie continued. "I understand it happened at that same motel where we visited you. My God! What do you think happened? Was it just a random shooting?"

A memory surfaced. "One of the cops did tell me there was another shooting a couple of blocks away. So it's possible. But that's pretty hard to believe."

"Well, I'm real sorry. If there's anything I can do, you just let me know."

I wondered how sincere the offer was. For one wild minute, I considered saying, "This hospital stay is going to be really expensive, because our insurance is shitty. Can you take care of the bill? Oh, and pick up the tab for his rehab, too, while you're at it?" But I simply thanked her and handed the phone back to Victoria.

I'd been too preoccupied to think about the financial crunch we were going to face until that moment. I thought unhappy thoughts, while Victoria Flores wound up her conversation with Lizzie Joyce. For the first time, I saw the full scope of the problem in front of me. I realized Tolliver's injury meant the end of our dream of buying a house, at least in the foreseeable future.

It was possible for me to be more depressed, which I would not have believed ten minutes earlier.

I told Victoria about the visit to Pioneer Rest Cemetery. She asked me a lot of questions I couldn't answer, but finally she seemed satisfied that she'd wrung every last bit of knowledge and conjecture out of me.

"I hope I can perform like they want me to," she said, having her own down moment. "I can't believe they came to me instead of some big agency, but now that I know the details, I can see why they called someone like me."

"It's been hard, the move to this area?" I asked.

"Yeah, there's a lot more business, but a lot more competition," Victoria said. "It's good to be close to my mother; she helps with my daughter. And the school MariCarmen's in here is better than the one in Texarkana. Plus, the driving distance isn't bad, and I still have business and a lot of contacts back there. It just takes me two and a half, three hours, depending on traffic and weather."

"We're never going to find Cameron, are we?" I said.

Victoria's mouth opened, as if she was going to tell me something. Then she closed it. "I wouldn't say that. You never know when a lead will pop up. I wouldn't string you along. You know that's true."

I nodded.

"It's always in the back of my mind," Victoria said. "All those years ago, when I came by your trailer and talked to Tolliver . . . I was just a rookie cop. I thought I could find her quick, and make a name for myself. That didn't happen. But now that I'm out on my own, I still look for her, everywhere I go."

I closed my eyes. I did, too.

seven

AFTER Victoria left, I sat down on the chair next to the hospital bed. My right leg felt wobbly. It's the leg the lightning traveled down that afternoon in the trailer when the thunder was rumbling outside. I'd been getting ready for a date; it was a Saturday, or a Friday. I discovered I no longer remembered all the circumstances, which was a real shock.

I did recall I'd been looking in the bathroom mirror while I used a hair curling rod, which was plugged into the socket by the sink. The lightning came in through the open bathroom window. The next thing I knew, I was flat on my back, half in and half out of the little room, and Tolliver was performing CPR, and the EMTs were taking over, and Matthew was yelling at them in the background. Mark was trying to shut him up.

My mom was passed out in their bedroom. I could see her sprawled across the bed if I turned my head to the left. One of the babies was screaming, probably Mariella. Cameron was standing pressed to the wall in the hall, her face soaked with tears and her expression distraught. There was a strange smell in the air. The hairs on my right arm were little crispy flakes. Nothing about me seemed to work.

"Your brother saved your life," the older man bending over me said. His voice sounded far away and it buzzed.

I tried to respond, but my mouth wouldn't work. I managed a tiny nod.

"Thank you, Jesus," Cameron said, the words almost incoherent because she was so choked up.

That scene in the trailer seemed more real to me than this Dallas hospital room. I could picture Cameron so clearly: long straight blond hair, brown eyes like Dad's. We didn't look that much alike, even a quick glance would tell you that; our faces were different shapes and so were our eyes. Cameron had freckles across her nose, and she was shorter, and her build was more compact than mine. Cameron and I both made good grades, but she was more popular. She worked at it.

I think Cameron would have managed much better if she hadn't been able to clearly remember the nice house in Memphis where we'd grown up, before our mom and dad had gone to hell. That memory also made her struggle to keep us up to a standard she held in her head. It made her crazy if we didn't look neat, clean, and prosperous. It made her nuts if anyone even suspected what our home life was like. Sometimes that frantic desire to keep up appearances at school made Cameron a little hard to reason with. To live with, truth be told. But she was absolutely loyal to her siblings, both step and full. She was determined to raise Mariella and Gracie as she deemed fit according to her shadowy memories of our respectable past. Cameron worked constantly to keep the trailer looking clean and orderly, and I was her deputy in that struggle.

Seeing Victoria had raised a lot of ghosts. While Tolliver slept, I remembered the years I'd expected to see my sister everywhere we went. I'd imagined that I'd turn around in a store, and she'd be the clerk who was waiting to ring up my purchases. Or she'd be the prostitute we passed on the street corner at night. Or she'd be the young matron pushing a stroller, the one with the long blond hair.

She hadn't been.

Once I'd even asked someone if she was named Cameron, because I was suddenly convinced that the young woman was my sister, a little aged and worn. I'd frightened her. I'd had to walk away quickly, because I'd known she would call the police if I said one more word.

In all those fantasies, I'd never once explained to myself how Cameron had gotten launched in this second life of hers, or why she hadn't called me or written me in all those years.

At first, I'd been convinced my sister had been abducted by a gang or sold into slavery, something violent and horrible. Later it had occurred to me that maybe she'd simply been fed up with her life: the tawdry parents and the tacky trailer, the sister who limped and looked abstracted, the baby sisters who never seemed to stay clean.

Most days, though, I was sure Cameron was dead.

I was yanked out of my unhappy reverie by the sudden appearance of one of the detectives from the night before. He came into the hospital room very quietly and stood looking down at my brother. Then he said, "How are you today, Miss Connelly?" in a voice that barely moved the air in the room, it was so hushed and even.

I stood up, because he made me nervous, with his silent entrance and hushed voice. He wasn't especially tall, maybe five foot nine, and he was thickset and had a heavy mustache flecked with gray. He wasn't anything like his partner, Parker Powers. This detective looked like a million other men. I tried to remember his name. Rudy something. Rudy Flemmons.

"I'm fine compared to my brother," I said, nodding down at the figure on the bed. "Have you got any ideas about who did this to him?"

"We found some cigarette butts in the parking lot, but they could have come from anyone. However, we bagged them just in case we ever get someone to compare the DNA to. Assuming the lab guys can get DNA." We did some more looking at the patient. Tolliver opened his eyes, smiled at me very slightly, and went back to sleep.

"Do you think they were really shooting at him?" the detective asked.

"They hit him," I said, a little confused at the question. Of *course* the shooter had been aiming at Tolliver.

"You think they might have been shooting at you?" Rudy Flemmons asked.

"Why?" That sounded stupid the minute it was out of my lips. "I mean, why shoot at me? You're saying you think the bullet hitting Tolliver was an accident, that it should have been me?"

"It *might* have been you," Flemmons said, "not *should* have been you."

"You're basing that on . . . what?"

"You're the dominant one in your little group of two," Flemmons said. "And your brother is strictly your support staff. You're the talent of the outfit. The chances are much higher of someone taking issue with you, rather than with Mr. Lang, here. I understand he doesn't have a girlfriend?"

This was the strangest policeman I'd ever talked to.

I sighed. Here it came again. "He does," I said.

"Who is she?" He'd even gotten out his little notebook.

"Me." Flemmons looked up, his eyes quizzical.

"Come again?" he said.

"He's not my brother by blood, you know." I was very tired of explaining our relationship.

"Right, you don't share parents," he said. He'd been doing his research.

"No, we don't. We're partners, in every sense of the word."

"Okeydokey. I got an interesting phone call this morning," Flemmons said, throwing the line away. I immediately became more alert.

"Yes? From whom?"

"From a detective on the Texarkana police force. Name of Peter Gresham. He's a friend of mine."

"What did he tell you?" I said and sighed. I really didn't want to hear yet another rehashing of my sister's disappearance. It had already been a "grieved about Cameron" day.

"He said there'd been a phone call about your sister."

"What kind of phone call?" There are more crackpots in the world than you can shake a stick at.

"Someone spotted her at the Texarkana mall."

I stopped breathing for a second. Then the air surged into my lungs in a choked gasp. "Cameron? Who saw her? Someone who used to know her?"

"It was an anonymous call. A male, calling from a pay phone."

"Oh," I said, feeling as though someone had punched me in the stomach. "But . . . how can I find out if that's true? Get that person to come forward? Is there any way?"

"You remember Pete Gresham? He was the primary on your sister's case."

I nodded. I did recall him, but not with much clarity. When I looked back on the bad, bad days immediately following Cameron's vanishing, they seemed like one big blur of anxiety to me. "He was a big guy," I said. I added, less certainly, "Wears cowboy boots all the time? He was losing his hair. He was young to be balding."

"Yeah, that's him. Pete's bald now. I think he shaves the little he has left in the hair department."

"So what did he do? About the phone call?"

"He viewed the security tapes."

"They tape inside the mall?"

"Some, and they tape the parking lot pretty good, Pete said."

"Was she there?" I thought I would scream if he didn't tell me.

"There was a woman who fits your sister's general description. But there's no clear shot of her face, and there's no real way to know whether or not it's Cameron Connelly."

"Can I see it?"

"I'll see if that can be arranged. Ordinarily, I guess, you'd want to drive over to Texarkana yourself, but with Mr. Lang here, and liable to stay in the hospital for a couple more days, maybe we can let you see them at our office."

"That would sure be wonderful if you can swing it," I said. "The round trip would be a long time to be away from him." I was trying to force myself to be calm.

Before I could stop myself, I bent over Tolliver and took hold of his hand. It was cold, and I told myself I'd have to ask the nurse for another blanket. "Hey, you," I said. "Did you hear the detective?"

"A little," Tolliver said. It was more of a mumble, but I could understand him.

"He's going to try to get the mall tapes here for me to see," I said. "Maybe we'll finally get a lead." It seemed incredible that Victoria and I had been discussing this very thing not an hour previously.

"Don't get your hopes up," Tolliver said, in a clearer voice. "This has happened before."

I didn't want to consider all the previous false sightings. "I understand," I said. "But maybe this time will be the charm, huh?"

"She wouldn't be the same," Tolliver said, his eyes fully open. "You know that, right? She wouldn't be the same."

I calmed down in a hurry. "Yes, I know," I told him. She would never be the same. Too many years had passed. Too much pain had been felt, too much . . . everything.

"If you need to go to Texarkana . . ." Tolliver began.

"I'm not leaving you," I said immediately.

"If you need to go, you go," he said.

"I appreciate that," I said. "But I'm not going while you're here in the hospital." I couldn't believe I said it, even as I listened to my own words. For years I'd been waiting to hear news of my sister. Now there was actually a lead, however odd and unreliable it sounded—and I was telling Tolliver I wasn't going to chase it down immediately.

I sat down in the chair by the bed. I laid my forehead against the cotton blanket that covered my brother. I'd never felt more committed.

Detective Flemmons had listened to our discussion with a blank face. He seemed to be reserving judgment on us, and I appreciated that, too.

He said, "I'll give you a call when we're ready."

"Thank you," I said, feeling a little numb.

When the detective was gone, Tolliver said, "It's only fair."

"What?"

"You got shot for me. Now I got shot for you, if he's right. You think the shooter was aiming for you?"

"Huh," I said. "The difference is, when I got shot, she almost missed me. I mean, it was just a graze. Whoever shot you did a better job."

"So," he said, "I get shot by more efficient people."

"I think that pain medication must be pretty damn good."

"The best," he said dreamily.

I smiled. It wasn't often Tolliver was so relaxed. I didn't want to think about Cameron anymore, because I didn't know what I wished for.

His dad knocked on the door of the room and stepped in before we could say yes or no. Our peaceful moment was shot all to hell.

Matthew was looking a little ragged, not too surprising considering how late we'd been up the night before; and he'd told me he'd had the morning shift at McDonald's. Clearly he'd taken the time to shower after he'd been at work, because he didn't have the distinctive McDonald's smell.

"Tolliver, your dad helped me while we called for an ambulance," I said, because I had to give the devil his due. "And he came to the hospital until they said you were out of danger."

"You sure he didn't shoot me, too?"

If I hadn't lived with Matthew Lang for several years, I would have been shocked through and through.

Matthew himself gave a good impression of a man hurt to the core. "Son, how can you believe that?" he asked, simultaneously wounded and angry. "I know I wasn't the best dad . . ."

"Not the best dad? You remember the time you held a gun to Cameron's head and told me you would blow her brains out if I didn't tell you where I'd hidden your stash?"

Matthew's shoulders slumped. I think he'd managed to forget that little incident.

"And then you ask me how I can believe you'd shoot me." If Tolliver's voice hadn't been so weak, it would have been hot with sheer rage; as it was, Tolliver's words sounded so sad I could have wept for him. "It's real easy to believe, *Dad*."

"But I wouldn't have done it," Matthew Lang said. "I loved that girl. I loved all of you. I was just a damn junkie, Tolliver. I was a mess, and I know it. I'm asking for your forgiveness, now that I'm clean and sober. I won't screw up again, son."

"It'll take a lot more than words to persuade us," I said, looking at Tolliver and seeing how exhausted he was after five minutes in his father's presence. "As long as we're bringing up happy memories, I can sure dredge up a few we haven't reminisced about in a while. You were there last night . . . okay. That was good. But it wasn't a drop in the bucket."

Matthew looked sad. His brown eyes were like a spaniel's, innocent and liquid with soft feelings.

I didn't believe he'd reformed for a second. And yet, I have to admit, I wanted to believe him. If Tolliver's father could really reform, really try to love Tolliver as he deserved to be loved, respect him as he deserved to be respected, it would be a wonderful thing.

The next second, I cursed myself for being pathetic, for being sucked in to even that extent. Since Tolliver was hurt and weak, I had to be extra vigilant. I was watching out for both of us, not just myself.

"Harper, I know I deserve that," Matthew said. "I know it'll take a long time to convince you both that I'm really sorry. I know I fucked up, over and over again. I know I didn't act like a real father. I didn't even act like a responsible adult."

I looked down at Tolliver to gauge his reaction. All I saw was a young man who'd been shot in the shoulder hours before, a man exhausted by the demands his father was bringing into the room.

"Tolliver doesn't need all this drama now," I said. "We shouldn't have gotten into this discussion. Thanks for your help last night. You should leave now."

To his credit, Matthew said goodbye to Tolliver and turned and walked out of the room.

"Okay, that's over with," I said, to fill the sudden silence. I'd taken Tolliver's hand, and he squeezed it, but he didn't open his eyes. I didn't know if he was truly asleep, but he needed to act like he was, so that was all right with me. Our stream of visitors seemed to have died out, and we had a few hours of that hospital boredom that I'd anticipated. It was almost a relief to be bored. We watched old movies, and I read a few pages. No one called. No one came to visit.

By the time five o'clock made its appearance on the big clock in his room, Tolliver insisted I needed to leave and check into a hotel, get some rest. After talking to his nurse, I finally agreed. I was almost walking in my sleep, and I wanted to shower again. All the little cuts on my face were sore and itchy.

I was extra careful with my driving as I stopped at a couple of hotels. I checked into one that had a room that was clean and ready and on the third floor. I hauled my bag in and slogged through the lobby and into the elevator, feeling an intense longing for a good bed. I was hungry, too, but the bed was the central item in my little daydream. My cell phone rang. I answered it because I thought it might be the hospital.

Detective Rudy Flemmons said, "You sound like you're just about asleep on your feet."

"Yes."

"We'll have those tapes tomorrow morning. You want to come by the station to watch them?"

"Sure."

"Okay, then. See you there at nine o'clock, if that suits you."

"Okay. What's happening with the investigation?"

"We're still canvassing the neighborhood to see if anyone saw anything last night when your brother was shot. The other shooting was on Goodman Street, and it was a case of a falling-out between thieves. It's possible the shooter in that incident was so jacked up after he took care of his buddy that he decided to take a shot at a good target as he drove by the motel. We think we found the spot where the shooter stood."

"That's good," I said, unable to drum up more of a reaction. The elevator opened its doors on my floor, and I stepped off and went down the hall to my new room. "Is that all you need to tell me?" I used the plastic card in the lock.

"I think so," the detective said. "Where are you now?"

"I just checked into a Holiday Inn Express," I said.

"The one on Chisholm?"

"Yeah. Close to the hospital."

"I'll talk to you later," Rudy Flemmons said, and I recognized the tone of his voice.

Detective Flemmons was a Believer.

People who meet me in my line of work fall into three categories: those who wouldn't believe me if I produced an affidavit signed by God, those who are open to the idea that there are strange things in this world that they might encounter (the "Hamlet" people, I call them), and the people who absolutely believe I can do what I do—and furthermore, they *love* that connection I have with the dead.

Believers are likely to watch *Ghost Hunters*, go to séances, and employ psychics like our deceased colleague Xylda Bernardo. If they aren't willing to go quite that far, they're at least open to new experiences. There are not many law enforcement people in the Believer category, not too surprisingly, since law enforcement professionals meet liars every single day.

I'm like catnip to Believers. I'm convincing, because I'm the real deal.

I knew that from now on, Detective Rudy Flemmons would show up more and more often. I was living confirmation of everything he'd ever secretly believed.

And all because I'd gotten struck by lightning.

I wanted to get in the shower, but I pulled off my shoes and lay down on the bed. I called Tolliver to tell him that I had to go by the police department in the morning, and that I'd come by God's Mercy afterward to tell him all about it. He sounded as drowsy as I felt, and instead of getting in the shower after I put my phone on the charger, I shucked off my pants and slid between the sheets.

eight

I woke up with a jerk. I lay there for a few seconds, trying to pin down the reason I was so unhappy, and then I remembered that Tolliver was in the hospital. I relived the moment he'd been shot with gruesome clarity.

Since I'd been shot through a window before, I had to wonder what it was with us and windows. If we stayed away from buildings, would we be okay? Though Tolliver had been a Boy Scout and had camped out with them, I didn't remember his particularly enjoying the camping experience, and I knew I wouldn't.

It was four thirty in the morning. I'd slept through the dinner hour and the whole night. Not amazingly, now I was wide awake. I piled up the pillows behind me and turned on the television, keeping the sound very low. Watching the news was out of the question: it's always bad, and I didn't need to witness any more bloodshed and cruelty. I found an old Western. It was phenomenally soothing to watch the good guys win, to see the hardened dance-hall floozies reveal their hearts of gold, and to observe that once upon a time, when people got shot and collapsed to the ground, they didn't bleed. This was a much better world than the one I lived in, and I enjoyed visiting it, especially in the wee hours of the morning.

After an hour, I must have fallen back to sleep, because I woke up again at seven o'clock, and the TV was still on. The remote was clutched loosely in my hand.

When I was showered and dressed and groomed, I went down to the complimentary breakfast buffet. If I didn't eat more regularly, I'd collapse. I had a big bowl of oatmeal and some fruit, and then two cups of coffee. I returned to the room to brush my teeth. Foundation was out of the question since my face was so cut up, but I did manage a little eye shadow and mascara. I made a wry face as I looked at the result in the bathroom mirror. I knew I looked like something the cat dragged in. I might as well give up on trying to improve my appearance.

It was time to go to the police station to watch the videos from the Texarkana mall. My stomach fluttered uneasily with suspense. I'd done my best not to think about the Cameron sighting, but I noticed my hands were shaking as I took my vitamins. I'd called the nurses' station to ask about Tolliver, and the nurse said he'd slept most of the night, so I felt all right about putting off a hospital visit until later.

The rest and food had really helped, and I felt much more like myself, despite my apprehension. The city police department was housed in a one-story edifice that looked like it had started out modest and taken steroids. It had obviously been added onto, and just as obviously it was bursting at the seams. I had a hard time finding a parking spot, and just when I got out of the car, rain came down.

At first it was a light sprinkle, but as I hesitated about getting out the umbrella, the downpour started. I whipped out the umbrella and unfolded it in record time, so I wasn't too wet when I got to the lobby.

One way or another, I've spent a lot of time in police stations. New or old, there's a sameness about them; they're just like schools and hospitals, in that respect.

There wasn't a good place to stow my dripping umbrella, so I had to carry it with me. It sprinkled raindrops all over the floor, and I knew the janitor would have a lot to do today. The Latina behind the counter was thin and muscular and all business. She used an intercom to call Detective Flemmons, and I didn't have to wait more than a couple of minutes until he appeared.

"Good morning, Miss Connelly," he said. "Come on back." He led the way into a warren of cubicles created by chest-high partitions, the kind with carpeting on them. As we went past, I noticed that each cubicle had been decorated to suit the person who used it. All the computers were dirty: smudged with fingerprints, their screens so dusty you had to peer at them to read the type. A hum of conversation hung over the bullpen like a cloud of smog.

This was not a happy place. Even though law enforcement people usually thought I was a fraud and a con, which meant that often I didn't get along with them individually, in the abstract I thought it was wonderful that anyone would choose to do this job. "You have to listen to people lie all the time," I said, following this line of thought. "How do you stand it?"

Rudy Flemmons turned to look back at me. "It's part of the work," he said. "Someone's gotta stand between regular people and bad ones."

I noticed that the detective didn't say "good" people. If I'd been a cop as long as Flemmons had, I wondered if anyone would seem truly good to me, either.

There was a sort of conference room at the end of the cubicles, with a long table surrounded by battered chairs. Video equipment was set up at one end. Flemmons darkened the lighting after I sat down, then he pressed a button.

I was so tense I felt like the room was humming. I stared at the screen, afraid I would miss something.

In the next minute, I was watching a woman who seemed to be in her late twenties or early thirties walk across a parking lot. Her face was not clearly visible. She was partially turned away. She had long blond hair. She was short. Her build was compact. I put my hand over my mouth so I wouldn't speak until I was sure about what I was going to say.

The scene shifted abruptly to a shot of the same woman walking inside the mall. She was carrying a shopping bag from Buckle. This clip was taken from the front, directly facing the woman. Though the film was grainy and she wasn't on it very long, I closed my eyes and felt my stomach plummet.

"It's not her," I said. "That's not my sister." I thought I would cry—my eyes got that hot feeling—but I didn't. But the shock of the anticipation and my subsequent disappointment (or relief) was immense.

"You're sure?"

"Not completely." I shrugged. "How could I be, unless I saw her face-to-face? It's been eight years or more since I saw my sister. But I can tell that this woman's face is rounder, and the way she walks is not the way Cameron walked."

"Let's watch again, to be completely sure," Flemmons said in a very neutral voice. I sat up straighter and watched again. This time it was possible to take more notice of the little things.

The woman in the parking lot film was toting a huge purse that I didn't think my sister would ever choose. Granted, people's tastes changed as they grew up and grew older, but I didn't think Cameron's choice of purses would be that drastically different. The shopping woman wore high heels with her dress slacks, and Cameron disdained heels for everyday wear. She could have changed her style in shoes as well as purses, though. I wasn't wearing the same accessories I'd had in high school. But the shape of the woman's face, and the way the woman in the film moved along at a fast clip with her shoulders hunched a little forward . . . no, I was sure this woman wasn't Cameron.

"Definitely not," I said, after the second viewing. I was a lot calmer now. The shock was over, and the reality of another dashed hope had settled in.

Rudy Flemmons looked down for a minute, and I wondered what expression he was concealing. "All right," he said quietly. "All right. I'll tell Pete Gresham. By the way, he asked me to tell you hello."

I nodded. Now that I'd seen this film clip, and I knew the woman in it wasn't my sister, I was very curious about the man who'd called it in.

I tried to ask some questions, but Detective Flemmons wasn't spilling any beans. "I'll let you know if more information comes in," he said, and I had to be dissatisfied with that.

I redeployed my umbrella and dashed back to the car, feeling the phone in my pocket vibrate as I shook the umbrella off and got into the driver's seat. I tossed the umbrella into the rear, slammed the door, and opened the phone.

"Mariah Parish did have a baby," Victoria Flores said.

"Should you be telling me that?"

"I've already talked to Lizzie Joyce. I'm tracking down the kid now. Since Lizzie hired me, I've spent hours on the computer, and I've gotten out and done some legwork. This whole thing is weird, I'm telling you. Since she said you could talk to me, I take that to mean I can talk to you, too." Victoria, who'd always seemed so closemouthed and prosaic, was practically bubbling.

"That doesn't exactly follow, but you know I'm not going to tell anyone." I admit, I was curious myself.

"Want to have dinner together? I figure you're not getting to chat to too many people since your sweetie's in the hospital."

"That sounds good."

"Okay, how about the Outback? There's one close to the hospital." She gave directions, and I said I'd meet her there at six thirty.

I was not a little surprised that Victoria was being so forthcoming. In fact, her interest in talking to me was almost odd. But the truth was, I was feeling lonely. It felt good to know someone wanted to talk to me. Iona had called exactly once to ask after Tolliver, but that conversation had been brief and dutiful.

Hospitals are all self-contained worlds, and this one was spinning relentlessly along on its own axis. When I got to Tolliver's room, he'd been taken away for tests, but no one could tell me what tests or why he was having them.

I felt oddly forlorn. Even Tolliver, confined to a hospital, wasn't where I thought he'd be. My cell phone rang, and I started guiltily. I wasn't supposed to have it on in the hospital. But I answered it.

"Harper? Are you all right?"

"Manfred! How are you?" I was smiling.

"I got the feeling you were in trouble, and I had to call. Is this a bad time?"

"I'm glad you called," I said, probably more fervently than I should have.

"Oh, well, then," he said. "I'll be on the next plane." He was only half joking. Manfred Bernardo, developing psychic, was younger than I by three or four years, but he'd never made any bones about how attractive he found me.

"I'm lonely because Tolliver got shot," I said, and immediately realized how egocentric that sounded. After I'd explained to Manfred what had happened, he got all excited. He was actually serious about coming to Texas to "give you a shoulder to cry on," as he put it. I was absurdly touched, and for a crazy minute I considered saying yes. It would be comforting to have Manfred around—piercings, tattoos, and all. Only picturing Tolliver's face as I told him what I'd done stopped me.

By the time Manfred was ready to hang up, I'd promised I'd call him if "things got any worse," which was vague enough to satisfy both of us. And he'd sworn he'd check in with me by phone every single day until Tolliver got out of the hospital.

I felt a lot more cheerful when I hung up. To make my day even brighter, an orderly wheeled Tolliver in right after I'd shut my phone. His color was better than it had been the day before, but I could tell he was very weak, just from the way he slumped in the wheelchair. Tolliver was ready to get back into the bed, though he hated to admit it.

After the orderly had made sure Tolliver was settled and comfortable, he left with that quick, quiet walk hospital staff members seem to acquire as part of their job description. Tolliver had had another

X-ray to check on his clavicle, he told me, and a neurologist had come in to verify that there hadn't been any nerve damage to the shoulder.

"Have you seen Dr. Spradling today?" I asked.

"Yeah, he came by earlier. He said everything looked okay. I kind of expected you an hour ago." Tolliver had completely forgotten that I'd told him I was going to stop by the police station.

I told him about the film I'd seen, how the woman differed from Cameron.

"I'm sorry," he said. "I was ready for it to be someone else, but I guess I've always got a little bit of hope." That was exactly how I felt.

"It wasn't, and I'm only wondering why someone thought it was her. I mean, who called the police? Who got Pete to look at the tapes? And this woman was close enough in appearance to Cameron to at least make Pete feel I should see the video. Was the anonymous caller someone who went to high school with Cameron and me, someone who was genuinely mistaken? Or was he some creep who just wanted to jerk us around?"

"And why now?" Tolliver said. He looked at me. I didn't have an answer.

"I hardly see how this could have anything to do with Rich Joyce and his caregiver," I said. "But the timing is really suspicious, huh?"

We couldn't think of anything else to say about this strange grouping of events. After a while, I found Tolliver's comb in a pocket of his jeans, which were hanging in the closet. They were a little stained. His shirt had been cut off of him. I reminded myself to bring another one to the hospital for the day he was released.

When I began to comb his hair, I found it was dirty, of course, and I tried to think of a way to wash it. With some improvisation, including a clean bedpan, an extra pad that they'd brought in case his shoulder leaked, and the little bottle of shampoo included in his admissions package, I managed. I also helped him shave and brush his teeth, and then I gave him a sponge bath, which turned unexpectedly bawdy.

He was very relaxed and sleepy—and happy—by the time that was over, and he said he felt much better. I combed his damp, dark hair and kissed his smooth cheek. He was going through a clean-shaven phase.

A nurse came in to give him his bath right after I finished, and she shrugged when I told her it was done.

Time in a hospital inevitably drags. Before I had a chance to tell Tolliver about Victoria's phone call, he fell asleep. I hated to wake him when the long day stretched in front of us. I napped myself. I struggled awake when Tolliver's lunch tray came at eleven thirty.

That was another exciting break. I cut up all his food—well, the little that required cutting—and put a straw in his drink for him so that he could eat one-handed. He was so happy to be getting real food instead of liquid that even hospital food was welcome, and he managed pretty well. When I was sure he'd had as much as he wanted, I rolled the table away and handed him the TV remote. I needed to go in search of food myself.

"You don't have to sit here all afternoon, you know," Tolliver said.

"After I eat, I'll spend the afternoon with you," I said in a tone that told him not to argue. "Then I'm meeting Victoria for supper. I probably won't come back after that."

"Good. You don't need to be cooped up all day. You'll probably want to have a run or try the hotel's weight room or something."

He was right about that. I'm used to sitting still for long periods, because we're in the car so much, but I'm also used to getting exercise every day, and my muscles were stiff.

I got a salad at a fast-food place, enjoying the bustle and purpose of the people in the restaurant. It felt odd to be alone, though I didn't mind so much after I watched (and listened to) a mother dealing with three preschool-age children at the next table. I wondered if Tolliver wanted to have children. I didn't. I'd already had the care of two babies, my little sisters, and I didn't want to go through that again. And I admitted to myself that while I didn't want to be pushed out of my sisters' lives, I didn't want to be in charge of those lives, either.

Even after I saw the youngest boy give his mother a spontaneous hug and kiss, I didn't warm up to the concept of carrying someone else inside my body. Should I feel guilty about that? Didn't every woman want to have her own child to love?

Not necessarily, I thought. *And God knows there are plenty of children in the world. I don't need to supply another one.*

Tolliver was awake and watching a basketball game when I walked into his room. "Mark called while you were gone," he said.

"Oh, gosh, could you reach the phone?"

"It was my big adventure for the day."

"What did he have to say?"

"Oh, that I'd made my dad feel bad, that he thought I was being an idiot for not welcoming Dad back to the land of the sober, with my arms open wide."

I debated with myself for a minute before deciding to say what I thought. "Mark has a real weakness for your dad, Tolliver. You know I love Mark, and I think he's a great guy, but he won't ever really get it, about Matthew."

"Yeah," Tolliver said. "You're right. He was nuts about Mom, and when she died, he kind of transferred that emotion to our dad."

Tolliver didn't talk about his mother a lot. Her death, from cancer, had to have been completely awful.

"I think Mark believes that Dad has to be good at heart," Tolliver said slowly. "Because if Dad isn't good, then he's lost his last parent. And he has to have that relationship."

"Do you think your dad is good at heart?"

Tolliver really thought about his answer. "I hope he's got some good left in him," Tolliver said. "But honestly, I don't think he'll stay sober, if he's really sober now. He's lied about it before, over and over. He always goes back to the drugs, and you remember that at his worst he'd take whatever anyone offered him. Now, I'm sure he must have been in a lot of emotional pain to need so many drugs to kill it, you know? But he abandoned us to whoever wanted to prey on us, because he had to drug himself. No, I can't trust him," Tolliver said. "And I hope I never do, because I'll be disappointed all over again."

"That was exactly the way I felt about my mother," I said, understanding completely.

"Yeah, Laurel was a piece of work," Tolliver said. "You know she tried to hit on Mark and me?"

I thought I might throw up the food I'd just eaten. "No," I said, my voice strangled.

"Yeah. Cameron knew about it. She came in on the, ah, critical moment. I thought Mark was going to die of embarrassment, and I had no idea what to do."

"So what happened?" I felt a deep and burning shame. I told

myself it was none of my concern, but it's hard to believe that when you hear a story about your own flesh and blood that makes you sick to your stomach.

"Well, Cameron dragged her mom into the bedroom and made her put some clothes on," Tolliver said. "I don't think Laurel knew where she was or who she was coming on to, Harper, if it makes a difference. Cameron slapped your mom a few times."

"Jeez," I said. Sometimes there are no words.

"We're out of it," Tolliver said, as if he was trying to convince himself.

"Yes," I said, "we are. And we have each other."

"It can't touch us anymore."

"No," I said, lying through my teeth. "It can't."

nine

THE restaurant where I met Victoria Flores was crowded, and servers were bustling back and forth. It seemed incredibly lively after the muted sounds of the hospital.

To my surprise, Victoria wasn't by herself. Drexell Joyce, Lizzie and Kate's brother, was sitting at the table with her.

"Hey, girl," Victoria said, rising to give me a hug. I was surprised, but not enough to pull back. I hadn't known we were on those terms. Somehow, this show was being put on for Drexell Joyce. I'd been picturing a relaxed dinner between two women who found out secrets for a living, not a strategy session with an unknown man.

"Mr. Joyce," I said as I sat down and stowed my purse under the table.

"Oh, please, call me Drex," he said with a broad grin. He poured a lot of admiration into his look. I didn't believe in his sincerity for a second.

"What are you doing away from the ranch?" I asked, with what I hoped was a disarming smile.

"My sisters asked me to come check with Victoria, here, see what she's found out and how the investigation's going. If we have a little aunt or uncle out there, we want to find that baby and make sure he's brought up right," Drex said.

"You're simply assuming that Mariah Parish's child was your grandfather's?" I found that astonishing, and I didn't try to hide it.

"Yeah, that's what I'm thinking. He was an old dog, no doubt about it, but he had a few tricks. My granddad liked the ladies, always did."

"And you think Mariah Parish would have been agreeable to his advances?"

"Well, he had a lot of charisma, and she might have thought her job depended on saying yes. Granddad didn't like to hear 'no.'"

Charming. I couldn't think of anything to say, so I didn't speak.

"So, how's your brother?" Victoria asked, her voice warm and concerned.

I was disappointed. I was sure now that Victoria had asked me here for some secret purpose of her own. She hadn't simply wanted my company, after all. "He's doing much better, thanks," I said. "I hope he'll be out of the hospital in another day."

"Where will you go next?"

"Tolliver usually handles our bookings, and I'll have to go over our schedule with him when he feels up to it. We had originally planned on staying here at least a week, so we could see our family."

"Oh, you got folks in this area?" Drex leaned forward, all interest.

"Yes, our two little sisters live here."

"Who's bringing 'em up?"

"My aunt and her husband."

"They live right around here?"

It could be true that Drex was simply fascinated by all things Harper, but I didn't credit his interest as personal. "Does your family spend a lot of time in Dallas?" I asked. "I saw your sisters the other day, and now you're here. That's lots of driving."

"We have an apartment here, and one down in Houston," Dex said. "We're on the ranch around ten months out of the year, but we all need to see the bright lights from time to time. 'Cept Chip. He loves running that ranch. But Kate and Lizzie sit on about ten boards apiece, from banks to charities, and those meet in Dallas."

"Not you?" Victoria asked. "You don't do charity work?"

Drex laughed, his head thrown back. I suspected that was so we could see his handsome jawline from another angle. I wondered what he would do when he got older and that jawline wasn't quite as firm. I know from my own experience that no one looks pretty in the grave.

"Victoria, I guess most boards are smarter than to ask me to be on 'em," he said. He had a down-home twinkle in his eye. Just one of the good ol' boy millionaires. "I'm not too good at sitting still, and I'd go to sleep if I had to listen to all them speeches."

How could Victoria listen to all this bullshit? She gave every appearance of being genuinely charmed by this asshole.

"But Victoria, to get back to the topic, how's the search going?" Drex asked, with the air of a man who had to abandon his bit of fun to return to grim business.

"Pretty well, I think," Victoria said, and I went on the alert. Victoria sounded calm and competent, and more than a little cagey. "I'm working on a complete biography of Mariah, and it's not as easy as

I thought it would be. What kind of background check did you run on her before she was hired to help your grandfather?"

"I don't guess Lizzie had that done," Drex said, sounding genuinely startled. "I think it was my granddad who did the hiring. Mariah was living in the house by the time we found out about it."

"But you'd considered hiring a housekeeper for him?" Victoria asked.

"He needed something more than a housekeeper, but less than a registered nurse," Drex said. "He needed an assistant. Really, she was like a nanny. Made sure he ate the right food, tried to monitor how much he drank. But he would've smacked us silly if we'd called her that. She took his blood pressure every day, too."

Victoria pounced on that. "Mariah had a nursing degree?"

"No, no. I don't think she had a degree at all. She was supposed to make sure he took his medicine, remind him about his appointments, drive him if he didn't feel well, call the doctor if she noticed anything off a list of warning signals they gave her. She was kind of our human Life Alert, at least that was the idea."

I exchanged a quick glance with Victoria. So I hadn't been the only one to detect a note of resentment in Drex's monologue. By now I wasn't convinced that Victoria was as interested in Drex as she'd appeared at first. Victoria was playing a deeper game than I could plot and execute.

"She saw her role a little differently?" I asked.

"Hell, yes. She saw herself as a watchdog, I guess," Drex said. He took a big swallow of his beer. He looked around to see if our server was within hailing distance. We'd placed our orders a few minutes before.

"Why did your family pay for her funeral and put her in the family plot?" I asked. It was a subject I'd wondered about a couple of times. "Where were her people?"

"We looked through all her stuff after she died, and we couldn't find anything with any names and addresses on it," Drex said. "Lizzie asked all of us what she'd said about her family, where she came from, and no one could come up with anything. We asked Chip, and none of his kinfolks could remember anything."

"What about her Social Security Number? As her employer, your granddad had to have that."

"He paid her under the table."

It baffled me why a man as rich as Richard Joyce would choose to do that. The Joyces had to have accountants and business people who would jump at the chance to be useful.

Drex said, "When Lizzie met Mariah, she told Granddad she thought Mariah wouldn't work out. Granddad thought she'd stay, but he could tell we didn't like Mariah that much. He didn't want to go to the trouble of setting something up, only to have to fire Mariah." He sounded defensive, and I could understand why. I exchanged a long look with Victoria.

"So your granddad hired someone he didn't know, paid her under the table, and didn't know anything about her previous work history, and he had her living in his house with him." If I sounded incredulous, pardon me. "Did you say you asked Chip to talk to his family after Mariah died?" I heard thunder and looked over at a window to see rain hitting the glass.

"Yes, they knew her. It was Chip who told us Mariah would be good for the job."

There was a long silence, while Drex looked around some more for our server and Victoria and I were absorbed in our own thoughts.

I didn't know what was going through Victoria's mind, but I was thinking that I hoped my family took better care of me than the Joyces had of their patriarch, Richard.

"How long has Lizzie been seeing Chip?" Victoria asked, as if she was introducing an entirely new topic, a little social side trip.

"Oh, man, years now. They knew each other from the ranch, of course. And they'd see each other when they were both rodeoing. After a few years, and Chip's divorce, they just clicked. He was at a rodeo in Amarillo, calf roping. She was barrel riding. She was having trouble with her trailer hitch, and he came up to help her."

"So Mariah had worked for Chip's family?"

"They were foster kids in the same house, and when she got out on her own, Chip recommended her to his distant cousin, Arthur Peaden, I think that was his name. The cousin died just around the time the doctors told Granddad that he needed someone at the house all the time. Chip suggested it and sent her to the house, my granddaddy liked her, and that was all she wrote. After we got over the surprise, we felt kind of relieved that we didn't have to interview a lot of people for the job. And Granddad got someone who'd had experience, but she wasn't going around in scrubs all the time making him feel like he was incompetent. She was nice looking, and she was always smiling. She was a great cook, too."

Drex got his fresh beer, and Victoria asked him some questions designed to get him to talk about himself. Drex was not the brightest guy I'd ever met, and Victoria was a sharp woman, so by simply sitting and listening it became easy to draw a picture of Drex's life. His dad had probably had a hard time accepting that his only son wasn't competent to handle the family affairs, but there was no denying that

Lizzie was not only the oldest but the sharpest. Katie, the middle kid, was wilder than either of her siblings. At least Drex thought so.

I was relieved when our food came. I was not a private investigator, and I wasn't being paid to absorb all these long stories about the Joyce family. By the time I'd eaten as much as I wanted, I was tired to death of Drex Joyce, and I wasn't happy at being in league with Victoria to pump this moron for information. However irritating I found her tactics, I could understand why Victoria had decided to include Drex as a guest at dinner. It was easier for us to alternate in the conversation so he didn't seem to understand where it was going, and presumably he told us more than he might have otherwise.

I also thought of a few questions that Victoria didn't.

I decided that Victoria had wanted to give Drex a choice of attractive women, and I was relieved that Drex had decided Victoria was more to his taste than I. I took a malicious pleasure in excusing myself early, before the waitress had asked about coffee and dessert. Victoria looked dismayed for a fleeting second, and then she said she'd talk to me the next day.

I thought not, not if I could avoid it. I dislike feeling used, and I was sure Victoria had deliberately planned the evening before she'd invited me. She could have been honest with me. I couldn't understand why she felt the need to resort to such a thing. Surely, if the Joyce family had hired her, they would cooperate with her in the most extreme way. Why hadn't Victoria gotten all this information already?

I drove back to the hotel feeling disgruntled. Since the rain had stopped, I decided it was time for some activity. I didn't like to run at night, but I really needed to do something physical. I hadn't had time to explore the area in any detail, but a block behind the hotel

I'd seen a large high school. Maybe I could run on its track, if the gate was unlocked. If I couldn't get in, there was a big bus yard across the road from the high school.

To my surprise, Parker Powers, the ex–football player turned cop, was sitting in the lobby.

"Were you waiting for me?" I asked, going up to him.

"Yes. Can we talk?" He gave me a very thorough look.

"What do you need?" I asked.

"I wanted to ask you a few more questions about your brother. There was a drive-by a couple of blocks away last night, and we're trying to find out if your brother's shooting was related. I hear he's doing well."

If he hadn't said that, I wouldn't have bitten. I'd seen that gleam in his eye. But if he was genuinely investigating Tolliver's shooting, I wanted to help him. I wanted to know who'd shot my brother. I wasn't going to talk about it in the public lobby anymore, though, and with that gleam in his eye, I wasn't going to ask him up to my room.

"I'm going for a run," I said. "Care to join me?"

"Sure," he said, with only a brief hesitation. "I've got running shorts in my car. You know, you really shouldn't be going out by yourself if someone is gunning for your brother. We have no idea why he was shot, yet. Might be related to the drive-by, might not."

"I'll be back in ten minutes," I said, and went upstairs to my room. I had a lanyard from which was suspended a clear plastic rectangular holder, and I put my hotel key and my driver's license into it. I put on my running shorts and T-shirt, and my running shoes. I was ready. I tucked the rectangle down into my shirt and bounced up and down on my toes a couple of times to make sure it was secure. I tucked my cell phone into my shorts pocket, zipped the pocket shut, and went back down to the lobby.

Parker was there, wearing ancient shorts and a ragged sweatshirt. I gave him a nod, and we went out to the parking lot and began stretching. I got the impression Parker hadn't run in a long time; probably the shorts and sweatshirt were his gym clothes, because I could see he worked his muscles, though a paunch was gaining ground on his waistline. I could tell he wasn't enthusiastic about the exercise, but he was enjoying watching me.

"Ready?" I asked, and he nodded, his mouth set in a grim line. He looked more like he was going to face the guillotine than a pleasant evening exercise session.

Off we went, down the sidewalk past a block of houses, then another block of houses, then the high school grounds. The outside lights were plentiful, and everyone seemed to be inside tonight. It was chilly, and there were still puddles here and there from the earlier shower. Cars went by with fair frequency, some of them clearly exceeding the speed limit and some of them at a crawl, but with a sidewalk, that didn't present any problem. I wondered if any of the drivers recognized my running partner.

The cold air felt good to me. I went at an easy pace, enjoying the stretch of my legs and the increased rate of my heart. The high school track was surrounded by a high fence, and it was locked, no big surprise. I led my companion across the road to the vast lot filled with school buses. Parker kept up with me, and I glanced sideways to see that he was smiling a little, pleased with himself. I picked up the pace, and the smile faded rapidly. Within four blocks of really running, Parker was wheezing for breath. He kept going because he was fueled by pride.

Even his pride ran out in the next half mile. There were three rows of buses, and we'd run from the road to the end of one row, up the other row, and we were rounding the end by the road to start running the length again. I was really moving and feeling good, but Parker stopped, hands on his knees, chest heaving. I ran in place. He waved a hand at me to tell me to keep on going. "Stay in sight," he said, biting each word out in turn.

I waved back at him and began running again. I wasn't half the runner my brother was, but that night I felt as swift and light as a bird, compared to Parker. I zoomed down the silent line of buses, smelling the puddles and the pavement, washed clean by the evening's rain. I glanced over my shoulder to see that Parker was walking after me at a good pace, but I was definitely getting into the "out of sight" range. With some regret, instead of rounding the bus line and starting up the middle again, I turned and began running back the way I'd come. There must have been another street beyond the bus lot, because from that direction, I could hear a car going slowly. At that moment, car lights came on behind me, shining in Parker's face and casting my own shadow in a long streak in front of me. I felt a jolt of fear, and I slowed down, not sure what to do. The sound behind me was definitely a car engine, idling . . . but it was drawing closer.

The detective, though it was clear his eyes were dazzled, picked up his pace and began trotting toward me. As he drew closer, he pulled up his sweatshirt and drew a gun. I didn't register that for a second, and then I thought he was going to shoot me. My steps faltered, hesitated. The car engine began to get closer.

"*Run,*" he bellowed.

I didn't understand anything, but I began moving faster and faster, my arms sawing the air to build up my momentum. When I reached him, Parker shoved me between two buses and swung to face the oncoming car, his gun at the ready. The car swerved as the driver presumably noticed the gun pointed in his direction, and then, with a screech of tires, accelerated madly, fishtailing out of the parking lot as it sped away.

"What?" I said. "What?" I jumped out from between the buses to confront my appointed savior, and threw open my arms. "*What?*" I yelled.

"Death threat," he said. His breathing was still irregular. "You got a death threat today. Didn't want you going out on your own. Easy target."

"Why the hell didn't you tell me that? So that's why you agreed to run with me."

"I didn't know you were a health nut," he said unfairly. "I was just supposed to make you aware of the situation, tell you about the drive-by."

"So instead of . . ." I started to sputter. Then I closed my eyes, gathered myself, and stood up straighter. "Do you have a name attached to this death threat?"

"No, it was a man's voice. He was saying he thought your work was the work of Satan, and so on. Said he didn't think you ought to be in Texas, and he was going to take care of that the next time he saw you. He mentioned your new hotel by name."

I was pretty offhand about the phone call until Parker Powers got to the "he mentioned the hotel" part. That was unnerving, and I knew I had to take this seriously.

"So do you think this car was his, or do you think you just scared the shit out of some teenagers parking back here?" My legs were getting stiff, so I bounced up and down gently on the balls of my feet, then stretched down to touch my toes.

"I don't know," Parker said, his voice gloomy. "I got a partial license number, though, and I'll run the plate."

I suddenly realized, actually understood, that this man had put himself in front of me when he thought someone was going to be shooting at me. The enormity of the act virtually smacked me in the face.

"Thank you," I said. All of a sudden, my knees were shaking. "Thank you for doing that."

"That's what we're supposed to do," he said. "We're supposed to protect. Lucky I didn't have to do much protecting. I might have had a heart attack." He grinned, and I was glad to observe that his chest wasn't heaving anymore.

"So, we should head back, huh? I guess this was pretty much a nonincident?" I didn't want to hurt his feelings, which was pretty absurd.

"No, I guess they left for good." He seemed relieved about that. "Let's go back to the hotel." He holstered his gun.

I knew there was no way I was going to get the policeman back up to a running pace. We were at least walking briskly when we left the bus lot and we passed the high school. Then we were in the residential area, and there was almost no traffic now. Everyone was home from work, no one was going back out tonight. The temperature had dropped a little, and I began to shiver. We had three blocks to go. We were in a little neighborhood where yards were a hobby. Even in the winter, there were trees with leaves, and bushes, and rock gardens decorating the small front yards. Parker Powers was asking me questions designed to calm me down, an inconsequential stream of inquiry about my running history, how long I ran each day, if my brother ran . . .

And just as I recognized that the shadow behind one of the trees was suspiciously man shaped, it began to move. A man stepped out from the tree, and I saw the streetlight glint off a gun. Parker Powers lunged toward me to shove me aside, away from the threat, and the gunman fired right at him and hit him in the chest.

Screaming would have been a waste of time. The only advantage I had was speed, and I jumped onto the tiny grass lawn and took off like a rabbit on meth. I heard footsteps behind me, even on the grass, and I tried to go behind the house and found there was a fenced-in backyard. It wasn't much of a fence, kind of a swipe at providing security. I grabbed the top of the fence and vaulted it, landing well, then chased across the dead grass and vaulted the other side.

It wasn't until later that I thought of everything that could have made me fall and break my leg.

I found myself in the next backyard, and I had a clear shot at the next street over. There were houses only on one side of the street. The opposite side was a narrow belt of trees with a ravine behind them, as near as I could tell in the spotty pools of light. I began running toward the hotel, running in earnest, flat out. It was much darker back here. I was afraid I would fall, afraid I would get shot, afraid the detective was dead. I knew I was going in the right direction, but I couldn't see the hotel because the street curved. I almost knocked on a door, but then I thought of the danger to the people inside that house, and I ran on. I thought I heard a noise ahead of me, and I dove to the side and crouched behind a car parked in a driveway. I was silent for a moment, listening, though my heart was pounding so loudly it was hard to make out external sounds.

I unzipped my shorts pocket, withdrew the cell phone, and flipped it open, keeping a hand curved around it to dim the light. I punched in 911, and a woman's voice answered. "I'm hiding in the driveway of a house, in the business park behind the Holiday Inn Express," I said, keeping my voice as low as I could. "Detective Parker Powers has been shot. He's lying out on Jacaranda Street. The shooter is after me. Please come quick."

"Ma'am? Did you say an officer's been shot? Are you wounded?"

"Yes, Detective Powers," I said. "I'm not wounded yet. I have to hang up." I couldn't be talking on the phone. I needed to be listening.

Now that my own breathing had moderated, I was sure I could hear someone else breathing, someone else stepping very quietly through the front yards. Someone who didn't want to be out in the middle of the street. Weren't any of these people aware of what was going on around them? Where were the armed householders with guns when you needed them? I didn't know whether to break and run, or stay where I was and hope he didn't find me.

I found the tension almost intolerable. Waiting crouched beside that car was one of the hardest things I'd ever done. I didn't even know if this quiet street went through. Maybe it dead-ended just around the slight curve. I'd have to plunge back through the yards so I could emerge on Jacaranda Street to get back to the hotel. There might be fences, there might be dogs . . . I could hear one barking now, and it sounded like a big one.

The footsteps, very quiet footsteps, came a little closer and then stopped. Could he see me? Would he shoot me in the next minute?

Then I heard the wail of sirens. God bless the police, God bless their lights and noise and guns. The shadow that had crept almost up to where I crouched made a rapid retreat as the gunman abandoned caution and ran back down the street in the direction I'd come from.

I tried to get up but I couldn't. My legs just wouldn't work. I could see the beam of a large flashlight coming closer and closer, and then it danced over me. It returned to fix me in its glare.

"Lie down with your arms extended!" said a woman's voice.

"Okay," I said. "I will."

At the moment, that seemed a lot better than standing up.

ten

IN the end, I went back to the hospital and spent the night with Tolliver. I simply didn't want to be by myself, and I felt safer around him even though he had been shot.

Detective Powers was still alive. I was profoundly glad to hear that, profoundly grateful that his courage would be rewarded in this life rather than the next. I had caught snatches of conversation from the cops around me, who'd pretty much treated me as if I weren't there.

"Powers is going to be all right," the female officer, who'd finally let me get up, had told me. "He's too tough to kill."

"All those years playing football, he's got to be tough," said one of the ambulance attendants who'd been summoned to have a look at me. He was taking his time packing up his stuff, having determined that I was pretty much okay.

"Yeah, those knocks in the head didn't do him any good, though," said another officer, a young guy with a shaved head. "Powers played one season too many."

"Hey, respect the detective," the older ambulance attendant said. "He's a good spokesman for the department."

Reading between the lines, I gathered that Detective Powers had been a recruitment point for the police since he'd been hired, and that had a lot to do with his promotion to detective. People were so thrilled to be questioned by a former football star that they told him things they hadn't planned on spilling, just to keep his attention. So he was not highly regarded because of his cleverness or innate ability, but because he was an asset and was always willing to share the spotlight. Plus, he was regarded as being a genuinely nice guy.

It was a pleasure to tell his cohorts how brave he had been, and a pleasure to see the pride they took in that. The fact that they thought he'd been pretty much of an idiot to go running with me—well, that was left on the back burner.

I had a few speckles of blood on my face, and I went into my hotel room to scrub them off. The female officer, Kerri Sauer, went with me, and she also volunteered to follow me over to God's Mercy, a gesture I appreciated.

"You ever watch Parker play?" she asked, as she watched me scrub his blood off with a washrag.

"No," I said. "Did you? You must have been a kid."

"I was. He was great. Him getting hurt, that was a terrible thing for the team. He did—still does—all kinds of stuff for kids at risk. He's a great guy. You had his location when you called. That saved his life. He's got a chance to make it."

It seemed counterproductive to point out that Powers probably wouldn't have gotten shot if he hadn't been with me. I nodded and buried my face in towel so she couldn't read my expression.

After I parked at the hospital and walked to the door, I waved to the patrol car, and it pulled out into the traffic. I had a crazy idea: if I couldn't make money finding bodies anymore, could I be a police officer? I wondered if I could even pass the physical. Usually my right leg was okay, but every now and then it gave me fits. And I got awful headaches. So probably law enforcement wasn't a career option for me. I shook my head and saw the movement reflected in the shiny walls of the elevator. I was just being silly.

I went through the hall on silent feet and opened Tolliver's door carefully. It was dark inside, though the light in the bathroom was on and that door had been left open a crack.

"Harper?" he said, his voice thick with sleep.

"Yeah, it's me. I missed you," I said, keeping my voice down.

"Come here."

I went to the bed, and I crouched to take my shoes off. "I'm going to sleep in the chair," I said very softly. "You go back to sleep."

"Climb in with me, on my good side."

"Are you sure that'll be comfortable for you? That bed's mighty small."

"I'm sure. I'd rather be crowded with you than have lots of room without you."

I felt tears begin to trickle down my cheeks, and I suppressed the sobbing sound that went with them.

"What's wrong?" He put his good arm around me after I'd crawled into the bed. I lay on my side to give him enough room.

"Nothing we need to talk about now," I said. "Sleep now. I just didn't want to be by myself."

"I didn't either," he said. And he fell back to sleep. After a few minutes, so did I.

The nurse who came in at five thirty in the morning was fairly surprised to find me there, in bed with Tolliver. Once she saw that we were both clothed and she could assume that Tolliver hadn't done anything to hurt his mending shoulder, she relaxed.

Tolliver looked a lot better in the morning light. Being with him had done me good, too. I felt a lot more confident. After he'd been bathed and shaved and he'd eaten breakfast, I told him the story of the night before.

He said instantly, "I have to get out of here," and actually began to sit up to get out of the bed.

"No, you aren't," I said sharply. "You're going to stay right here, where no one can get at you, until the doctor says you can go."

Tolliver said, "You're in danger, baby. We've got to find somewhere to put you, somewhere safe." He'd abandoned the idea of leaving, I was relieved to see, mostly because the movement had been enough to make him cold and sweaty.

"That sounds good," I said. "But I just don't know where that would be."

"You could leave," he said, a little wildly. "You could go up to St. Louis, to the apartment."

"And leave you here by yourself? Not too likely."

"You could leave the country."

"Oh, hush. I'm not going to spend the money to fly to Europe or whatever, just because someone shot at guys while I was around."

"You got a *death threat*," Tolliver said, as if I was mentally slow or hard of hearing.

"I *know that,*" I said, mimicking his tone accurately. He gave me a narrow-eyed glare. "Seriously, Tolliver, I think someone's just trying to spook me. I mean, you got shot and then poor Detective Powers. But couldn't that shooter have hit me, just as easily, if I'd been the real target? I'm not so sure anymore that I simply got lucky both times. I'm thinking maybe the shooter is just trying to scare me."

"I don't particularly like the results of someone trying to scare you any more than I like the idea of someone trying to really kill you," Tolliver said, indicating his hospital bed pointedly.

"True enough." It appeared we were at an impasse.

Dr. Spradling appeared and asked Tolliver the usual questions. It seemed clear that Tolliver was out of danger, and the doctor talked about dismissing him, provided Tolliver had someone to take care of him at home. I raised my hand, to indicate I was that person.

"What about traveling?" I asked.

"By car?"

"Yes."

"I wouldn't. He needs to rest for at least two days before you travel. I'm thinking of giving him an antibiotic drip, but if you promise to stick to what I say faithfully, if you promise to keep him in a room and quiet, then I'll make it oral antibiotics and release him tomorrow."

"Okay," I said. "I promise."

"Then if he continues to improve, doesn't run a fever, tomorrow."

I was delighted to hear it. Tolliver looked relieved, too. When the doctor had left, I said, "I guess I'd better go back to the hotel to take a shower and eat something."

"Can you wait until Mark gets off work? He could go with you."

"I'll go by myself. I can't stay shut in a room the whole time, Tolliver. I've got to get out and get things done." I didn't want Mark to get shot, too.

"Who do you think is doing this?"

"I know it sounds ridiculous, but I wondered if it was someone who got obsessed with me on the website, some nut who decided he didn't want me to be around other men. Or maybe it's a coincidence that I was with men both times. Maybe this guy is a really bad shot and was trying to get me. Maybe it's someone who just wants to rattle me and see what I do."

"Why now? There's got to be a reason."

"I don't know," I said, losing patience. "How would I know? Maybe the police will come up with something. Having one of their own shot is a powerful incentive to find the bad guy. God knows they asked me to tell them every single thing I've done in the past few days, over and over. I'll tell you something else I have to do—I have to go see the detective who got shot."

Tolliver nodded. He turned his face away from me, to look out the window. The day was cold and clear, the sky so bright a blue that it hurt to look at it. It was an achingly beautiful day. And here we were, shut inside a hospital and peeved with each other.

I stepped over to his bed, took his hand. It was unresponsive in my grasp. "I have to shower and eat, and I have to go see the detective," I said. "After that, I'll be back. If I keep moving, I'll be fine. No one can follow me 24-7. Right?" I hated to sound wheedling, but I did.

"I need to get out of here," he said.

"Yes, and you will, soon. The doctor said so. Just don't do anything crazy and fall, okay?"

There was a sketchy knock at the door, and as our heads turned, a short man walked in. He was extraordinary looking—all in black, with platinum spiked hair and piercings in his eyebrow, his nose, and (I knew from the past) his tongue. He was younger than me, somewhere around twenty-one, and he was slim and oddly handsome.

"Hello, Manfred," Tolliver said. "I never thought I'd say this, but I'm glad to see you."

eleven

MANFRED seemed a little hurt that I had protested against his coming with me. "You don't think I can be helpful?" he asked, his blue eyes looking a shade too forlorn.

"Manfred," I began, exasperated, "I just don't know what to do with you."

"I have some very good ideas," he said. He waggled his eyebrows.

He was making it funny, but he was serious. I never doubted that at my slightest response, Manfred would be booking us into the nearest hotel as fast as he could whip out his wallet.

The thing was, I'd have to pay for the room, because that wallet was probably empty. I didn't know how Manfred was getting by. His grandmother, Xylda Bernardo, had been a colorful old fraud, but she'd had the genuine gift. It just didn't always speak to her when she needed it to, and when she didn't hear the real voice, she'd make one up. She'd made a poor living at it. She had a flare for the dramatic that had led to some pretty unconvincing overacting.

Manfred was much cannier. And he had the gift, too. I didn't know the scope and depth of Manfred's psychic ability, but I had a feeling that as soon as Manfred found his level and honed his gift, he'd be making money. As far as I knew, that hadn't happened yet.

"First," I told him, ignoring his innuendo, "I've got to go to my hotel and shower and change. Then we'll go to the other hospital, the one where they took Detective Powers."

"The Dallas Cowboy? Parker Powers?" Manfred's face lit up in a wonderful way. "I read an article in *Sports Illustrated* about him, when he became a cop."

"I would never have guessed you were a football fan," I said. Life is a process of reevaluation, isn't it?

"Are you kidding? I *love* football. I played in high school."

I eyed him dubiously.

"Hey, don't let my size fool you," Manfred said. "I can run like nobody's business. And it was a little high school, so they didn't have much choice," he added honestly.

"So what position did you play?"

"I was a tight end." And he said it absolutely straight. Manfred did not joke about football.

"That's really interesting," I said, and I meant it. "Manfred, not to change the subject, but why'd you decide to come all this way after I said I could handle it?"

"I got the feeling you were in trouble," he said. He looked sideways at me, and then straight out the windshield of his car. We'd decided that if I were being followed (an idea that still seemed incredible to me) taking Manfred's beat-up Camaro might throw my stalker off the trail.

"Really? You saw that?"

"I saw someone shooting at you," he said. His face was older all of a sudden. "I saw you fall."

"Did you . . . You didn't know for sure I was alive when you came into Tolliver's room, did you?"

"Well, I'd watched the news, and I didn't see anything indicating you'd been killed. I did hear that a Garland policeman had been shot. They weren't releasing his name then. I hoped you were okay. But I wanted to see for myself."

"So you drove all this way." I shook my head, marveling.

"I wasn't that far away," Manfred said.

There was a little silence, while I waited for him to continue.

"Okay, I'll bite," I said. "Where were you?"

"I was in a motel in Tulsa," he said. "I had a job there."

"You're officially in the business now?"

"Yep. I've got a website, the whole nine yards."

"How does it work?"

"It's twenty-five dollars for an answer based on one question. Fifty dollars for a consult if they give me their astrological sign and age. And if they want me to travel to them for a private reading, it's . . . a lot more."

"How are you doing?" I'd definitely been wrong about Manfred's finances.

"Pretty well," he said, with a slight smile. "Of course, I'm building on Xylda's reputation. God bless her soul."

"I know you must miss her."

"I really, really do. My mother is a very nice woman." He said that with the air of someone doing his duty. "But my grandmother gave me more love, and I took care of her as much as I could. My mother had to work all the time, and I don't remember my father, so Xylda was my real . . . she was my home."

That was a great way to put it.

"Manfred, I'm so sorry about Xylda. I think of her often."

"Thanks," he said, his voice lightening in a conscious attempt to brighten the dark conversation. "She liked you, too. She liked you a lot."

We were silent for the rest of the ride.

While I showered and changed, Manfred walked down to the place where Parker Powers had been shot the night before. He wanted to see if he could pick up anything there, and he knew I'd be more comfortable if he wasn't in the room while I was cleaning up. I appreciated both ideas. When he knocked on the door, I was dressed, as made up as my healing face would permit, and braced for our next stop. Manfred set his GPS so we could get to the hospital where Parker Powers was a patient. It was called Christian Memorial. I didn't understand why he'd been taken there instead of God's Mercy, where Tolliver was. Tolliver and Parker had both had gunshot wounds, so it couldn't be the level of trauma the emergency room could handle.

I was impressed with Manfred's GPS, and I'd been thinking of getting Tolliver one for his birthday, so we talked about that on the way to Christian Memorial. I didn't want to think about the visit I was about to pay. Fortunately, we had to watch out for everyone else on the road, and that distracted me.

Every city in the world thinks it has the worst traffic. Dallas has grown in such a hurry, and so many people who move to the city haven't driven in an urban area before, that I think Dallas may be right when it claims its traffic is pretty awful. This congestion extends to the dozens of towns that cluster right around Dallas's outskirts. We were maneuvering among those towns now.

When we'd exhausted small talk about the GPS, Manfred asked me about the case we'd been on before we'd come to Dallas. "Fill me in on your last few days" was the way he put it. "You know this shooting is related to something you've done recently. I don't see how the Carolina case can be related."

I agreed with him. Since Manfred was a colleague, I explained to him about what had happened at Pioneer Rest Cemetery. I wouldn't have broken my unwritten bond with the Joyces, but I'd come to believe they were probably involved in what was happening. More importantly, I knew Manfred would keep it to himself.

"So there are two ways you can go with that," he said. "You can pursue the missing baby, which one of the men you met may have fathered—though I guess that kid isn't a baby anymore, it'd be in school—or you can pursue the possibility one of them threw the rattlesnake at Rich Joyce, startling him into a heart attack."

"There are those two possibilities," I said, relieved to be talking about the whole situation. "And there's the fact that Tolliver's father has shown back up, and he's trying to reconnect with Tolliver. And the girls. And there's the weird thing that after all these years, someone's reported a Cameron sighting."

I filled Manfred in on our family business.

"So this might have to do with your little sisters, somehow. Or with your missing sister. What if this has something to do with Cameron?"

I was startled. "Why would it?"

"There's a caller claiming to have seen Cameron. Then another caller threatens you. Two anonymous phone calls. Those sure might be linked, don't you think?"

"Yes," I said slowly, considering it for the first time. "Yes, of course they could." If I hadn't put this together before, blame it on the fact that people near me kept getting shot. "So this might have to do with Cameron."

"Or with the caller knowing this was the surest way to get you away from Tolliver. Maybe he thought you would leave, go to Texarkana. He couldn't have counted on the police being willing to show you the tape at the police station." There was silence for a long minute. "Uh, Harper," Manfred said. "You sure—for real—that the woman you saw in the tape wasn't your sister?"

"I'm sure," I said. "Her jaw was different, and the way she walked was different. True, she was blond and she seemed the right height. True, I don't know why anyone would claim to have seen her when the case is cold and no one's looking anymore."

"You're . . . I guess you've always been convinced that Cameron is dead?"

"Yes, always." I said that firmly, as if there were no doubt in my mind at all. "She would never let me worry like this, not for all these years."

"But you said you two had it real hard at home."

"Yeah, real hard." I took a deep breath. "She wouldn't do that," I said. I packed my voice full of conviction. "She loved all of us, all the kids."

"So your stepdad resurfaces, and suddenly there's a Cameron

sighting," he said, tactfully abandoning the possibility of my sister's voluntary disappearance. "Isn't that quite a coincidence, too?"

"Yes, it is," I said. "And I don't know what to make of it. I've never thought that he killed her. Maybe I should have considered it. But he was visiting a jailbird friend of his, a guy he did business with, and the time frame excluded Matthew."

"What kind of business?"

"Drugs, and whatever else they could do to raise money." I had to stop to remember. Crazy. I would have never believed I'd forget any detail of that day. "That afternoon Renaldo and Matthew were going to take scrap iron to the recycle plant to get some money. But I don't think they ever made it.They started playing pool."

"What was the friend's full name?"

"Renaldo Simpkins." I was very unhappy that I had to struggle to recover that memory. "He was younger than Matthew, and he was a nice-looking man; I remember that." I tried to picture his face. "Maybe Tolliver will remember," I said finally. I felt that in forgetting even the most minute circumstance of that day, I was betraying the memory of my sister. For the first time, I appreciated the records of that day that the police would have, and Victoria Flores, too.

We pulled into the parking lot of yet another hospital. Christian Memorial was maybe a little newer than God's Mercy, though nothing in that area was very old. We walked into the lobby and asked the lady in the pink smock if she could give us directions. She gave us a practiced smile that aimed at being warm and welcoming. "Detective Powers is up on the fourth floor, but I warn you, it's mighty crowded up there. You may not get to see him."

"Thanks," I said, smiling back just as brightly. We made our way across the lobby and into the elevator, where Manfred's facial decorations attracted a certain amount of attention. He seemed oblivious to the startled and fascinated looks that came our way. When the doors opened on the fourth floor, we were confronted by a sea of faces, and the predominant clothing color was blue. There were cops in several different uniforms standing around, and there were men and women who could only be detectives. There was also a football player or two.

Though it hadn't occurred to me to leave Manfred downstairs, I immediately realized I'd made a mistake bringing him up here. He attracted no little attention, and none of it was positive. I stiffened my back. Manfred was my friend, and he had as much right to be here as anyone. A tall woman with broad shoulders and a thick head of brown hair came up to me. She was in charge. She'd be in charge no matter where she was.

"Hello," she said. "I'm Beverly Powers, Parker's wife. Can I help you?"

"I hope so," I said, feeling hesitant. Somehow, I hadn't foreseen this crowd and all these eyes fixed on me. "I'm Harper Connelly, and Parker was shot when someone tried to kill me. I'd like to thank him. This is my friend Manfred Bernardo, who's driving for me today while my brother's in the hospital."

"Oh, *you're* the young woman," Beverly Powers said, looking at me with a lot more interest. "I'm so glad to meet you. You understand, there are all kinds of stories going around about why you and my husband were out there together, and I very much hope you'll tell me exactly what happened."

"Of course I will," I said, surprised. "There's no big mystery about it."

She waited, her eyebrows raised to indicate she was ready. I was taken aback, since I realized she meant me to tell her here and now.

Everyone around us was listening, though they were all trying to look like they weren't. Out of the corner of my eye, I saw that Manfred had retreated to a spot against the wall. He was standing with his hands folded together, his eyes on me and his stance alert. He looked like an undercover operative of some kind. I was sure that was his intent. The man was a chameleon.

"My brother had been shot two nights before," I explained, trying to pick my words carefully. "And Detective Powers came to the scene then. He and Rudy Flemmons. Detective Flemmons came to see me at my brother's room in the hospital the next day to give me some information, and then last night, when I went back to my hotel, your husband was there. When I told him I was going for a run, since I'd been cooped up with my brother in his hospital room all day, he said he'd run with me, since he wasn't convinced the shooter had actually meant to hit my brother." There was definitely no point in mentioning Powers's avid eyes. "He thought the person who shot Tolliver might have been aiming for me, and someone had called in a death threat for me that day. I guess neither one of us took that seriously enough, which was our big mistake—and for that, I'm so sorry. My only excuse is that I've gotten threats before, and they were always nothing. Your husband said he had his running clothes in his trunk, and he changed in his car, and we started out running. He got winded pretty quick—excuse me, he just hadn't run in a long time, I guess." To my surprise, my audience had relaxed considerably while I was telling Beverly Powers how her husband had come to be shot, and when I described how winded he'd gotten, a few people actually laughed, and a smile flickered across Beverly Powers's face.

I suddenly understood: Mrs. Powers and Parker's fellow officers had thought I'd been having an affair with him. My no-frills explanation had dispelled that suspicion. They weren't really amused; they were relieved.

"We were running up and down the aisles of that big bus depot across from the high school on Jacaranda." I saw some nods out of the corner of my eye. "We heard a car come into the lot, and Detective Powers and I both thought it was after us, but then it sped away. We decided we better go back to the hotel, and we were walking on the street going back. This guy jumped out from behind some bushes and fired. I don't know if he was trying to hit me or your husband, but Detective Powers shoved me aside real quick. That meant he caught the bullets. I'm really sorry. He was so brave, and I feel awful about him getting hurt so badly. I called 911 as soon as I could."

"That saved his life," Beverly said. Her face was round and sweet, but her eyes were another matter. Whatever sport she'd played, this woman had been a ferocious competitor.

I was profoundly glad I hadn't been having an affair with her husband.

"Please, come see him," Beverly said.

"Is he conscious?"

"No," she said, and I understood by the way she said that one word that there was a good chance Detective Powers would never be conscious again.

Taking my hand, the tall woman led me to a glass-walled room, and I looked at her husband. He looked awful, and he was out of it. I didn't know if it was the medication, or if he was in a deep sleep, or if he was maybe in a coma.

"I'm sorry," I said. He was going to die. I'm not always right—death can hang over people like a shadow without ever descending—but with Detective Powers, I was pretty sure. I hoped I was wrong.

"Thanks for giving me a little longer with him," she said. We stood for a moment in silence.

"I've got to get back to my brother," I said. "I appreciate your talking to me, and letting me see him. Please tell him thanks for what he did for me."

I patted Beverly's shoulder in an awkward way and eased my way through the crowd over to Manfred, who took my hand and pressed the elevator button. The door opened immediately, and we stepped into an empty elevator. I was praying for the doors to shut out the painful scene.

"I'm glad you came with me," I said. "That must have been pretty nerve-wracking for you."

"Oh, no, I love going into a pen of lions wearing a sign that says *Edible Lamb.*" Now that we were alone, Manfred's bland mask relaxed into a face that was just as relieved as mine must have been.

Our hands were gripping so tightly that I could feel his bones against mine. Even as I realized I was in pain, he eased his hold on me.

"That was an adventure," he said, in a more normal voice. "What next? Alligator wrestling?"

"No, I thought we'd go eat lunch. Then I need to go back to Tolliver's room and sit with him." We were in the car and driving over to the hotel when Manfred asked, "Did the doctor say when Tolliver would be released?"

"He'll get out tomorrow. I'm sure I'll have to do some nursing. Maybe I should see if I can get a suite at another hotel, instead of the room I've got now. We might be there for a week or so, because the doctor said Tolliver had to stay quiet. He'll be in the bed a lot, and I don't want to bother him."

"You're definitely settled with Tolliver, then? He's the one?" Manfred asked, his face suddenly serious.

"He's the one," I said. "He's been the one since I met him. Of course, you were always my fallback position." I tried a smile. To my relief, he returned it.

"I'll have to cast my net wider," he said dramatically. "Maybe I'll haul in a mermaid."

"If anyone could find a mermaid, you'd be the one," I said.

"Speaking of mermaids, are you checking the mirrors for tails? Or are you just scared of my driving?"

"I'm hoping I can tell if someone's following us. That's happened here, and for the life of me, I can't spot anyone. It's good I don't want to be a detective." Manfred tried to watch, too, but he didn't notice a car that was doing everything we did. In Dallas traffic, that wasn't decisive, but at least I felt a little better.

When we reached the hotel, I collected my stuff and checked out, after first calling another chain hotel down the block to see if they had a suite-type room available. They did, and I booked it under Tolliver's name. The anonymous caller had known I was in this hotel, and though it wouldn't be hard to find me again, I might as well not make it completely easy. I reserved the suite for six nights, figuring I could always check out earlier if Tolliver was doing well enough to leave town. I also called Mark, to tell him where we'd be. Then Manfred drove me to the new hotel and helped me carry in Tolliver's bags as well as mine.

We went out to eat after that, to a family-style restaurant with a long salad bar. It was about time I ate something that wasn't actively bad for me, and I loaded up my plate with salad and fruit. A little to my surprise, Manfred did, too.

My companion was a great believer in conversation. Or at least, he enjoyed talking while I listened. I wondered how well Manfred fitted in with his peers, because he needed to say a lot of things out loud that he maybe hadn't had a chance to say, mostly about Xylda and how much he missed her, the things she'd taught him, the odd items he'd found stored away in her house.

"Thanks for showing up today," I said when there was a lull in the chatter.

He shrugged. He looked half proud, half uncomfortable. "I knew you needed me," he said and found something else to look at.

"I'd like you to meet some of these people and tell me what you get from them," I said. "If I can think of a way to make it look natural."

He looked all too happy about the prospect of doing me a favor.

"Of course, if you need to go home, I'll understand," I said.

"No," he said. "I do a lot of my business on the Web now, and I don't have any readings scheduled for this week. I brought my laptop and my cell; that takes care of me. What am I looking for?" The sense of fun faded from his face, and I was looking at an older person than the Manfred I was used to.

"You're looking for whatever you can tell me about these people," I said. "Someone shot Tolliver. Someone shot Detective Powers, though I guess they were trying to hit me. And I think it was one of these people. I want to know why."

"Not who?"

"Well, of course that, too. But the 'why' is pretty important. I need to know if I'm the target or not."

He nodded. "I get it."

We drove back to the hospital, and Manfred dropped me off at a side entrance, the closest to providing concealment that the hospital offered. I scooted inside and made my way to the bank of elevators off the lobby. I didn't think anyone was paying any particular attention to me, and no one seemed to be loitering. Everyone I looked at seemed to have a purpose, and no one spoke to me.

When I got back to Tolliver's room, I found him sitting up in the chair. I felt a wide smile spread across my face.

"Oh, you got adventurous," I said, beaming at him.

"Hey, I'm no slacker," he said, but he smiled back. "Hearing I might get out made me feel better than any of the drugs. How was your trip across the city with the amazing Manfred?"

I told Tolliver about our visit to Detective Powers. "Once they all understood I wasn't sleeping with him, they were all relieved," I said.

"When he gets better, you can tell him his fellow officers thought he was a real dog."

"I don't think he's going to get better," I said. "I think he's going to die."

Tolliver took my hand. "Harper, that's not up to us. All we can do is hope he pulls through."

That was such a sweet thing to say; maybe not the words so much as the way Tolliver said it. I could tell he loved me. I cried a little, and he let me without saying anything patronizing, and then I helped him back into bed because he was tired. We should have been talking about who shot him, but at the moment we were simply too flattened.

Mark and Matthew came in together an hour later.

We were watching an old movie, and we were actually enjoying it, but I switched it off to be polite. As they stood together at the foot of the bed, I noticed that Mark and Matthew were much more alike in looks than Tolliver and his dad were. The shorter, thicker build, the square faces . . . All three men had the same coloring, but other than that, Tolliver definitely looked more like his mom. I'd only seen pictures of the first Mrs. Lang, but she'd had Tolliver's much narrower face and thinner build.

I wondered if they wanted me to leave.

Tolliver didn't give me any signal one way or the other, and though I half expected Matthew to tell me he wanted to talk to his sons alone, he didn't say a word about it, so I stayed.

After the usual inquiries into Tolliver's recovery and when he'd get out of the hospital, Mark said, "I wondered if you'd like to come back to stay with me, at my house, I mean. While you get better."

"Your house," Tolliver said, as if he'd never heard of such a thing. We'd been to Mark's house exactly once. He'd had us over to dinner, and he'd ordered out. It was an absolutely standard three-bedroom ranch with a fenced-in backyard.

"Yeah, why not? Since you and Harper are . . ." Here he made a kind of indeterminate gesture, meant to indicate that we were sleeping together. "That means you can share a bed, so there'll be room."

"So, Dad's staying in the other room now?" Tolliver didn't look at his father as he spoke to Mark. He'd sure picked up on that little indicator.

"Yes, he is," Mark said. "It just made sense, since his job doesn't pay a lot, and the bedroom was empty."

"I already got us a suite at a hotel," I said. I made sure my voice was both quiet and neutral. I didn't want to make this a confrontation.

But it looked as though I wasn't going to get my wish.

"Listen," Mark said, flushing up as he did when he was angry, "you butt out, Harper. This is my brother, and I get to ask him to stay with me. It's his call. We're family."

Not only was I angry now, too, I was hurt. I didn't care if I ever got called a member of Matthew's family, but Mark and I had shared a lot of woe together. I thought we kids had been our own family. I could feel my own face reddening.

"Mark," Tolliver said sharply, "Harper is my family. She's been my family for years now. Yours, too. I *know* you remember how we had to stick together."

Mark looked down at the floor, conflict making his face really distressing to watch.

"It's okay, Mark," Matthew said. "I understand what they're saying. You-all did have to band together. Laurel and I weren't exactly up to making a family work. We were together, but we weren't a real family. Tolliver's right."

Overkill, I thought.

"Dad," Mark mumbled, like he was seventeen again. "You tried to keep us together."

"I did," Matthew said. "But my addictions got in the way."

I tried very hard not to roll my eyes. Drama 101. Tolliver was watching Matthew confess—yet again—and his face was unreadable.

There were still times when I couldn't tell what Tolliver was thinking, and right now was definitely one of those times. He might be softening toward his father, or he might be planning how to kill him. At the moment, I would vote for the killing.

"Please, Tolliver, give me a chance to get to know you again," Matthew pleaded.

There was a long silence. Mark said, "Tol, you remember when Gracie got so sick? You remember, Dad took her to the hospital? And the doctors gave her antibiotics and she came home so much better?"

I'd forgotten about that. It had been a long time ago. Gracie had been very little, maybe only four months old. How old had I been? Fifteen? It had been hugely embarrassing to have a baby sister, I remembered, because that was plain evidence that my mother and her husband were actually having sex.

It's amazing what can embarrass you at fifteen.

I knew something about babies by then, because we'd already had the care of Mariella. My mother had been a little better when our first half sister was born, though, and she'd done at least some of the everyday care. We'd been able to leave Mariella with her during the school day, for example. That was out of the question when Gracie was born, underweight and sickly. Why they didn't take Gracie away from Mom in the hospital, I don't know. We had almost prayed that someone would take the baby or that Mom would come to her senses and give Gracie up for adoption.

Neither of those things had come to pass. So Cameron and I had taken turns babysitting for other families, and the boys had earned money, and Matthew had chipped in, too. We'd been able to take the girls to day care while we were out of the house.

Then Gracie, who'd always had trouble with her breathing, had gotten really bad. I couldn't remember much about it, except being scared. We'd been so impressed that Matthew had taken her to the hospital.

"Are you saying I should make friends with Dad because one time, *one time*, he acted like a real father?" Tolliver said, and I let myself exhale. He wasn't fooled.

"Oh, Tolliver." Matthew shook his head, grief written in big letters on his face. "I'm trying to stay straight, son. Don't harden your heart against me."

It took everything I had not to speak, but I was proud that I could hold my tongue. For a second, my heart went to my throat, because I thought I detected a weakening in Tolliver's face. "Goodbye, Mark. Dad. Thanks for coming by," he said, and I breathed out a silent sigh of relief.

The two visitors looked at each other, then at me. They obviously wanted me to leave the room, but I wasn't going to do it. After a moment, they could tell I was staying put.

Matthew said, "If you need our help transferring Tolliver to the hotel, just call Mark's number and leave a message, Harper. We'll be glad to do whatever we can."

I nodded.

Mark said, "I'm sorry we can't all . . ." His voice trailed off miserably. "Jeez, I wish you two could forgive and forget."

I found this incredible. I had no response to make to my stepbrother, but I had something to say to my stepfather. "I learned some of the basic lessons of my life under your neglect, Matthew. I don't hate you, but I'm sure not going to forget. That would be under the category of really, really stupid."

Matthew looked directly at me, and for a second I saw his undisguised dislike before he pulled the repentant mask back over his true face.

"I'm sorry you feel that way, Harper," he said smoothly. "Son, you'll be in my prayers."

Tolliver looked at him silently. Then his father and his brother turned and left the room.

"He hates me," I said.

"I'm not so sure he feels any different about me," Tolliver said. "If I fall down three flights of stairs, don't call them. I love Mark and he's my brother, but he's back under Dad's thumb, and I don't trust him at all."

twelve

I left the hospital after dark, and I drove around for a while until I was sure there was no one behind me. I was so new to worrying about being followed that I'm sure there could have been five cars following my trail and I might not have realized it, but I did my best. I parked close to the hotel entrance, and I practically ran into the lobby. The suite was on the second floor, and I waited in the hall until I was sure no one was in sight to watch to see which door I unlocked.

I unpacked and did a little ironing. I optimistically checked over Tolliver's clothes, picking out something he could wear home. I figured he wouldn't be comfortable stretching his arm up to pull on a T-shirt or polo shirt, so I decided on a sports shirt and jeans. I put them in a little bag. I was ready.

After I'd watched the news, I called down for room service. I was glad there was a restaurant attached to the hotel, because I didn't want to go out by myself. I was a little surprised I hadn't gotten a call from Manfred offering to join me for supper, but whether or not I had a companion, I was hungry. I ordered a Caesar salad and some minestrone, figuring that should taste good even if the cook wasn't hugely talented.

I hustled to the door when the expected knock came, but I paused before flinging it open. In my experience, the server knocking at the door always said, "Room service." This one hadn't.

With my ear to the door, I listened. I thought someone on the other side might be doing exactly the same thing.

Of course I should look to see who was standing there. But weirdly, I found myself scared to put my eye to the peephole. I was afraid the shooter was standing out there with a gun, and he'd fire through the door if he had proof I was inside. I knew if you were alert you could tell when the person in the room was looking out, and for the life of me, I couldn't make myself do it.

I heard the elevator down the hall, and I heard the ding as it arrived at my floor and the sound of the doors opening. There was the rattle of the cart, a sound I recognized, and I heard someone shift positions right outside my door. Yes, someone was still there. But after a second, my caller walked rapidly away. I put my eye to the peephole, but it was too late. I didn't catch a glimpse of whoever had been at the door.

The next second there was a much firmer knock, and a woman's voice said, "Room service." The peephole verified that this was in fact a server with a cart, and I opened the door without hesitation once I saw how bored she seemed.

"Did you see someone walking away from my door?" I asked. I didn't want to seem too paranoid, so I added, "I was taking a nap, and I thought I heard someone knock right before you did, but by the time I made it to the door, they were gone."

"There was someone walking the other way," the woman said, "but I didn't see his face. Sorry."

That was the end of that, apparently.

I was pretty angry with myself. I should have looked through the peephole. Maybe I would have discovered it was a stranger who'd gotten the wrong room number. Maybe I would have seen Manfred, who knew I was in this hotel. Or maybe I would have seen the face of my enemy.

Disappointed in my fearful self, I turned on the television set and watched a rerun of *Law and Order* while I had my soup and my salad. The sun never sets on *Law and Order*, and if I'd seen that episode too many times, there was always *CSI* in any of its incarnations. There is plenty of justice on television, but not so much in the real world. Maybe that's why so many of us like television so much.

I ate slowly, and found that I was trying to chew quietly so I could listen for noise at the door. This was silly. I put on the chain and the night bolt, and with that measure of reassurance, I felt better. After I'd eaten, I looked out very carefully before I pushed the cart into the hall, and I retreated into the room and locked up again. There were no doors leading to other rooms, and on the second floor I felt no one could get in the window. But I drew the drapes.

And I stayed isolated in the room until the next morning.

It was no way to live.

Tolliver looked even better the next day, and the doctor said he could check out of the hospital. He gave me a list of instructions. The wound was not supposed to get wet. Tolliver was not supposed to lift anything with his right arm. He was supposed to have some physical therapy on the arm when he got home. (I supposed in our case that would mean when we returned to St. Louis.) Of course the discharge process took forever, but eventually we were both in the front seat of our car together, and I'd buckled Tolliver in.

I started to say, "I wish we could just leave," but then I thought that might make Tolliver feel bad. We had to follow the doctor's orders, so we had to stay a few more days. I was increasingly eager to leave Texas. I'd thought we might start house hunting this trip, and instead I wanted to pack our stuff into the car and drive like hell.

Tolliver looked out the car window as though he'd been in prison, as though he hadn't seen restaurants and hotels and traffic in years of solitary confinement. He had on the jeans and button-up shirt I'd brought him, and he looked a lot more like himself than he had in the hospital smock.

He caught me looking sideways at him. "I know I look like hell," he said, matter-of-factly. "You don't need to tell me."

"I was thinking you looked really great," I said innocently, and he laughed.

"Right," he said.

"I've never gotten shot before. Not really. Just grazed. Was it really like a big fist hitting you? That's the way they always describe it in books."

"If the really big fist travels all the way through you, making you bleed and causing some of the worst pain you've ever felt, yeah," he said. "It hurt so bad I wanted to die for a minute."

"Gosh," I said. I tried to imagine pain that intense. I'd been hurt, and hurt badly, but when the lightning had struck, I hadn't felt anything for a few seconds, except that I was in another world, and then back in this one. After that, I'd pretty much hurt all over. My mother had told me that childbirth was horribly painful, but I'd never experienced that.

"I hope that never happens again," I said. "To either of us."

"Have you heard from anyone?" he asked.

I thought that was an odd way to put it. "Who, specifically?" I asked.

"Victoria came to the hospital last night," he said.

I held my tongue for a second. "Should I be jealous?" I asked when I could manage the appropriately light tone.

"Not any more jealous than I am of Manfred."

Uh-oh. "Then you'd better tell me all about it."

We pulled up at the hotel then, and our talk was postponed while I went around the car to open Tolliver's door. He rotated his feet out, I pulled a little with my hand under his good arm, and out he came. He made a face, and I knew the process had hurt. He moved away from the door, and I shut and locked the car. We went into the hotel slowly. I was more dismayed than I cared to show when I realized just how shaky Tolliver was.

We got through the lobby just fine, then into the elevator. I was trying to keep my eyes on Tolliver in case he needed support, and also trying to watch out for some approaching trouble, so I felt like a demented woman, with my eyes darting here and there and then back to my patient.

When we were actually in our room, I heaved a sigh of sheer relief and helped Tolliver lie down on the bed. I pulled a chair up to the bed, but that felt too much like the hospital, so I lay down beside him and turned on my side so I could look at him.

He took a minute to get settled. Then he turned his head so his eyes would meet mine.

"This is so much better," he said. "This is better than anything."

I agreed that it was. In the spirit of welcoming him back to the nonhospital world, I unzipped his pants and gave him some physical therapy he hadn't expected, which pleased him so much that after kissing me, he fell asleep, and so did I.

We were wakened by a knock at the door. I found myself wishing for a door that I could lock, a door no one could knock on. I should have put out a Do Not Disturb sign. Tolliver stirred, and his eyes opened. I rolled off the bed, straightened myself up and ran a hand through my hair, and went out of the bedroom and through the living room to see who was there. This time, I mustered up my courage and looked through the peephole.

To my astonishment, since I hadn't told anyone in the police department where we were staying now, Rudy Flemmons was outside the door.

"It's the detective," I said. I'd gone back to the doorway into the bedroom. I was stupid with sleep. "Rudy Flemmons, not the one that got shot."

"I'd assumed that," Tolliver said and yawned. "I guess you better let him in." He zipped his jeans and I buttoned them, and we smiled at each other.

I let Detective Flemmons in, and then I helped Tolliver out to the living room to share in the conversation. Tolliver sat carefully on the couch, and Flemmons took the armchair.

"How long have you two been here?" he asked.

I looked at my watch. "Well, we checked out of the hospital about an hour and a half ago," I said. "We came right here and took a nap."

Tolliver nodded.

Rudy Flemmons said, "Have you seen your friend Victoria Flores in the past two days?"

"Yes," Tolliver said right away. "She came by the hospital last night. Harper wasn't there, she'd already left. I guess Victoria stayed for about forty-five minutes, and then she took off. That must have been about . . . man, I don't know, I was taking a lot of stuff for pain. I think around eight o'clock. I haven't seen her since then."

"She never came home last night. She'd left her daughter, Mari-Carmen, with her mother, and her mother called the police when Victoria was late picking the child up. Normally, the police wouldn't really think much of that, an adult woman being late picking up her kid, but Victoria used to be on the Texarkana force and some of us know her. She was never late to anything involving her kid, not without calling and explaining. Victoria is a good mother."

I could tell from his face that he was one of the Garland cops who knew her well. I thought maybe he knew her *very* well. "Have you found anyone who saw her later than my brother?"

"No," he said, his voice heavy and depressed. "I haven't."

At least no one could imagine that Tolliver had leaped from his hospital bed, subdued Victoria, and stowed her under the bed until he could bribe the janitor to dispose of her body.

"Her mom hasn't heard from her at all?"

The detective shook his head.

"That's awful," I said. "I . . . That's awful."

I remembered Tolliver had been about to tell me a story involving Victoria when we'd gotten to the hotel. I was sitting on the couch beside him, and I turned my head to catch his eyes. I raised my eyebrows in query. Would he bring it up?

He gave an infinitesimal shake of his head. No.

All right.

"What did you two talk about? Did Victoria give any indication of what she was working on, or where she planned to go after she left the hospital?"

"I'm afraid we mostly talked about me," Tolliver admitted. "She asked questions about the bullet, about whether the place where the shooter had fired from had been found, if there'd been any other random shootings that night—you-all told Harper there'd been one real close to the motel, right?—how long I was going to have to stay in the hospital, stuff like that."

"Did she say anything personal?"

"Yes. She said that she'd dated a guy for a while, a guy on the force, and they'd recently broken up. She said she'd reconsidered, and she was going to call him last night."

I hadn't expected such a dramatic reaction. Detective Flemmons turned white as a sheet. I thought he was going to pass out. "She said that?" he said, and almost choked on the words.

"Yeah," Tolliver said, as startled as I was. "That's almost word for word. I was surprised, because we'd never talked about her love life before. We weren't that close, and she didn't like to talk about personal stuff, either. You know the cop she was seeing?"

"Yes," Flemmons said. "It was me."

Neither of us had anything to say, or any idea how to respond, when we heard that.

Flemmons was there for at least another quarter hour, and he asked Tolliver about twenty more questions, getting every detail of the conversation he'd had with Victoria, but Tolliver never elaborated on what Victoria had told him. I was surprised—and not a little worried—that Tolliver was playing the situation so close to the vest.

I told Rudy Flemmons about the mysterious person at my door the night before, the person who'd knocked before room service came. I didn't really think that person had been Victoria Flores, but I wanted to tell someone that the little incident had occurred.

At last, Detective Flemmons got up to leave. I felt incredibly relieved when I'd shut the door behind him. I waited, listening, and after a moment I heard him go down the hall to the elevators. I heard the ping of the arriving elevator, and then the whoosh of the doors as they opened and shut. I even opened our door and looked around to make sure no one was there.

I was getting paranoid as hell, but I thought I had good reason.

"Tell me," I said. Though Tolliver was looking very tired and got up laboriously so I could help him back to the bed, I was determined to hear what he'd been about to say when Rudy Flemmons had come to our door.

When he was flat on his back, Tolliver said, "She asked me if I believed the Joyces really wanted to find the baby Mariah Parish carried, or if I thought they wanted to kill the child."

"Kill the child," I said, stunned. Of course, I got the idea right away. "A Joyce baby would inherit at least a fourth of the estate, I guess. An heir of the body, isn't that the phrase? If the lawyer who drew it up used that phrase, the kid would inherit whether it's legitimate or not. I don't suppose there's any question of Rich Joyce marrying Mariah on the sly?"

Tolliver shook his head. "No, he would have married her legally, not in some made-up ceremony. He was a four-square kind of guy, according to Victoria. And if the baby was his, he'd own up to it. If he'd known about it."

"She was sure about that?"

"She was sure because she'd interviewed a lot of people who'd known Rich Joyce, people who'd been close to him. They all told Victoria that Lizzie Joyce is like her granddad, no-nonsense and basically honest, but Kate and Drex are all about the money."

"What about Chip, the boyfriend?"

"She didn't mention him."

"Victoria'd found all of this out already?"

"Yeah, she'd been busy."

"Why'd she tell you all this? I'm guessing it wasn't because she thought you were cute, since she was thinking about getting back together with Rudy Flemmons."

"Because she thought one of the Joyces had shot me. That's why she told me."

"Okay, I'm still not following."

"They all think you know more about Rich Joyce's death than you said at the graveside. They're upset because you identified Mariah's cause of death and raised the question of the existence of a baby at all. They're afraid, I guess, that you'll find the baby's body."

"Victoria didn't think the baby was alive? She thought someone had killed the baby?"

I felt sick inside. I've seen and heard of bad things, evil things, because of this "gift" the lightning left me. In the past, so many babies died; so many things could go wrong, things that are rare now. I'd stood on many tiny graves and seen the still, white faces, and it never failed to be a sad moment. The murder of a child was the worst of crimes, in my book, the absolute rock bottom of evil.

"That's what she was assuming. She couldn't find any birth record. So maybe Mariah had the child by herself."

"Oh, what kind of woman doesn't go to the hospital when she feels her time's there?"

"Maybe one who can't," Tolliver said.

I felt my lips compress with disgust and horror. "You mean someone wouldn't let her go to the hospital? Or simply allowed her to die of neglect?" I didn't need to say that was cruel and inhuman. Tolliver shared my feelings.

"It's possible. That's the best explanation for her having died after childbirth, and there being no record of the child or a hospital stay for her."

"And if it wasn't for me . . ."

"No one would ever have known any of this."

Put that way, I guess it was no surprise that someone wanted me dead.

thirteen

I ran in place on the treadmill in the "exercise room," the hotel's token nod to fitness. At least it was in an enclosed area, which right now meant "safe." I'd woken up early, and I could tell by his breathing that Tolliver was deep in dreamland.

I had a better picture of why all these awful things were happening around me, but I didn't have any idea what to do about it. I had nothing to take to the police, nothing, and the Joyces were rich and connected. I didn't know if all of them were involved, or if the shooter and the murderer (I considered both the deaths of Mariah Parish and Rich Joyce to be murders) were one and the same and acting alone. The three Joyces and the Joyce boyfriend were all capable people with guns, almost undoubtedly. Maybe I was stereotyping, but I didn't think a western rancher like Rich Joyce would teach his granddaughters how to ride rodeo and neglect to teach them how to shoot, and Drex would have to learn as a matter of course.

The boyfriend, too. I knew the least about Chip Moseley. He looked like a good match for Lizzie; he was just as lean and weather-beaten, and he looked competent and down-to-earth. He was skeptical of my claims, but he could join most of the people I met in that respect.

I was drenched with sweat when I began my cooldown. I walked for ten more minutes, then I dried my face with a towel and went back to the room. I was beginning to hate hotel rooms. I wouldn't have thought there was much of a domestic gene in me, but I wanted a home, a real home. I wanted a bedspread that wasn't synthetic. I wanted sheets that only I had slept on. I wanted to keep my clothes folded in a drawer; I didn't want to fish them out of a suitcase. I wanted a bookcase, not a cardboard box. We had those things in our apartment, but even the apartment didn't have any air of permanency. It was just a nicer rental than the hotel rooms.

In the elevator, I took a deep breath and shoved all those thoughts into a bucket in the corner of my mind. I put a heavy lid on the bucket and weighted that lid down with a rock. Lots of imagery, but I wanted to be sure I wasn't distracted at this crucial time when someone was gunning for us. I had to be extra strong with Tolliver sidelined.

Rudy Flemmons was standing outside the room, raising his hand to knock.

"Detective," I called, "hold on a minute."

He stayed in position, one hand raised in a fist, and I knew from the way he was standing that something was very wrong.

I came up to him and examined his face, or at least his profile. He didn't turn to look at me.

"Oh, no," I breathed. "Listen, let's go in the room." I reached past him to unlock the door, and we entered. I flicked on the light, hoping I wasn't waking Tolliver, but then I saw that the light was on in the bathroom and I knew he was up. I knocked on the door. "Hey, you okay in there? We've got company."

"This early?" he asked, and I knew he'd had a bad night.

"Honey, just get out here," I said, and hoped he got the message.

He did, and in thirty seconds he'd come out and made his way over to the seating area. I could tell by the way he was moving that he wasn't feeling good. I hurried to bring him some orange juice from the little refrigerator. There wasn't any point in offering some to Rudy Flemmons, who was sunk in a state that I assumed to be misery or extreme apprehension. I didn't know him well enough to tell exactly; I just knew it was bad.

It must have been an unpleasant way for Tolliver to start the day, but he eased back on the couch.

"Tell us why you're here," Tolliver said.

"I think Victoria's dead," Rudy Flemmons said. "Her car was found this morning, in a cemetery in Garland. Her purse was in it."

"But you haven't found her body?" I said.

"No. I was wondering if you would come take a look."

This was sad, and it was also professionally awkward. In view of his obvious misery and our friendship with Victoria, I wasn't even thinking about money. I was thinking about the rest of the cops out there who would decide that my arrival on the scene was Rudy Flemmon's anxiety taking an extreme form.

But there wasn't much I could say except, "Give me ten minutes."

I jumped into the shower, soaped up and rinsed off, brushed my teeth, and pulled on my clothes. I put on boots; not high-heeled fashion boots, but flat, waterproof Uggs. The weather had been intermittently rainy, and I didn't want to get caught by surprise. Though I hadn't watched the forecast that morning or checked the paper,

I noticed Rudy was wearing a heavy jacket, and I bundled up accordingly.

There was no question of Tolliver coming. That idea suddenly hit me in the face when I was ready to go out the door. Sloppy weather, cemetery conditions: not ideal for someone recovering from a gunshot wound.

"I'll be back as soon as I can," I said, with a terrible pang of anxiety. "You don't do anything. I mean, get back in bed and watch TV. I'll call you if anything happens, all right?"

Tolliver was as stricken by the belated realization that I was going out on a work call alone as I was. "Get some candy out of my jacket pocket," he said, and I did. "Don't do anything that's going to hurt you," he said severely.

"Don't worry," I said, and then I told Rudy Flemmons I was ready to go, though that was far from the truth.

On the ride through the misty rain, in the heavy morning traffic, we were silent. Rudy called someone on the radio to tell them we were on the way, and those were the only words spoken in fifteen minutes.

"I know you charge for this," he said suddenly, as he pulled in behind a long line of cars on a road through a huge cemetery, the modern kind that forbids headstones. I was being bombarded by the vibrations of the corpses, coming from all directions. They were all intense, since this was a relatively new burial ground. I thought the oldest was maybe twenty years in the ground.

"Not an issue. Please don't mention it again," I said, and got out of the car. The last thing I wanted to do was debate prices while I was looking for this sad man's girlfriend.

You would think that if I knew the person it would be easier, but it isn't. Otherwise, I would have found my sister long ago. The dead clamor for attention with equal intensity, and if Victoria was out here somewhere, she was simply part of the chorus. It was hard to avoid the graves that called for my attention, and it was incredibly painful to be here without Tolliver. I had no anchor.

Common sense, I told myself. I went as close to the abandoned car as I could. One technician was peering at the tire treads, in a desultory way that told me the major work had been done. There were cops searching the landscaped graveyard, which was on rolling ground. It was a common layout for a modern place: there were areas defined by the tall statue in the middle, like an angel garden or a cross area, to help visitors navigate to the correct gravesite. I had no idea what method was used, whether the plots radiated out from the central sculpture or if you got to pick your site within that area. The place was looking pretty full—lying room only. There was a caretaker's shed in the distance and a chapel in the middle, a sizable marble structure that probably held a mausoleum and a columbarium. Across the width of the grounds I could see a funeral taking place as the search for Victoria Flores went on around me.

Hoping profoundly that no one would notice me, I closed my eyes and reached out. So many signals to sort through, so many clamoring to be recognized; I shuddered, but I persevered.

Freshest. Freshest. I needed something brand spanking new. That is, someone who'd passed over yesterday or even a few hours ago. There, out in front of me. I opened my eyes and walked to a grave still strewn with funeral flowers. I closed my eyes again, reached down.

"No," I muttered. "Not her." I was not surprised to find the detective at my elbow. "This is Brandon Barstow, who died in a car wreck,"

I told him. I reached out again. I felt the pull coming from the caretaker's shed. Very fresh.

"Here we go," I said, to the air in front of me, and I began walking. I watched my feet, because when I was tracking, it was easy to forget where my feet were going. Rudy Flemmons was right behind me, but he didn't know how to help me. That was okay; I could make it by myself.

The grass was wet and the pine needles made the ground slick in some spots. I knew where I was going; now there was no more uncertainty.

"They looked over here already," the detective said.

"Someone's here, though," I said. I already knew the bottom line on this search. "They're going to try to say I knew this somehow," I muttered, "and they'll try to keep me here."

The body wasn't in the shed itself, or right behind it. The ground behind the shed sloped down to a drainage ditch, where earth and grass thinly covered a culvert. Victoria was in the culvert; her body had been stuffed up inside, and it wasn't visible at all. But I could tell she was there, and I could tell she'd been shot and had bled out.

Rudy looked down uncomprehendingly, and I pointed to the mouth of the culvert. There was nothing for me to say. He scrambled down the slope and fell to his knees. He bent over and peered inside.

And he yelled.

"Here! Here!" he bellowed, and they all came running, every law enforcement person on the scene, including the guy who'd been examining the vehicle. Rudy was thinking, I suppose, that there was a chance she was still alive, but he was just dreaming or staving off the truth. I can't find the living.

I got out of their way, and went back to Victoria's abandoned car.

The trunk was standing open. I found myself staring down into it, trying to look uninterested. There were file folders, lots of loose ones and some in a bundle bound together with a huge rubber band. The top one was labeled *Lizzie Joyce*, and before I could think about what I was doing I picked up the bundle and tossed it in Rudy's car. There were still plenty of file folders left, I told myself—and I also told myself that we owed it to ourselves to find out about our enemies.

I saw afterward that this had been the wrong action to take, incidentally. I should have left things to the police. But at the moment, it seemed a natural, even clever, tactic. That's all I can say in my own defense. One of these people was shooting at us; I had to find out which one was the most likely.

I got into Rudy's car. He had an old jacket tossed into the backseat, and I pulled it into the front and bundled it around me as though I were cold, which wasn't far from the truth. After a few minutes, a uniformed guy came up and said he was supposed to take me back to the hotel. I had put on the jacket and zipped it up with the files inside, by that time. I got out of Rudy's car and climbed into the squad car.

The uniform, a man in his thirties, had a shaven head and a grim face—not too surprising, considering the circumstances. He said exactly one thing to me on our drive. "As far as we're concerned, we found her during our search," he said, and he gave me a look that was supposed to make me quake in my boots. It was easy to nod in agreement. I must have looked cowed, because he didn't speak after that.

I made a clumsy job of getting out of the car because of the files. He must have wondered if I was physically disabled in some way, but it didn't soften his attitude any. With my arms wrapped across my middle I strode into the hotel, blessing the automatic doors that allowed me to keep my hands in place, my contraband secure, as I made my way to the elevator.

My hands were cold, and I had a hard time fishing out my plastic key card and putting it in the lock the right way, but the door opened and I almost leaped into the room.

"What happened?" Tolliver called instantly, and I hurried into the bedroom. The maid had been in, and the bed had been made; he was in clean pajamas and lying on top of the bedspread, with the blanket from the foldout couch spread over him. The curtains were open on the dismal gray day. It had begun raining while I was in the elevator. That would complicate things at the cemetery. Raindrops were sliding down the window glass. I went up to the bed, leaned over it, and pulled the bottom of Rudy Flemmons's old jacket open. The files landed on the bedspread with a thud.

"What have you done?" Tolliver asked, not in an accusatory way, but more as if he was simply interested. He clicked off the television and reached out for the bundle, but I was there ahead of him. I pulled off the rubber band, putting it aside for future use, and I handed him the top file, the one labeled *Lizzie Joyce.*

"So she was there," he said. "Dammit, she loved her little girl. This is getting worse and worse. Did it take long to find her?"

"Ten minutes," I said. "A patrolman brought me back."

"You stole the files?"

"Yeah. Out of her trunk."

"How likely are they to come looking?"

"Don't know how hard they'd looked before everyone scrambled to see if she could be revived. Maybe they'd already taken pictures." I shrugged. I couldn't undo it now.

"What are we looking for?" he asked.

"We're trying to find out which one of these people is most likely to be the one who shot you."

"Then you have my undivided attention," he said.

I took off my wet, muddy boots, climbed up on the bed with him, and started in on Kate's file while he tackled Lizzie's.

An hour later I had to take a break and call room service for some coffee and some food. Neither of us had had breakfast, and it was now almost eleven.

We'd learned a lot.

"She was really good," I said. I'd never appreciated Victoria before, but I did now. In a very short time, she'd amassed a lot of information and interviewed quite a few people.

Tolliver was grateful to get a cup of coffee, and he was also glad to get a bran muffin. I slathered it with butter for him, an unusual indulgence. He chewed and swallowed and took another sip of coffee. "God, that tastes good after hospital food," he said. "Lizzie Joyce is a colorful woman, even more colorful than she seemed that day at the cemetery. She really is a barrel-riding champion, several times over, and she's won a lot of other rodeo titles. She was rodeo queen in her teens, all over the state, looks like, and she was also an honor graduate from high school and ranked thirtieth in her class at Baylor."

I didn't know how many people were in a Baylor class, but that sounded pretty damn good to me. "What was her major, just out of curiosity?"

"Business," he said. "Her dad was already grooming her to take over from him. The Joyces own a huge ranch, but the bulk of his money came from oil in the big boom, and it's since been invested, a lot of it overseas. There is a corps of accountants who just look after

Joyce holdings. Victoria says they all keep watch over each other, too, so no one can embezzle; or at least, they won't get away with it if they do. The Joyces also have a big interest in a law firm founded by an uncle."

"So, what do they do?" I asked.

Tolliver understood what I meant, which was kind of amazing. "They donate a lot of money to cancer research; that's what took Rich Joyce's wife. They maintain a ranch for disabled children. That's their big charity. It's open five months a year, and the Joyces pay the salaries of the staff, though they accept donations, too. Then they have the main ranch, which the boyfriend, Chip Moseley, is in charge of running. They live there, when they aren't in the Dallas apartment or the Houston apartment. I haven't read the boyfriend's file yet."

"I'll get to it next," I said. "Kate, also known as Katie, is not as smart as her sister. She flunked out of Texas A&M, after majoring in partying, sounds like. In her teens, she had a couple of arrests for driving under the influence, and she smashed the windows on a boyfriend's car when they broke up. Since then, she's grown up a little, apparently. She works on the small ranch set up for the disabled children, she organizes fund-raisers for that ranch, and she shops. Oh, she did a stint as a volunteer at the zoo."

That just sounded boring.

Chip Moseley was more interesting. He'd come up from the rank and file. His parents had died when he was little, and he'd gone into a foster home, which happened to be on a working ranch. He'd learned to rodeo and made a name for himself. Right out of high school, he'd gotten a job on the Joyce ranch. He'd gotten through one marriage and fell in with Lizzie. He'd worked his way up and taken night courses, and now he managed the cattle operations at the ranch and he'd been "dating" Lizzie for six years. Aside from a minor brush with the law when he was in his twenties, he was clean. He'd been arrested in a bar brawl in a dive in Texarkana. To my surprise, I recognized the name of the place. My mother and stepfather had gone there from time to time.

I was tired of reading by then. I flopped back on my pillow. Tolliver told me what was in Victoria's file on Drex, though I had surmised most of it after ten minutes in Drex's company. The only male Joyce had been a disappointment all the way around. He'd gotten his high school girlfriend pregnant and they'd had a runaway marriage, followed by a divorce in six months. Drex supported the baby and its mother. Drex had joined the Marines right after he'd turned eighteen (take that, Dad!) and he'd made it through basic until he'd developed ulcers. Or maybe the ulcers he'd already had had gotten worse. Anyway, he'd left the service honorably, and gone on to drift around, doing this and that on his father's big ranch. He'd also worked with the disabled kids from time to time, and he'd worked in one of his dad's friend's businesses for a couple of years in an office job. It wasn't clear exactly what he'd done there.

"Probably not much, and probably not well," Tolliver said. "I don't think he's ever gone to college."

"I feel sorry for him," I said. I yawned. "I wonder how old Victoria's mom is. I wonder if she can bring the kid up on her own. Who's the dad? Did Victoria ever say?"

"I wondered if it was my father," Tolliver said, and I froze in the middle of another yawn.

"You're not kidding," I said. "You mean it."

"Yeah," he said. "Victoria was around a lot after Cameron disappeared, you know. But when I figured it out, the timing was wrong.

I think he was already in jail by the time the baby was conceived. I never could figure out why women thought he was so attractive."

"I sure don't," I said, with absolute sincerity.

"Well, good thing. You like men taller and thinner, right?"

"Oh, you bet, bay-bee. I love those string beans!"

Our hands clasped, and I snuggled closer to Tolliver on the bed. There was a little silence while we watched the rain hit the window of the room. The skies had decided to let go in earnest. I felt sorry for everyone who might still be out at the crime scene, and I decided they should be grateful to me for finding Victoria earlier, in time to get her body out of the culvert. I thought about the Joyce family, the kids who had grown up to be typical rich adults, as far as I could tell. They did some things that were quite good, but it was the bad things I was interested in. I thought it was significant that none of them had managed to sustain a happy marriage—though they were all in the prime age range, and one of them might make it yet. I was just about to shake my head over the truism that being rich didn't mean being happy, when I had the unpleasant realization that Mark, Tolliver, Cameron, and I had hardly turned out to be fulfilled citizens, either. Cameron was in some unknown place, Mark had never had a serious girlfriend that I knew of, and Tolliver and I . . .

"Do you really want to get married?" I asked him.

"Yes, I really do," he said without a second's hesitation. "I'd do it tomorrow, if we could. There's no doubt, is there? Do you have any worries about us being right for each other?"

"No," I said. "I don't. You're sure far from the commitment-phobic guys in the magazines, Tolliver."

"You're not anything like the women in the men's magazines, either. And that's a compliment."

"We sure know each other," I said. "We've probably seen the worst of each other. I can't imagine trying to get through life without you. Does that sound too clingy? I can try to be more independent."

"You are independent. You make a lot of decisions, every day," he said. "It's just easier for me to make the practical arrangements. Then you do your specialty. Then we leave, and it's my turn again."

Somehow that didn't sound completely even.

"Where's Manfred?" he asked, suddenly, as if someone had poked him with a needle.

"Gosh, I don't know. He told me to call him if I needed him. He didn't say where he was going or what he was going to do when he got there."

"He really has a crush on you."

"Yeah, I know."

"How about it? If I was to vanish, would you take up with the Pierced Wonder?"

He said that in a teasing voice, but he wanted a reply. I wasn't foolish enough to actually ponder the question and answer it seriously. "Are you kidding? That'd be like having hamburger after having steak," I said loyally. I admitted to myself that there were days when I sure craved a hamburger, and I didn't doubt there would be times when Tolliver eyed other women with appreciation. If he could just keep that urge to the eyeing level, I could do the same. I knew who I loved.

"So, after reading the files, which one do you favor in the role of shooter?" he said more cheerfully.

"Any of them could have done it," I said. "It's depressing to think that. But faced with losing a substantial hunk of a fortune, I imagine any of them could have decided hell no. Even Chip Moseley. He's got to have hopes of marrying Lizzie, after all these years of being together. And it wouldn't be human, not to count on all that money. He'd have a better idea of the size of the Joyce estate than most boyfriends might have, since he runs the big ranch. I'll bet he sees a lot of other financial papers, too, on the various Joyce businesses."

"Yes, I'm sure he does. I'm inclined to dismiss the idea that it's Lizzie, since she was the one who called you in. She had to know that there was a chance you were really able to do what you say you can, so if she was the killer, she'd never have risked it. She'd know that her granddad's death—well, it wasn't an out-and-out murder, but the snake triggered the heart attack and the snake wasn't flying through the air by accident. Someone pitched it at him. Maybe they thought it would bite him, and that would be all she wrote, but instead Rich had a heart attack, which was even better. All the person watching had to do was prevent him from getting to his cell phone. Mission accomplished."

"That was cold," I said, "and the person able to do something like that is really vicious."

"Do you think that the shooter was aiming at me, or at you?" Tolliver asked. "I realize there's no real way to know, but that would sure be interesting."

"Especially for you."

He laughed, just a little, but it was a sound I'd missed.

A knock at the door interrupted me as I'd started to frame an answer.

We both sighed. "I'm tired of having people knock at our door and come in to tell us bad stuff," I said. "We're sitting targets, here in a hotel." I didn't know how it'd be any different if we had our own home, but somehow I felt it would be.

I used the peephole, and to my surprise I saw Manfred. Since we'd just been talking about him, I felt a little self-conscious when I opened the door to let him in. And he flashed a very aware look at me, a look that said he knew he was on my mind.

"How's the invalid?" he said. Tolliver came out of the bedroom then, and Manfred said, "Hey, bro! How's getting shot?"

"Overrated," Tolliver said. We all sat. I offered Manfred a Coca-Cola or a bottle of water, and he took the Coke.

"I heard about the private eye," Manfred said. "She was working for you-all after your sister got taken, right?"

I was surprised that he knew that; I couldn't remember having mentioned it in his hearing. "Yes," I said. "She was. How'd you hear that?"

"It was on the news. About her book." I looked at him questioningly. "Did you know Ms. Flores was writing a book? She didn't tell you?"

"No," I said, though Tolliver was silent.

"Yeah, it was going to be called *Private Eye in the Lone Star State,* and she had gotten an offer on it."

"For real?" I was thunderstruck.

"Yeah, for real. Cameron's case was the one that made her decide to quit the force and become a private eye. Her continuing search for Cameron is the big story in the book."

I didn't know what to think of that, how to react. There was no real reason I should feel betrayed, but I did. It's particularly unpleasant to think that, for the price of a book, anyone who's inclined is going to be privy to the most agonizing event in your life.

"Did she tell you this last night?" I asked Tolliver.

He nodded. "I was going to tell you, but then Rudy Flemmons came to get you," he said.

"You've had time since."

He hesitated. "I wasn't sure how you would take it."

"I wish I'd stolen a manuscript instead of the files," I said, and Manfred's eyes turned to me with interest.

"What files did you steal? Do the police know you have them? Who are they about?"

"I stole some files out of her trunk," I said. "The police would probably make me into mincemeat if they knew I'd taken them. They're about the Joyce family."

"There's not one on Mariah Parish?"

"No," Tolliver said. "Should there be?"

"Actually, no," Manfred said, "since I have it right here." With a typical Bernardo flourish, he opened his jacket and pulled out a file. He'd carried his exactly like I'd carried mine, but he just had the one.

"Where the hell did you get that?" Tolliver sat forward on the couch. He was looking at Manfred as if Manfred had revealed he had a baby hidden in his coat, with a mixture of horror and admiration.

"Late last night, I went by her office, and the door was open," Manfred said. "My inner sense had told me it was important to talk to her. But I was too late. I'm assuming this was before she was reported missing. I went inside, and I asked the spirits if there was something there I should find, something that pertained to . . . anyone I know."

We were both gaping at him by that time, and not because of the "spirits" reference. "Victoria's office had been rifled?" I said, thinking that was an unfortunate word to spring to my mind.

"Yes," he said. "It had been searched really thoroughly. But not thoroughly enough." He paused for dramatic effect. "I was drawn to her couch," he said, and the moment was somewhat ruined by Tolliver's snort. "Well, I was," said Manfred, looking very young for a moment. "Someone had tossed the cushions off, but it was a sofa bed like the one I slept on at Grandma's, and I pulled it up, and the file was stuck down in there. Like maybe someone had been knocking at the door, and she'd pulled up on the handle just a little and slid the file inside."

"And I notice you had no trouble making off with it." Tolliver's voice was so dry it could have been toast.

"No," Manfred admitted. He had a sunny smile, the only sunny thing about this day.

"We've robbed a dead woman," I said, abruptly appalled at what I'd done. "And we've taken some clues away from the police."

"We're trying to save your life," Manfred said.

Tolliver gave the psychic a hard, sharp look, and I thought he would say something, but he only nodded. "The more important question is, who was at her office door?" he said. "Manfred, can you help us with that?"

Manfred looked smug. "As it happens, I may be able to. While I was in her office, I took a nail file from her pencil caddy. That's a personal thing, has some skin cells still on it. I'm going to use that for a reading, and see what I can get. May be helpful, may not. You can't count on it; that's why so often those of us in the business are less than honest."

We didn't disagree. Most "psychics" were frauds, even the real ones who had a genuine gift. Psychics have to make a living, and if you have to earn your money by sitting in a storefront telling Mrs. Sentimental that Fluffy is purring in paradise, that's what you do when your gift is giving you nothing to go on.

"What do you need to do to get ready?" I asked. Every practitioner I've encountered has his or her own process.

"Not much," he said. "No loud sounds. Close your eyes for a while, till I get into it."

That was easy enough. Tolliver and I closed our eyes, and his hand came over to cover mine. It was possible to drift away, wondering where Manfred was in the stream of otherness, the state between waking and sleeping, between this world and the next world. That was the place I inhabited when I looked down at the bones in the earth, and that was the place Manfred was exploring now. It's not too hard to get there, but sometimes it can be hell getting back.

The room was silent except for the low rush of warm air coming from the heating system. After a minute or two, I was sure it was all right to open my eyes. Manfred's head lolled back. He was so relaxed he seemed boneless. I'd never seen Manfred in action. It was interesting and spooky.

"I'm worried," Manfred said suddenly. I had opened my mouth to tell him everything was okay, when I realized Manfred was not making conversation. He was interpreting Victoria. "I'm sitting in front of the computer. I've gotten lots of information in a very short time, and it's going to give me enough to go on. I have lots of ideas. If Mariah died by accident, and that's what Harper said, then the baby has a much better chance of being alive. Who would place the baby? Where would that person take a baby? Drop it off at an orphanage? So I'll call all the orphanages in Dallas and Texarkana and in between. I can ask them if they received a baby Doe around Mariah's death date. Maybe I can call a few tonight."

Wow, Victoria really had been a good investigator.

"I'm worried," Manfred said, and his head moved restlessly. "I've talked to all the Joyces and to the boyfriend. I've compiled a list of the rest of the household staff who worked for Rich Joyce while

Mariah was there. But I don't know how far I'll get. I can't do any more tonight. I think someone followed me to the office. Rudy?" Manfred pantomimed someone holding a cell phone. "I hate to leave a message, I haven't talked to you in so long. But I think there's someone following me, and when you're lucky enough to have a cop as your friend, you should call them when you're in a fix like this. I don't want to lead them to my mom's when I pick up MariCarmen. Well . . . 'bye. I'm leaving the office in about ten minutes. I got some phone calls to make." Half the time Manfred was telling us, though in the first person, what Victoria had been thinking, and half the time he seemed to be speaking as if he were in Victoria's body.

Now Manfred's hands were moving. It was clear he was performing some task, but I couldn't interpret his gestures. I looked at Tolliver and raised my eyebrows in a question. Tolliver pointed at the stack of files on the coffee table. After a moment, I understood. Victoria was tamping papers into a neat stack, then closing them into a folder and stacking it on the others. Then she got a rubber band out of a drawer and worked it around the stack. "Put this in the trunk," she whispered. "Come back, make the calls." There were slight movements in Manfred's feet and shoulders that suggested Victoria (through Manfred) was going outside, opening the trunk, tossing in the files, shutting the lid, moving back into the office.

This was a very strange experience. Enlightening, but strange.

"Someone's coming," Victoria/Manfred muttered. "Huh."

I understood better, now, why I made people so nervous after they saw me in contact with that other part of the world, the unseen part that was so hard for most people to access. I could feel the tension in Tolliver's hand.

Again, little twitches of Manfred's body suggested that Victoria's movements were happening in his head. He made a definite yanking gesture. I was sure he was pulling open the sleeper couch to insert Mariah's folder. She—no, Manfred—turned her head to look at something, very abruptly, and then Manfred's eyes flew open with a look of complete terror on his face.

"I'm going to die," he said. "Oh, my God, I'm going to die tonight."

Fourteen

IT took at least fifteen minutes for Manfred to completely come out of walking Victoria through her last moments.

"Who did she see?" Tolliver asked.

"I don't know," Manfred said. "I couldn't see them."

"Well, a hell of a lot of good that did us," Tolliver said, and I put a hand on his shoulder (his good one, let me point out) and squeezed.

"It did a lot of good," I said. "We know what Victoria was thinking, and we know someone did kill her because of the case, or at least we know that's what Victoria thought or she wouldn't have hidden that particular file. She was thinking something might happen to her office, thought someone was after her, so she had already put the other Joyce files in her car to keep them safe. She didn't believe anyone would hurt her personally, but she called her former boyfriend, Rudy Flemmons, to come watch her back. He didn't answer, or he didn't get the message in time, and that's why he's all bent out of shape now."

"We know those things, but they don't do us any good." Tolliver was determined to be a butthead.

"Maybe once we look at Mariah's file, they will."

Manfred was looking tired, and older. He seemed very alone. I felt a pang of pity for him, and then I had to tell myself not to overdo it. Pity and a vague physical attraction were not enough motivation to imperil my relationship with Tolliver. I knew without a doubt that Manfred needed to find someone else.

I found myself wondering what kind of woman would be good for Manfred, and then I realized the answer had to be *Anyone besides me.*

By then it was almost five o'clock, and I called room service and asked them to send up some food and some coffee before I reached down to pick up the file. I opened it to the first page, the fact sheet with Mariah's background information, and read it carefully. Then I passed the fact sheet to Tolliver, and he began studying it. While we looked through the information Victoria had gathered on Mariah, Manfred began reading the Joyce files.

"Mariah Parish wasn't what she seemed," I said, which was an understatement.

Tolliver shook his head. "She sure wasn't. If the Joyces had checked her credentials more closely, they wouldn't have hired her."

It wasn't that Mariah had been deceitful. She'd been an orphan, as she'd said. She'd been taking care of another ill elderly man, Arthur Peaden, before she came to Rich Joyce. She'd done a good job, too, because there were glowing testimonials from Art Peaden's survivors about how kind Mariah had been, how conscientious, while she was taking care of their father.

She'd also been taking college classes over the computer. Eventually, she'd gotten evenings off to attend classes in person. And in the fullness of time, she'd graduated from college with a degree in economics and business.

Mariah had had her own online trading account, and it had been a busy one. At first, she'd lost some money, but more recently, even in the financial downturns the market had taken recently, she'd held steady. The adult babysitter had been profiting from her job to a degree no one would have imagined.

"Wow," said Tolliver with some admiration. "She was learning all the tricks of the trade."

"I guess her 'client' talked in front of her, and his friends and family talked in front of her, and she profited by everything she heard."

"Caregiver by day, stock market trader by night," Manfred said. "You gotta admire her nerve and determination."

"And sneakiness," I said, wrinkling my nose. "Isn't that kind of deceptive?"

"I don't know," Tolliver said after a long pause. "Is it? She didn't *say* that she was an uneducated, ignorant woman who couldn't get a better job. She let her employers think so, but that's the persona she adopted. She was really smart, and she was determined to put that to use the best way she knew how."

"Smart," Manfred said. He sounded approving.

"Two-faced and not really honest."

"Ah, sour grapes," Manfred said, smiling. "You haven't gotten to raid the brains of your dead people to get stock tips."

"What an opportunity I've missed," I said, deadpan. "I need to find a cemetery and look for the grave of a financial wizard, see if he can give me ideas in what I see of the last few moments of his life."

"That's kind of what Mariah did," Manfred said.

When I thought about it, he wasn't too far off. "I wonder if it was a conscious plan or something that just evolved." I looked at the picture of the young Mariah, who'd had bangs and a chin-length bob. Red hair and freckles, brown eyes, and a cute nose; all she needed was a straw hat, overalls, and an egg basket on one arm. There'd been steel under all that unsophisticated cuteness.

"I bet she talked real country," Manfred said. "I bet she made sure she did."

Deeper and smarter than her surface suggested, Mariah Parish had crafted a way to survive and prosper. And she'd provided good care to those who'd employed her. "Not bad, Mariah," I said, toasting her with a coffee cup. Our sandwiches had come, and we were all eating like we'd been starved for days.

"Until she got pregnant," Tolliver said.

"And I wish we knew the name of the father," I said. "That's the million-dollar question."

"Not so much who the actual dad was," Manfred corrected, "as who thought he *might* be the dad."

"I don't suppose—?" I gestured at the picture. "Manfred, do you think you could find out anything about her, your way?"

"Nah, not without something of hers," he said. "Since I never met her in life."

"The dad might have been Rich Joyce himself, or Drexell, or even Chip Moseley." I was thinking out loud.

"Or anyone else, as long as one of them thought there was a chance he was the dad," Tolliver said.

"So she had sex with one of these guys, we're assuming. If she had sex with Rich Joyce, think of what a coup it would be if she was going to have his child! Sure, he'd had a stroke, but he had recovered well and he was definitely active and in his right mind. This child would presumably have equal rights with the other kids, and Lizzie, Kate, and Drexell would be out millions of dollars." I picked up another triangle of club sandwich and bit into it, then had to dust crumbs off my shirt. "Was Drexell still married nine years ago?"

"Don't remember. I'll have to check his file." Manfred flipped through some pages. "Yes, he was. So was Chip."

"So," Tolliver said, stretching his legs out in front of him. He propped his feet on the coffee table, now littered with papers and plates and glasses. "Why now? Why did all this happen now? Mariah and Rich Joyce are both eight years in their graves. Why now?"

"Because Lizzie Joyce started reading Harper's website after the case in North Carolina," Manfred said, as if the answer was simple. "She wanted the latest and greatest. And what Lizzie Joyce wants, she makes happen. We don't know how many arguments her family and friends put up against getting Harper here. We don't know how many times they told her she was a fool."

"If what I saw is any estimate," Tolliver said, "she wouldn't take real kindly to that at all. She wanted Harper to come, and she had the money to make it attractive to us. Then came the worst part, her huge mistake. She didn't direct Harper to Rich's grave right away. She let Harper wander and read other graves, and Harper landed on Mariah's. Lizzie either had to believe Harper or disbelieve her, and since she'd spent good money to bring Harper, she decided to believe her. So now Lizzie knew that Mariah had been pregnant, and that her death probably could have been prevented; or at least, the birth took place under circumstances that weren't straightforward and aboveboard, so she didn't have as good a chance of recovering.

And the baby wasn't in the coffin with her, so something happened to it. Also, the death certificate said infection, but not what kind, so I'm wondering if the doctor who signed it was in on the secret."

"That's something we can look up," I said. "We can find him and ask him questions. Is there a copy of the death certificate in Mariah's file?"

Tolliver was looking tired, I realized, and it was Manfred who located the copy of the certificate. "Dr. Tom Bowden," he said. I called information for the little town next to the Joyce ranch, but he wasn't listed. Next, I tried Texarkana, but no Dr. Tom Bowden was there. Manfred went into our bedroom and came back with the huge phone book. He looked up "Physicians" in the Yellow Pages, and he told us with an air of triumph that there was a Dr. Bowden listed.

"We'll have to go see him tomorrow," I said. "Tolliver needs to rest."

"Oh, gosh, sure," Manfred said, disarmingly apologetic. "Sorry, Tolliver. I was forgetting you were on the disabled list."

Tolliver scowled. "I'll get better every day," he said.

"Of course," Manfred reassured him. "In the meantime, since I still have plenty of energy, I'll track down this doctor's office."

"Are you sure you ought to do that?" I said. "Maybe it wouldn't be such a good idea."

"Ah, I'll just have a look-see," Manfred said. "I've got that GPS now, so I better put it to good use. Thanks for supper." He put the cart out in the hall for me as I helped Tolliver up. For the first time in hours, Tolliver took some pain medication along with his other pills. I chided myself silently for not realizing how tired he was getting.

I helped him with the undressing process, and he was finally settled in bed, covers pulled up, with his pajama bottoms on and a full complement of medicine. I found *Law and Order* and settled in. Tolliver was asleep in ten minutes or less.

My brain was tired. I'd thought about the Joyces, about Mariah Parish, about poor Victoria and her daughter. Other people had filled my head all day, and I had to add Rudy Flemmons's grief on top of that. I didn't want to think anymore, or bear the burden of other people's emotions. It was a sheer relief to go out into the living room area and watch the stupidest movie I could fine. I also painted my toenails and fingernails. I called my little sisters and talked to them for twenty minutes, before Iona said they had to get in the bathtub. Iona tried to steer the conversation over to my relationship with Tolliver, but I kept on course and didn't go there. I hung up feeling pleased with myself, a good feeling to have after the unhappy events of the past few days.

Thinking of unhappy events, I called the hospital and asked about Detective Powers. The switchboard connected me to the waiting room, and I asked the man who answered if I could speak to Beverly Powers.

"She can't come to the phone. Parker just died," said a man's voice, and he hung up the phone. He was crying.

No matter how often I told myself I hadn't killed Parker Powers, I knew he would not have died if he hadn't been trying to protect me.

There was no magic formula that I could use to make this all better. There was no philosophy that would diminish the pain his family and friends were feeling. There was no way I could erase the memory of his collapse, the blood pouring from his wound, the way I'd cowered in the shadow of the car. That was especially galling, that I'd had to hide from the man who'd done such a despicable thing.

That was pride speaking; it only made sense to hide when someone was trying to kill you. Of course it did.

I had this image I needed to conform to, though, maybe culled from the comic books I'd read as a child or the tough-woman fiction I read now. Every female private eye and cop was able to protect citizens without a second thought, able to shoot the evildoer after tracking him down. Every comic-book heroine was able to perform fearlessly, able to commit acts of heroism in the cause of protecting mankind.

I'd let myself be protected by a broken-down, none-too-bright ex–football player, and it had killed him.

He knew he was in danger. He knew that was his job. He was willing to take the risk, my common sense told me.

And I was willing to let him, I had to admit. I tried to think of something else I could have done. If I'd insisted on running by myself, would he still have followed me? Maybe. What if I'd decided to stay in the hotel? Yes, he'd still be alive. I had a terrible responsibility to Parker Powers.

I hoped I would not fail again.

Fifteen

I slept that night, but not well. It was reassuring to hear Tolliver's breathing as I tossed and turned. When light crept under the heavy curtains and I permitted myself to get out of bed, I felt used up, exhausted before the day even began. I made myself run on the treadmill again, hoping to drum up some energy with the exercise. That strategy didn't work.

Assuming Manfred had tracked down Tom Bowden's current office, I decided to drop in on Dr. Bowden this morning. It would probably be easy to get past the receptionist, because the mirror told me I looked anything but well. Though we hadn't set a definite time the night before, Manfred knocked very quietly on our door just as I finished dressing.

Tolliver, just up, had woken as grouchy as a bear. He was about as much fun to be around as a bear, too. Manfred was petty enough to emphasize Tolliver's invalid status with obnoxious cheerfulness and many wishes for Tolliver's recovery. Manfred was glowing with health and energy. When you added the lights bouncing off his silver piercings, he practically sparkled.

Manfred liked to talk in the morning.

As we drove to the office building Manfred had scouted the night before, he told me that his grandmother's will had left everything to him. That had surprised his mother, who was Xylda's only daughter, but after her initial disappointment, she'd seen the justice in it, since Manfred had taken care of Xylda her last couple of years.

"Xylda had a . . . ?" Then I stopped, embarrassed. I'd been on the verge of expressing amazement that Xylda had had an estate to leave.

"She had a little cash stashed away, and she owned a house," Manfred said. "It was my good luck that it was in the downtown area, and the school district needed the ground it stood on to build a new gym. I got a decent price. Like I told you before, I found all kinds of weird shit when I was cleaning out all the accumulated stuff. I put everything I wanted to keep into storage until I decide where to base myself."

"So you're going to make your living in your grandmother's business, but do most of your work via email and phone?"

"That's the idea. But I'm open to new adventures." He glanced over at me and waggled his eyebrows.

I laughed, though reluctantly. "If you can make even a faint pass, given the way I look today, I think you're nuts."

"Didn't sleep last night?"

"No, not a lot. Detective Powers died."

Manfred's cheer was wiped off his face as if he'd used an eraser. "That's crappy. I'm sorry, Harper."

I shrugged. There wasn't anything to talk about; I'd thought everything there was to think during the course of the night, and Manfred had sense enough to recognize that.

DR. Bowden's office was in a four-story building, an anonymous glass and brick cube that could have held anything from an accounting firm to a crime syndicate. We ran through the pouring rain to reach the sliding glass doors on the south side of the building.

As we entered, I saw a husky gray-haired man leaving the lobby by another set of doors, his jacket held above him to avert the rain. As the automatic doors swooshed shut behind his back, I thought his walk looked familiar. I looked after him for a moment, then shrugged and joined Manfred at the lobby directory. We discovered Dr. Bowden was on the third floor. He was listed as a GP.

Dr. Bowden had a modest office in that modest building. The waiting room was small, and there was one woman behind the sliding glass panel. Her workstation was messy, almost chaotic. She seemed to be the receptionist, the scheduler, and the insurance clerk, all rolled into one. Her short hair was dyed a deep red, and she wore black glasses that tilted up at the outer corners. Maybe she was aiming for retro.

"Trying to make a fashion statement," Manfred muttered, I hoped too low for her to hear.

"Excuse me," I said, when she didn't look up from her computer. She had to know we were standing right there, since there was only one other person in the waiting room, a man in his sixties who was extremely thin. He was reading a *Field and Stream* magazine.

"Excuse me," I said again, more sharply than I'd intended.

"Oh, sorry," the receptionist said. She took an earpiece from her ear. "I didn't hear you."

"We'd like to see the doctor," I said.

"Do you have an appointment? Do you have a referral?"

"No," I said, and smiled.

Nonplussed, she looked past my shoulder at Manfred, as if hoping to find someone who could explain the phenomenon of a person trying to see a doctor without an appointment.

"I'm with her," he said helpfully. "We both want to see the doctor. It's about a personal matter."

"You're not the daughter-in-law—are you?" The red-headed woman was full of delighted, horrified anticipation.

"Sorry, no." I hated to burst her bubble.

"He won't see you," she said. She'd switched to a confiding tone. Maybe it was Manfred's facial decoration that had won her heart. She was obviously a woman who liked strong style. "He's very busy."

I looked around at the one patient, who was trying to appear oblivious to the interesting conversation we were having. "That's not the impression I get," I told her.

"I'll check, though," she said, as though I hadn't spoken. "What's your name, please?"

I told her. Before she could ask, I said, "This is my friend Manfred Bernardo."

"What's this in reference to?"

She'd never understand the long version. "It's about a case he had around eight years ago," I said. "We want to discuss his findings with him."

"I'll tell him," she said, and rose to her feet. "You'll have to wait your turn."

We did, and when the thin man had left and no one had taken his place in the waiting room, we waited some more.

Pointy Glasses could tell we weren't going to leave, and apparently the doctor decided against sneaking out without seeing us. When we'd been there forty-five minutes or longer, he appeared at the door into the examining area. Dr. Bowden was in his sixties, bald except for a gray fringe. He was one of those anonymous-looking men you'd have trouble describing. You could meet him six times in a row and you'd still have to ask his name.

"All right, I have a moment now," he said. He preceded us into his office, a small room crowded with bookcases, papers, home-stitched framed needlework ("Doctors leave their patients in stitches"), and photographs of himself with a short, very plump woman and a boy. The boy grew up to be a young man in the photos, and then there was a wedding picture of the grown-up son with his own wife.

He settled himself behind the desk, giving a good impression of a busy and prosperous man who was sparing us a few minutes out of the goodness of his heart.

"My name is Harper Connelly, and this is my friend Manfred Bernardo," I said. "I'm here about a death you certified eight years ago, the death of a woman named Mariah Parish."

"I'd been warned you were coming," he said, which startled the hell out of me. "I can't believe you'd have the sheer effrontery to show up here."

"Why not?" I said, completely at a loss. "If Mariah Parish was murdered, it completely changes a very complicated situation."

"Murdered?" He looked as astounded as I was, now. "But I was told . . . I was told you were alleging that Mariah Parish was still alive."

"No, I've never said that, and I don't believe it. Who told you that?"

But the doctor didn't answer. He looked very concerned, but not as hostile. "You aren't here to dispute my filing a death certificate?"

"No. I know Mariah Parish is dead. I'm just wondering why you didn't fill in the cause of death correctly."

Tom Bowden flushed, and it didn't look good on him. "Do you represent her family?"

"She didn't have a family," I said. "We represent the detective who's looking for her baby." Which, in a way, was true.

"The baby," he said, and he aged five years in thirty seconds.

"Yes," I said, very sternly. "Tell us about it."

"You know how influential the Joyces are," he said. "They could have ended my career; they could have sent me to jail."

"But they didn't," Manfred said, his voice just as severe as mine. "Tell us."

We had no idea what was going on, but it was good to look like we did.

"That night, the night she died, of course I was still practicing in Clear Creek," Dr. Bowden said. He swiveled in his chair to look out of his window. "It was raining that night, pouring, like it is today. I think it was in February. I'd never treated any of the Joyces; they had their own doctors in Texarkana and Dallas and didn't mind driving to go to one of their doctors, miles away." Bitterness crossed his face and left its tracks. "I knew who Rich Joyce was, everyone in town knew him. He was one of those rich men who acts like they're just like everyone else, you know? Old pickup truck, Levis? Like he didn't have enough money to drive any vehicle he wanted!" The doctor shook his head at the foibles of someone who could have anything preferring instead to stick with something plain and familiar.

"Was it Rich Joyce who came to your house?"

"Oh, hell, no," Tom Bowden said. "It was one of the hands, I think. I don't remember what his name was." He was lying. "He said Mr. Joyce's housekeeper was sick, needed me, and they'd pay me extra if I'd come out to the house. Of course I went. I didn't want to, but it was my duty, and there was the prospect that I'd get in good with Richard Joyce. I'm not going to pretend I wasn't hoping for that."

He could have tried to pretend that all day long, and it wouldn't have convinced me. I felt Manfred shift beside me, wondered if he was trying to suppress a laugh.

"What happened?" I asked.

"I went out there in his truck, and we got out in the rain. We went through this big empty house, and we got to a bedroom, and in it was this young woman. She was in bad shape. She had just given birth. Evidently, her labor had started unexpectedly, and from what the man said to me, she hadn't even known she was pregnant."

I tried to absorb that, couldn't. "But you went out there knowing that you were going to treat a pregnant woman, right?"

He shook his head. I didn't know if he was trying to say that he hadn't known, or that he didn't want to talk about it. I suspected he didn't want to add to his feeling of guilt by admitting that he'd known he was going out to the Joyce house to treat a patient under conditions he had to know were illegal or pretty damn near.

"What did she say?" I asked.

"She didn't say much of anything. She was having a very hard time. She was very sick, very sick. Her temperature was high; she was sweating, shaking, and very unsteady. Almost incoherent. I couldn't understand why the man hadn't taken her to a hospital, and he told me that she didn't want him to, that she wasn't supposed to be having the baby, it was a real unpleasant family situation. He told me that the baby was the product of incest." Dr. Bowden's mouth folded up in a way that left no doubt as to how uncomfortable the word made him. "He said she was some kind of favorite of old Mr. Joyce, and she wanted to have the baby without him knowing, and then she would go back to her job and give the baby up for adoption. Her memories were too bad for her to want to keep it."

And you believed this? I wanted to say, but knew I couldn't break the flow of this confession. This was coming more easily than I ever would have believed, and I could only imagine that Tom Bowden had wanted to tell this story for years. I had a fleeting wonder about the kind of background this man must have, to have fallen for any of this. Of course, you had to add in the big dollop of greed that had influenced him.

"She didn't have any family," Manfred said, and after a second Dr. Bowden understood what Manfred was saying. He looked down at his desk fixedly. I could have hit Manfred for his interruption; at the same time, he'd only said what I was thinking.

"I didn't know for sure," Bowden muttered. "The man who'd brought me out to the ranch—I thought he was Drexell Joyce—the son. I figured the baby was probably his. Maybe he was ashamed to tell his grandfather that he'd been cheating on his wife; he was wearing a wedding ring, and Ms. Parish wasn't."

"Did she talk to you?" I said.

"What?"

"Mariah. Did she talk to you?" It seemed a simple enough question to me, but Tom Bowden was shifting uneasily in his black leather chair.

"No," he said, and I sighed. Manfred raised a finger, just at the edge of my vision. He thought the doctor was lying again.

"So what happened?" I said, not seeing how we could get him to be honest unless we started beating on him.

"I cleaned the woman up, with some difficulty," Dr. Bowden said. "I wanted to call for an ambulance and I told the man so again, but he told me that was out of the question. I went to get my coat to use my cell phone, but he'd taken it out of my coat pocket, and he wouldn't let me have it. I had to treat the patient, and I didn't have time to fight with him about the phone. She was clearly in the end stages. Even if I could've gotten her to a hospital within the hour—and the nearest hospital was that far away, incidentally—she wouldn't have made it. She had a massive infection."

"You're saying she died that night."

"Yes. About an hour and a half after I got there, she died. She got to hold the baby."

We all sat silent for a moment. "So, what happened then?" Manfred said.

"The man asked me to examine the baby, and I found that she was okay, a little feverish, but nothing serious. Other than that, physically, she was fine."

"The baby was a girl."

"Yes, yes, she was. Small, but as far as I could tell she would be okay, if she got the proper course of treatment. He asked if I had the right stuff to give her. He was going to take the baby directly to the adoptive parents. I actually had some antibiotics with me in my bag, samples a salesman had given me. I explained the dosage and administration to him, and he carried the baby out of the room. That was the last I saw of the infant. The mother expired then."

Expired. "And what did you do after that?"

He sighed, as if the complexity of relaying his story was too much for him to bear. "I told the man that we had to call into town. We had to report the death. We had quite an argument. He didn't seem to understand that it was the law, that the law had to be followed."

Since you'd already bent it so far out of shape, I thought. "But he let you call, finally?"

"He agreed, as long as I didn't mention the baby. So the funeral home came to get the poor young woman, and I signed the death certificate." His shoulders slumped. He'd finally told the worst thing, in his view, and now he could relax.

"You said she'd died of . . . ?"

"Massive infection due to a ruptured appendix."

"And no one questioned that?"

He shrugged. "No family came forward. The Joyces sent me a check to pay my bill—no more—and after that, if anyone who worked for them got sick, they came to me for treatment."

It had been very clever of them not to offer Dr. Bowden an outright bribe. I was sure the bill he'd sent had been stiff, and they'd paid it just as they would have under normal circumstances. That had reassured the doctor. And since his practice wasn't flourishing, they'd thrown him a big bone.

"With a setup like that, why'd you move to Dallas?" Manfred asked. Again, I wouldn't have gotten into that, but again, I'd underestimated the doctor's elasticity.

"It was my wife. She couldn't stand Clear Creek," he said. "And

I've got to say, no one there got along with her, either. We were having some real wars at home. About six years ago, I got to talking to a doctor I'd never met before at an AMA meeting. He had a practice in Dallas. He told me his office was coming empty, did I want to take over the lease. It was at the previous price, much lower than new tenants were paying. And he'd throw in the equipment, too, because he was going overseas to a new job at an American consulate in Turkey or somewhere like that."

Could he really not see how set up that had been? It was like someone attaching a string to a dollar bill and then setting it out on the sidewalk, so he could drag it away and get a passerby to follow the path of the money.

"Jeez Louise," said Manfred. He almost continued, but fortunately he decided to keep his mouth shut.

"Thanks," I said, after I'd tried to think of more questions to ask. "Oh, did someone else come here this morning, asking about Mariah Parish?"

"Ah . . . yes, as a matter of fact."

Why the hell hadn't I thought to bring pictures of the Joyces with me? I'd done well so far, for someone who didn't know squat about being a detective, but this was a huge mistake I'd made.

"Who was he?"

"Said his name was Ted Bowman."

Oh, not that that was anything like Tom Bowden, oh, no.

"And he wanted . . ."

Tom Bowden looked troubled, or rather, more troubled. "He wanted to know the same things you two wanted to know, but not for the same reason."

"What do you mean?" I asked.

"It was like he already knew the whole story. He just wanted to know how much *I* knew about who was involved."

"What did you tell him?"

"I told him I had no idea who the man who brought me to the house was, that as far as I could tell, the last time I saw the baby she was fine, and that I'd never talked to anyone else about that night."

"And he said?"

"He said that was good news; he'd heard the baby had died and he was glad to know that she had survived. He said I better forget about that night, and I told him I hadn't thought about it in years. He warned me that someone else might come asking questions, and he told me whoever came would be someone who was just trying to create trouble by saying Mariah Parish was still alive."

"What did he tell you to do about that?"

"He told me it would be in my best interest to keep my mouth shut."

"But you talked to us anyway."

For the first time, Tom Bowden met my eyes. "I'm tired of keeping the secret," he said, and I believed him. "I got divorced from my wife anyway. My practice isn't doing too well, and my whole life hasn't turned out like I thought it would. I date this downward slide from that night."

He'd told the truth that time, I was sure. "And what did this man look like?" I asked.

"He was taller than your friend here"—Dr. Bowden nodded condescendingly toward Manfred—"and a good bit stockier, big muscles and chest. Dark hair, in his forties or fifties. Graying a little."

"Visible tattoos?"

"No, he was wearing a rain jacket," Dr. Bowden said, in the tone of one pointing out the obvious. His attitude was creeping back. Evidently, crying time was over. I tried to think of more questions to ask him before the well dried up. "You really don't know the name of the man who took you out to the ranch house?" I found that hard to believe, in a little town like Clear Creek. I said so.

He shrugged. "I hadn't been in town that long, and the ranch people keep to themselves. This man said he worked for Mr. Joyce, and he was driving a ranch truck. He may have given me a name, but I don't remember it. It was a stressful evening. Like I said, I suspected he might be Drexell Joyce. But I'd never met Drexell, so I don't know."

I'll bet it had been a stressful evening. Especially for Mariah Parish, whose life might have been saved if the ambulance had come for her . . . if anyone had been humane enough to call one.

I was a little surprised that she hadn't been outright murdered, and the baby along with her. At that time Rich Joyce had still been alive, and maybe the fear of what he'd say and do if his caregiver disappeared in his absence had been the deciding factor. He'd miss Mariah, even if no one else would. And Rich Joyce wouldn't let go if he decided something strange was up.

Maybe the child had been stowed in someone's home as a bargaining chip of some kind. Maybe one of the ranch hands was raising her. I could make up all kinds of stories in my head, but none of them was more likely than another.

"Where was Rich Joyce that evening?" Manfred asked.

"The man just said he was gone," Bowden said. "His truck wasn't there."

"He didn't know his caregiver was pregnant? He didn't notice?"

Bowden shrugged. "That never came up. I don't know what she told Mr. Joyce. Some women just don't show that much, and if she was trying to hide it . . ."

Manfred and I looked at each other. We didn't have any other questions.

"Goodbye, Dr. Bowden," I said, standing. He couldn't hide his relief that we were leaving.

"Are you going to the police?" he asked. "You know, even if they exhume poor Ms. Parish, they won't be able to tell a thing." He was regretting having talked to us. But he was also relieved. This guy had had a hard time for the past eight years, living inside his own skin. I, for one, was glad of that.

"I don't know," Manfred said, very thoughtfully. He'd had the same reaction. "We're considering it. If the child came to no harm, it's possible you may keep your license."

A horrified Dr. Bowden was staring at us as we went down the hall and out through the waiting room. There were three more patients there, and I felt sorry for them. I wondered what kind of care the doctor would give now that he was definitely on the upset side. He'd had two visits in one day about an event he must have hoped was buried forever; that would be enough to rattle any man, even one made of better stuff than Tom Bowden.

"That guy is a human sewer," Manfred said when we were in the elevator. He was very angry, his face red with strong emotion.

"I don't know if he's quite that bad," I said, feeling at least ten years older than my companion. "But he's weak. And he's a joke, based on the standards a doctor ought to uphold."

"I wouldn't be so surprised if it was the 1930s," Manfred said, surprising me. "That sounds like a story you'd read in a collection of old ghost stories. The knock on the door in the middle of the night, the stranger who comes to take you to a mysterious patient in a big house, the dying woman, the baby, the secrecy . . ."

I was goggling at Manfred when the doors opened on the ground floor. That had been exactly what I'd been thinking. "Do you believe what he told us was the truth? If we both think he was telling us a story that sounds incredible, maybe it is. Maybe it was a pack of lies."

"I don't think he's a good enough liar," Manfred said. "Though some of what he told us was lies, of course. How has he made it this far? Didn't he know that someday, someone would come asking questions? He has to be at least a little smart because he's a doctor, right? Not everybody can make it through med school. And his license was there on the wall, I read it. I'm going to check up on it. Maybe we need another private eye."

"No, not considering what happened to the last one," I snapped, and then felt contrite. "I'm sorry, Manfred. I'm glad you went with me. It's good there was another set of ears listening and another pair of eyes seeing. Did you believe the main outline of his story? You're the psychic."

"I did believe him," Manfred said after a perceptible pause. "I went back over it in my head, and I think he was telling us the truth. Not all the truth; he did know who the man who came to get him was, for example. And I don't think the man hid his phone; I think he told the doctor he absolutely couldn't make a phone call, and I think he told him that in a threatening way. A really good threat would be enough to flatten a guy like Dr. Bowden. I also think the guy had warned the doctor what to expect at the house. Doctors don't go out now with big bags, like my grandmother said they did when she was little. I think Dr. Bowden knew to take medication for a woman who'd just had a difficult birth, and something for the baby, too."

That made a lot of sense. "You're right. So who do you think came into town to get the doctor? Who made that mysterious drive out to the empty big house? Who took the baby? Whoever took Dr. Bowden to the ranch, he was wearing a wedding ring."

"Oh, that's right. Good for you for remembering. Well, we know that Drexell was married for a while, and we know that Chip was, too. Could have been either one, or even someone we haven't met yet."

We drove back to the hotel, stopping along the way to eat a fast-food lunch. I got a grilled chicken sandwich and didn't eat the fries. I was trying to eat better; I'd feel better if I did. We didn't talk much over the food. I don't know what Manfred was thinking, but I was trying to trace the niggling feeling I'd had when I'd first seen the Joyce party get out of their trucks at the Pioneer Rest Cemetery. I'd thought I'd seen them before, at least the men. Where would I have seen them? Could they have come by the trailer when we were all living there? There had been so many people in and out . . . and I'd tried so hard to dodge them.

I had to put that idea on the back burner when we returned to the hotel to find Tolliver in a real (and rare) snit. He'd tried to take a shower, and during the course of covering his shoulder with a plastic bag, he'd banged it against the wall, and it had hurt, and he was angry because I was gone so long with Manfred. He'd ordered lunch from room service, and then he'd had a hard time managing taking the cover off the drink and unrolling his silverware, with one good hand. Tolliver clearly had a grievance, and though I was prepared to coddle him until he was in a better frame of mind, I got into my own snit when he told me that Matthew had called to check on him, and when he heard Tolliver's tale, Matthew had said he was coming to visit since I'd left Tolliver all by himself.

I was mad at Tolliver, and he was mad at me—though I knew this was all because I'd gone on an errand with someone besides him. Normally, Tolliver is not temperamental, and not irritable, and not unreasonable. Today, he was all those things.

"Oh, Tolliver," I said, my own voice none too loving. "Couldn't you just suck it up until I got back?"

He glared at me, but I could tell he was already sorry he'd said anything to his dad. It was too late, though. Apparently, McDonald's was being amazingly forgiving in its work schedule, because in just a few moments Matthew was knocking on the door.

When Matthew came into the living room and walked over to his son while I was still holding the door open, my eyes followed him, and I froze with my hand still on the door. Matthew was the man I'd seen leaving Dr. Bowden's office that morning. He'd been going out the doors across the lobby as we'd been entering. Same clothes, same walk, same set of the shoulders.

Manfred's eyes followed mine, and his widened. He asked me a silent question. After a moment, I shook my head. There was no point in having a confrontation—at least, my scrambled head couldn't instantly see any advantage.

If Matthew admitted he'd been there, he'd simply tell us that he was visiting another doctor, or a lawyer, or an accountant, in the same building, for whatever reason. It would be hard to disprove. But his presence in Tom Bowden's building was more coincidence than I could bite off and chew.

It had never occurred to me that Matthew's reappearance in his children's lives had anything to do with the Joyces.

Instead of joining the three men, I went into the bedroom and sat on the side of the bed. I felt as if someone had just slammed a car door on my legs, when I was only half in. I tried hard to focus on one idea out of the dozens that were suddenly percolating in my head. My whole world had shifted, and regaining my balance in that world was almost impossible.

Mariah Parish was dead. She had died in childbirth.

Rich Joyce was dead. He'd been shocked to death, if you could call it that.

Victoria Flores, whom Lizzie Joyce had hired to investigate Mariah's death, was dead, too.

Parker Powers, who'd been investigating the case, was dead.

My stepfather had been to the doctor's office, the doctor who was present when Mariah Parish had died.

And what else had happened only a couple of months after the mysterious birth of the mysterious baby eight years ago?

My sister Cameron had vanished.

sixteen

I went into the bathroom and locked the door. I closed the toilet lid and sat on the toilet. I didn't turn on the light. I didn't want to see my reflection.

Matthew was somehow connected to the Joyces, though I had no idea how. And he was also Cameron's stepfather. And as near as I could ascertain, not that long after Mariah Parish's baby had been born, Cameron had disappeared. It had never, ever occurred to me that anyone in our family had anything to do with Cameron's disappearance. When the police had questioned my mother and Matthew, and Mark and Tolliver and me, I had raged at them because they were wasting time that should be spent tracing the real killer or killers.

I had suspected the boys at our high school, particularly Cameron's last boyfriend, who hadn't taken their breakup with good grace. I'd suspected Laurel and Matthew's druggie friends. I'd suspected a random stranger, any stranger, who'd seen Cameron walking home alone and decided to rob her/rape her/abduct her. I'd suspected the guys who'd sometimes blown wolf whistles at us when we'd been out together. I'd constructed hundreds of scenarios. Some of them were wildly implausible. But they all gave me a possible answer to the terrible mystery of the disappearance of my sister, an answer that didn't involve feeling even more pain from another personal loss.

I felt a deep conviction that even if I couldn't see the connection, even if it seemed incredible, two such incidents could not happen that close together without there being some kind of connection, not if the same man was involved in both incidents.

Was I grossly overreacting? I tried to think, though my brain was cloudy with rage. My stepfather knew something about the Joyces. He knew enough to know the name of the doctor who'd "treated" Mariah Parish.

He *knew*. And I believed he also knew what had happened to my sister. All these years, he'd kept it from me.

I felt it in my bones.

I couldn't go into the living room and grab him by the neck. He was too strong for me. Tolliver wouldn't let me kill his father. Probably even Manfred, who had no personal stake in the matter, would feel obliged to intervene. But Tolliver was weak and injured, and Manfred would leave sooner or later.

It took all the self-control I could muster to break away from seriously considering how to kill my stepfather.

For one thing, it would be wrong. Maybe. For another thing, a much more important thing, I didn't know enough. I wanted to find my sister's final resting place. I wanted to be sure I knew what had happened to Cameron.

To that end, I had to be prepared to tolerate Matthew's presence.

I worked on it, there alone in the dark. I schooled myself to be strong. And then I got up and turned on the light and washed my face, as if I could wash the new knowledge off of it and return to what had been my happy ignorance.

I went out into the living room, having to move slowly. I felt I'd been kicked in the ribs—fragile, and sore with the suspicion and loathing I carried inside.

I could tell immediately that Matthew wanted Manfred to leave so he could talk to his son alone, and Manfred had not wanted to leave until he spoke to me again. He looked from Matthew to me as I came into the room, and he shuddered. Whatever Manfred saw in me, neither Tolliver nor Matthew could see. That was a good thing.

"Manfred," I said. "I'm sorry I flaked out on you. Thanks for going with me today."

"No problem," Manfred said, leaping to his feet with an alacrity that told me how anxious he was to get out of this hotel room. "Would you like to go out and get a cup of coffee with me? Or do you need me to take you to the store? Got enough . . . potato chips?" He was reaching, there. We never ate potato chips. I felt a smile twitch at the corners of my mouth. "Thanks, Manfred." I debated quickly inside myself. Manfred wanted to talk to me about what I now realized was our mutual recognition of Matthew, but I didn't know yet what I was going to do. Better to avoid the tête-à-tête until I had made a plan. "I guess I'll stick around here in case Tolliver needs me."

I hugged him, acting on an impulse. His bones felt small as my arms circled his body. Somewhat hesitantly, he hugged me back. He was floundering under the psychic image he'd gotten from me. If he could see anything like the way I felt, then he'd seen something awful and murderous. "Don't do it," he said into my ear, and I let go of him and stood back.

"Don't worry, we'll be fine," I said reassuringly. "I'll call you if I need help, I promise."

"Well . . . okay. I do have some readings to work on this afternoon. But my cell phone's always charged up and in my pocket. 'Bye, Tolliver. Mr. Lang." And with a last hard look directly into my eyes, Manfred was out the door, walking swiftly down the hall without a backward glance.

"What a flake," said Matthew. "Tolliver, you hang out much with people like that? He must be a friend of yours, Harper."

"He is a friend of mine," I said. "His grandmother was, too." I felt really strange, kind of out of myself. Matthew was sitting beside Tolliver on the couch, so I took the chair. I crossed my legs and wrapped my hands around my top knee. "It was really messy outside this morning, wasn't it, Matthew?"

He looked surprised. "Yeah, traffic was a bitch. It always is in Dallas. Raining, too."

"Did you have errands to run this morning?"

"Oh, a few things I had to do. I have to be at work at two thirty."

Was he really working at McDonald's? Or was he meeting one of the Joyces? Had he always been in their pay?

And the man I loved most in the world, the only person I truly loved, was this man's son.

That might bother Tolliver, but it didn't make any difference to me. More than most people, I understand the difference between the children and the parents. I had been brought up by the same woman who'd neglected her two little girls so much that her older children had had to take care of them.

I liked to think I'd turned out a little better than my mother.

And yet, if I killed Matthew Lang, would I be any better than my mother?

Well, at least I'd have made my decision with a clear head.

That's hardly true, said my saner self. *Aren't you so choked with hatred that you can't even swallow?*

True. But wasn't it better to kill someone when you really hated them? Was there a virtue to waiting until you were calm and collected?

I'd certainly have a better chance of getting away with it. And of living a life with Tolliver, rather than getting friendly with a bunch of women in prison. That was how my mother had lived out her life . . . and I wasn't like my mother. I wasn't.

I'm sure my expression was strange while I was going through this process, though it wasn't really continuous, but flashing through my head in flickers.

Judging by Tolliver's face, he clearly wanted to ask me if I was all right, but just as clearly he didn't want to do that in front of Matthew. Matthew was sitting turned toward Tolliver so his back was mostly to me, which was a good thing.

I tried to blank out my mind so I could listen to them talk. Matthew was asking Tolliver if he'd ever thought of finishing college, if he'd consider enrolling in one of the many colleges around the Dallas area when we moved here. He thought Tolliver would be able to find a good job if he got his degree, and then he wouldn't need to live off of me anymore.

Trust Matthew to plant a poisonous spin on our relationship. Tolliver looked shocked. "I don't live off of Harper," he said.

"You don't have a job other than traveling around with her while she does . . . whatever she does," his dad said.

"I make sure she gets there to do that job," Tolliver said. I realized it wasn't the first time he'd had this conversation; it was just that none of the previous times he'd had it were in my hearing. I was almost shocked out of my shell of hatred. "If I weren't with Harper, she couldn't do that job at all."

"He's absolutely right," I said. "I get sick when I work, and without Tolliver, no telling what would happen to me." I tried to make my words a simple statement of fact. I didn't want to sound defensive when there was nothing to defend.

"You can tell yourself that," Matthew said to Tolliver, ignoring me, "but you know a man's got to make his own way in the world."

"Like you did?" I said. "You made your own way by selling drugs, by letting your wife auction me off to the highest bidder? You made your own way by giving up a law practice to go to jail instead?"

Matthew flushed. He couldn't pretend I wasn't there. "Harper, I'm trying to be a good father. I know it's too late, and I know I did things that make me sick to remember, but I'm trying to mend my relationship with *my son*. I know he 'loves' you, but sometimes you just have to butt out and let me talk to him."

You could hear the quotation marks around "loves."

Tolliver said, "Harper never has to butt out. I do love her. It is too late, and you did things that made all of us sick to our stomachs. You would have let Harper die if I hadn't been there that day when the lightning hit."

I felt a rush of relief. Some small part of me was frightened that someday Tolliver would listen to his dad, would believe him, would be suckered again.

"Mark, at least, will let me talk to him," Matthew said, getting up.

He was going to leave, and I still hadn't killed him. I was going to let him walk out.

I had to. I had only my bare hands. And I had to discover what he'd done with Cameron, and why he'd done it. I didn't think he'd wanted to have Cameron sexually. Some of his friends had wanted to have sex with us, but not Matthew. At least, I was fairly sure of that. But there was a reason, and I had to know it. I stood up, my hands clenched at my sides, debating whether or not to hit him.

Matthew picked up on the hostility in the way I was standing. I guess if you spend time in jail, you're on the alert for stuff like that. He edged around me on his path to the door. "I don't know what's wrong with you today, Harper. I'm just trying to mend fences, here."

"Not working," I said through clenched teeth.

"Yeah," he said, with a nervous laugh. "I can see that. Son, I'll talk to you later. I hope you're better. Call me if you need me." And he was out the door and it shut behind him. And he was still alive.

"Sit here," Tolliver said, his voice so low I almost didn't hear him. "Sit here, and tell me what's in your head."

"He was at the doctor's office building," I said. "Your father was there, this morning, going out the door across the lobby as we were coming in."

I stood still until Tolliver processed that. Then he patted the couch beside him again. "Okay, let's figure it out," he said, and I could have done handstands and cheered, because he got it completely.

I told Tolliver about Dr. Bowden. I related the doctor's story, adding my own commentary. And he listened, God bless him, he listened to every word without interrupting. He abandoned his snit as quickly as he could toss it overboard. I told him how glad I was that Manfred had been there, had heard the same story, because otherwise I'd find it hard to believe it myself.

"So why did that lead to you wanting to disembowel my dad?"

"Because I don't believe in coincidences that huge. What was Matthew doing in that office building? He had to have been seeing Tom Bowden. And why would he know about Tom Bowden? He had to have had a connection with the Joyces, or at least whichever of them wanted to keep Mariah's pregnancy and the birth of the child secret."

"But did he *have* to?" Tolliver asked. "I mean, did Dad really have to have been in cahoots with the Joyces, one or all of them? We don't know who it was who took the doctor to the ranch that night. But we do know, from Victoria's files, that Chip Moseley was arrested in Texarkana once, so we can assume he was there pretty often. And we know that the Joyce family had some doctors there, according to Tom Bowden, so they had some connections there, too. That's a slim tie, but it's a tie."

"And when we met the Joyces, I thought the two men looked familiar. Just a little."

"Chip and Drex?"

I nodded. "I know that doesn't seem as conclusive, because I can't place them firmly. But most people I'm that fuzzy on, it's because they came to the trailer, and I hate to remember that time. Plus, I tried not to look, because I knew it was dangerous to know who was buying and selling drugs."

"Yes," Tolliver said heavily. "It was dangerous, every day, to be living there."

"So all this is why I think your dad is involved. And I'm wondering if he got in touch with Mark so Mark's intervention would lead to your dad's getting to see you."

Tolliver mulled that over. "Could be," he said. "I would never answer his letters or take his phone calls, so he might have used Mark. He'd know I'd never lose touch with my brother." There was a little pain in Tolliver's face; even now, he'd had a tiny flicker of hope that his dad was trying to do the right thing, that Matthew had really and truly reformed.

"But what *happened*?" I asked, frustrated. "Why was he involved with the Joyce family? And how did Cameron get involved in that?"

"Cameron? Why do you think he would hurt Cameron? Not my dad." Tolliver shook his head. "He had an alibi, remember. At the time the old woman saw Cameron getting in the truck, Dad was playing pool with that asshole and his girlfriend."

"I remember that guy," I said. "Come on, let's get you into the bed. We can talk about it tomorrow."

seventeen

TOLLIVER was stunned and exhausted. I had to help him climb into the bed. I called room service for some soup and salads for both of us after I got him settled. I sat on the side of the bed while we waited for the food to come.

"I can believe a lot of bad stuff about Matthew," he said, "but I don't believe he hurt Cameron."

"It had never occurred to me, either," I said. "Honestly, I don't want to believe it. But if he did have a connection to her disappearance and he's been letting us wonder all these years, I want him to die." With Tolliver, I wasn't going to worry about how saying such a thing would make him think of me. He knew me. Now he would know me a little better.

Tolliver understood. "He'd deserve to die, if he hurt Cameron," he said. "But there's not one single thing to tie him to Cameron's disappearance, and he had no motive at all. For that matter, we don't have any proof that he's involved in the mess with the Joyce family. We need something more than the sight of a man's back as he walks out of a public building."

"I understand," I said—and I really did, even if I hated his logic. "So we have to figure out a way. We can't go on living our lives unless we get rid of this, one way or another."

"Yes," said Tolliver, and then he closed his eyes. Amazingly, he fell asleep.

I ate supper by myself, though I saved his in case he woke up to eat it. After I was through with my salad, I did something I hadn't done in at least a year. I went out to our car, opened the trunk, and got my sister's backpack out of it. Back inside our room, I sat on the couch and unzipped the backpack. We'd thought it was so cute when Cameron picked it out. It was pink with black polka dots. Cameron had gotten a black jacket and black boots, and she'd looked wonderful. No one had to know that everything had come from the secondhand shop.

The police had finally let us have the backpack, after six years. It had been fingerprinted, turned inside out, examined microscopically . . . for all I knew, they'd x-rayed it.

Cameron would be very nearly twenty-six now. She'd been gone for almost eight years.

It was late spring when she'd been taken. She'd been decorating the school gym for the prom. She'd had a date with—oh, God, I couldn't remember. Todd? Yes, Todd Battista. I couldn't remember if I'd had a date or not. Probably not, because following the lightning strike, my popularity had plummeted. My new ability had thrown me completely out of whack, and it had taken me almost a year to adjust to the buzz of dead people. And then I'd had to learn how to conceal my strange ability. During that awful time, I'd earned a well-deserved reputation for being very strange.

She'd been so late that day. And that wasn't like Cameron. I remembered making my mother rouse enough to watch the girls, whom I'd collected from day care. Though it wasn't smart to leave them alone with her, I couldn't take them with me. I hurried down the road, past all the other trailers, following the route we always took coming home.

Tolliver and Mark had been at their respective jobs, and Matthew, as it turned out, had been playing pool in the home of one of his wonderful friends, a junkie named Renaldo Simpkins. The police would never have believed Renaldo, but his girlfriend, Tammy, had been there, too, and she said she'd walked in and out of the room at least five times during the pool game. She was sure that Matthew had never left between around four and six thirty. (The six thirty was firm, because that was when she'd gotten a phone call from a neighbor, telling her that there were police cars all around the Lang trailer, and Matthew better get his ass home.)

Around five thirty, I'd found my sister's backpack—the one now sitting before me on a hotel coffee table—by the side of the street. It was a residential street lined with very small houses. About half of them were abandoned. But there was a woman living in the house across the street from the spot where I'd found Cameron's backpack. Her name was Ida Beaumont.

I'd never talked to Ida Beaumont before, and despite all the times I'd walked past her house, I don't think I'd ever seen her out in her yard. She was afraid of all the teenagers in the neighborhood, and maybe she had good reason. This was a part of town where even police looked over their shoulders. But I met Ida Beaumont that day. I'd walked across the street and knocked on her door.

"Hi, I'm sorry to bother you, but my sister hasn't come home from school and her backpack is there, under that tree." I pointed over to the bright splotch of color. Ida Beaumont peered at it, her eyes following my finger.

"Yes," she said cautiously. She was in her early sixties, and the newspaper articles told me later that she was living on some kind of disability check and what remained of her dead husband's pension. I could hear her television going. She was watching a talk show. "Who's your sister?" she asked. "Is she that pretty blond girl? I see you two walking home all the time."

"Yes ma'am. That's her. I'm looking for her. Did you see anything happen over there this afternoon? She would have been coming home sometime within the past hour, I think."

"I stay at the back of the house, mostly." Ida seemed to put emphasis on that, because she didn't want to be seen as a busybody. "But I seen a blue pickup, an old Dodge, about half an hour ago. The man in it was talking to a girl. I couldn't really see her, she was on the other side of the pickup. But she got in, and they took off."

"Oh." I tried to make sense of this, tried to remember if anyone we knew had an old blue pickup. But no one popped up in my memory. "Thanks. That was about half an hour ago?"

"Yes," she said, very positively. "Yes, that was when it was."

"She didn't look like she was . . . like he was making her do it?"

"I couldn't say about that. They talked, she got in, they left."

"Okay. I appreciate your taking the time to talk to me." And I

turned and walked back across the street. Then I reversed myself. Ida Beaumont was still standing at her doorway.

"Do you have a phone?" I asked. We lived in a neighborhood where you couldn't take that for granted.

"I do."

"Will you call the police and tell them what I just told you, about my sister? Ask them to come? I'll be standing over there, by the backpack."

I could see reluctance in Ida's face, knew the older woman was wishing she hadn't come to the door. "All right," she said finally, exhaling loudly. "I'll call 'em." And without closing the wooden door, she went to a telephone that was mounted on the wall. I could see her dialing the police, and I could hear her part of the conversation.

I'll say this for the police: they were there very quickly. Initially, of course, they were doubtful about Cameron really being missing. Teenage girls often found better things to do than go home, especially to a home in this neighborhood. But the abandoned backpack seemed to speak to them, to testify that my sister hadn't been willing to leave.

Finally, I'd broken down crying, explained to them that I had to get home, that my mom couldn't be trusted to take care of my sisters, and that had made everything more serious, right away. They let me call my brothers, who both left work immediately to come home. That neither Mark nor Tolliver was skeptical that Cameron had been abducted also convinced the police that my sister hadn't gone away willingly or intentionally.

Going into the trailer with the cops would have been humiliating under any other circumstances. But I was so frightened by then that I was only glad they were there. They saw that my mother had passed out again on the couch and that the girls were crying. She'd started to put a diaper on Gracie and hadn't finished taping it shut. Mariella was trying to mash some banana for Gracie (who'd just started eating real food) and she was standing on a chair to reach the counter. It was clean, or at least as clean as an old dilapidated trailer could be, but of course we were very crowded in there, and the sheer amount of stuff made it look incredibly cluttered.

"Is it always like this?" asked the younger cop, looking around him.

"Shut up, Ken," said his partner.

"Cameron and I try," I said, and I began crying again. My bitterness ran out of me in a stream of explanation. I'd already realized, on some level, that our life there was over, so the pretence was over, too.

While I cried and talked, I was getting Gracie diapered and making a peanut butter sandwich for Mariella. I mashed the banana for Gracie and mixed it with a little formula and put it in a bowl for her. I got her little spoon out of the drainer. My mother never moved, except once. Her hand went out to the spot where Gracie had been, and she patted the air vaguely. I put Gracie in her infant seat and began feeding her, pausing from time to time to wipe my face.

"You take care of your sisters," the older cop said in a friendly way.

"My brothers make enough to take them to day care while we're at school," I said. "We've tried real hard."

"I can tell," he said. The younger cop turned away with his mouth pressed together and his eyes hot. "Where's your daddy?" he asked after a minute.

"My stepfather," I corrected automatically. "I have no idea."

When Matthew got home, he acted stunned that the police were there, agonized that Cameron was missing, appalled that his poor wife had slept through such hubbub and turmoil.

This had never happened before, he told the cops. There were several more at the trailer by now. One of them had arrested Matthew before, and he snorted derisively when Matthew finished his performance.

"Yeah, buddy," the officer said. "And where were you this afternoon?"

Later, Tolliver and I sat together on the couch after my mother had been taken to the hospital. Mark paced, as much as you can pace in a trailer. A woman from Social Services had come to get our sisters. Matthew had been arrested because he had some joints in his car. The drugs were the excuse the cops used; I think they just wanted to arrest him after they saw the trailer and talked to me. Mark and Tolliver had confirmed everything I said: Mark very reluctantly, Tolliver with a matter-of-fact air that said a lot about our lives. But I found Mark crying outside that night, after the police had gone. He was sitting in the lawn chair right at the bottom of the trailer steps, and he had his face in his hands.

"We tried so hard to stay together," he said, as if he had to explain his distress.

"That's all over now," I said. "That's all gone, now that Cameron's been taken. There's no more hiding things now."

For a month after that, Cameron had been "seen" numerous times around Texarkana, in Dallas, in Corpus Christi, in Houston, in Little Rock. A teenage panhandler in Los Angeles had been hauled in because she looked like Cameron. But none of those sightings had ever come to anything, and her corpse had never been found. I'd gotten excited about three years after she'd gone, when a hunter had found a girl's body in some woods around Lewisville, Arkansas. The corpse—what there was left of it—was female, and the right size to be Cameron. But after close examination, the bones appeared to be that of a woman somewhat older than my sister, and the DNA wasn't a match. That body had never been identified, though when they'd let me close to her I'd known she'd been a suicide. I didn't share that, because I had limited credibility with the police.

Tolliver and I had started our traveling by then, and we were building up our business. It had taken a long time for word of mouth to get around and for the Internet to pick up on what I was doing. The cops thought I was a scam artist. The first two years were very difficult. After that, my career took on a certain momentum.

But now was not the time to think about my own journey, but about Cameron's. I touched the backpack lovingly, and I took out everything inside. I'd examined every item a hundred times. We'd leafed through every page of the textbooks inside, looking for a message, a clue, anything. All the notes Cameron had been passed by other students were stuffed in a pocket, and we'd pored over them, trying to read something in them that would tell us what had happened to our sister.

Tanya had wanted Cameron to notice how stupid Heather's outfit was, and Tanya had also remarked on the fact that Jerry had said that Heather had had SEX with him when they'd gone out the weekend before. Jennifer thought that Cameron's brother Tolliver was HOT, and was he dating anyone? And wasn't Mr. Arden a stupid idiot?

Todd had wondered when he should pick her up for the prom,

and would she be getting dressed at Jennifer's house, like she had last time?

(If Cameron could manage it, she got her dates to pick her up somewhere else. I didn't blame her at all.)

There'd been a note from Mr. Arden, asking Cameron to tell her parents that one of them needed to come up to the school and explain that they knew the attendance policy. Just bringing a signature back to the school from home wasn't enough. (Mr. Arden had told the police that Cameron had missed his class once over the acceptable limit, and he'd wanted to lay eyes on one of Cameron's parents to make sure someone was aware that Cameron couldn't skip any more or she might not graduate.)

She hadn't been skipping the class out of senior giddiness. It was her last class of the day, and sometimes we had to leave early to pick up the girls at day care if Tolliver or Mark couldn't.

Of course, all the teachers we'd had had professed their shock and horror at our living conditions, except Miss Briarly. Miss Briarly had said, "And what would you have had us do? Call the police so the kids wouldn't have even had each other?"

That was exactly what the press thought Miss Briarly should have done, and she'd gotten reprimanded by the principal. It had made me so angry. Miss Briarly had taught Cameron her favorite class, advanced biology. I remembered how hard Cameron had worked on her senior project about genetics, charting the eye colors of everyone in the neighborhood. She'd gotten an A. Miss Briarly had given me the paper after Cameron's disappearance.

Ida Beaumont had had to tell her story over and over. She'd become such a recluse, as a result, that she'd stopped answering her door and got a church lady to deliver her groceries.

My mother and Tolliver's father had been sentenced to jail on multiple charges of child endangerment and assorted drug offenses.

Tolliver had been given permission to move in with Mark. I'd gone to a foster home, where I'd been treated very decently. It had been marvelous, to me, to be in a home where the floors were solid, where I only had to share a room with one other girl, where everything was clean without me having to clean it personally, and where study time was mandatory. I still sent the Clevelands a Christmas card every year. They'd let Tolliver come to visit me on the Saturdays he wasn't working.

By the time I graduated, we'd developed our plan for using my weird new talent to make our living. We'd spent hours at the cemetery, practicing and exploring the limits of my strange ability. Even weirder than our plan was the fact that this had actually been a very happy time in my life, and I think in Tolliver's, too. The biggest flaw in that new life was the loss of all my sisters. Cameron was gone, and Mariella and Gracie had moved away to live with Iona and Hank.

I opened Cameron's math book. She'd been taking precal; she'd hated it. Cameron had poor math skills. She was good at history, I remembered. She'd liked that. It was easier to study people's lives when they were all dead, their troubles all past. Cameron was a good speller, and she'd enjoyed all her science classes, too, especially the advanced biology class she'd been taking.

The newspapers had gone on and on about the sad condition of the trailer, the depravity of Laurel and Mark, the arrest records of their frequent visitors, the lengths we kids had gone to in our attempt to stay together. Truthfully, I don't think our home was so very unusual. In the unspoken way kids communicate, we'd learned of a dozen or more kids in our school who had it just as bad or worse.

People often can't help being poor, but they can help being bad. We were unfortunate in having parents who were both.

I flipped open one of my sister's notebooks. Her class notes were still in place. The grubby ruled pages covered in her handwriting were all that I had left of her. Cameron had been the only one, besides me, who could remember the good days—the days when our mom and dad were still married and they hadn't started using. If my dad was still alive, I doubted he'd remember much of anything.

I shook myself. I was not going to get maudlin. But it was necessary to think about the day Cameron had vanished. If she'd gotten into that pickup voluntarily, then I might as well forget about tracing her. Not only would that make her a stranger to me, but there would be no body to sense, unless something had happened to her in the meantime. If Cameron was dead, ironically enough, one of these days I might find her.

I wondered if Ida Beaumont was still alive. I'd been so young then, she'd looked positively tottering on the edge of her grave. Now, I realized she had been no more than sixty-five.

Obeying an impulse I couldn't fathom, I called information in Texarkana and discovered that she still had a listing. My fingers punched in the number before I could even explain to myself why I was doing this.

"Hello?" a creaky voice said suspiciously.

"Mrs. Beaumont?"

"Yes, this is Ida Beaumont."

"You may not remember me," I said. "I'm Harper Connelly."

Dead silence.

"What do you want?" the voice said.

That wasn't exactly the question I'd anticipated.

"Are you still in the same house, Ms. Beaumont? I was thinking I might come by to visit you," I said, making this up on the spot. "I was thinking I might bring one of my brothers."

"No," she said. "Don't come here. Don't ever come here. The last time you came, I had people knocking on my door all day and night for weeks. And the police still come by. You stay away."

"We have some questions to ask you," I said in a voice that I hoped was pitched somewhere between anger and simple determination.

"The police have already asked me plenty of questions," she snapped, and I knew I'd gone the wrong way. "I wish I'd never answered the door that day when you come knocking."

"But then you couldn't have told me about the blue truck," I said.

"I told you, didn't I, that I didn't see the girl clearly?"

"Yes," I said, though in my mind, over the years, I'd pretty much disregarded that. I was missing a girl, she'd seen a girl get into a pickup, and Cameron's backpack was there on the spot.

Over the line, I heard a deep sigh. Then Ida Beaumont began speaking. "A young woman started coming by from Meals on Wheels about six months ago," she said. "Those meals, they're never any good, but at least they're free, and sometimes they bring enough to last another day. Her name's Missy Klein."

"Okay," I said, since I had no idea what else to say. My heart was sinking into my stomach, because I knew this was going to be bad.

"And she said to me, she says, 'Mrs. Beaumont, you remember all those years ago when you saw a girl getting into a blue pickup?' And I says, 'Yes, sure, and it was a curse to me.' "

"All right." The dark feeling grew inside me.

"So she tells me it was her, getting into the truck with her boyfriend, who she wasn't supposed to be seeing because he was in his twenties."

"It wasn't my sister."

"No, it wasn't. It was that Missy Klein, and now she brings me Meals on Wheels."

"You never saw my sister."

"No, I didn't. And Missy, she tells me that the backpack was sitting there when she came along and got in his truck."

I felt like a ton of bricks had fallen on me. "Have you told the police?" I said finally.

"No, I don't go calling the police. I suppose I should have, but—well, they come by to see me every so often, take me back over that day. Peter Gresham, he comes by. I figured I'd tell him the next time he stopped in."

"Thank you," I said. "I wish I'd known this before. But thank you for telling me."

"Well, sure. I thought you'd be mad at me," she said, which I thought was kind of amazing.

"I'm glad I called. Goodbye," I said. My voice was as numb as my heart. Any minute now, the feeling would come back. I wanted to be off the phone with this woman when that happened.

Ida Beaumont was saying something else about Meals on Wheels when I clicked my phone shut.

Lizzie Joyce called me then, before I could think through the implications of what I'd just heard. "Oh, my Lord," she said, "I can't believe Victoria is dead. You were a friend of hers, right? You-all went way back? Harper, I'm so sorry. What do you think happened to her? You think it had anything to do with looking for the baby?"

"I don't have the slightest idea," I said, though that wasn't the truth. I didn't think Lizzie Joyce had anything to do with Victoria's murder, but I thought someone close to her was involved. I found myself wondering why she'd called me. Lizzie Joyce, wealthy beyond imagining, didn't have a BFF to call? Where was the sister, and the boyfriend, and the brother? Why didn't she call all the people she sat on boards with, the people who worked for her, the people who did her hair and polished her nails when she was going somewhere fancy, the people who set up the barrels for her competition practice?

After I'd listened for a minute, I realized Lizzie wanted to talk to someone she didn't have to brief, someone who had known Victoria; and I was the person who fit the bill.

"I guess I'm going to the firm of detectives my granddad's company always uses," she said. "I thought it would be helpful to talk to a woman out on her own, someone who wasn't up on our business, not involved in the family saga. But I think I caused her death. If I'd gone to our usual firm, she'd still be alive."

There was no rebuttal to offer on that. "How come you have a private detective firm on call?" I asked instead.

"Granddaddy started that when he became the head of a big enterprise. More than a rancher. He liked to know who he was hiring, at least for key positions." Lizzie sounded surprised that I needed to ask.

"So why didn't he get them to check out Mariah Parish?"

"Granddaddy had met her when she worked for the Peadens, and when he needed someone, and she was free, it seemed like a natural fit. I guess he felt like he knew her and didn't need to have her investigated. After all, she wasn't going to be writing checks on our account or anything."

He wouldn't have trusted her with his checkbook, but he would trust her to cook his food without poisoning him, and he would trust her to clean his house without stealing his possessions. Even suspicious rich people have their blind side. Given what we'd learned about Mariah from reading her file, I found that ironic.

I hadn't known that Rich Joyce had actually met Mariah before she moved into his house. Drexell hadn't mentioned that at our dinner with Victoria. Maybe Rich had seen a good way to sneak a mistress into his house under his kids' eyes. Maybe his friend who'd first employed Mariah had told Rich he'd been bedding her. Nudge nudge, wink wink. Here's a good woman who can cook, count your pills, and warm up your sheets, Rich. And she can stay right there in the house.

"And you didn't even think about investigating her the way you would any other employee?"

"Well," Lizzie said, clearly uncomfortable, "she and Granddaddy had everything worked out by the time we knew about it. He was sure in his right mind, so we didn't say anything."

All the Joyce grandchildren had been scared of the patriarch. "You didn't have her checked out afterward?"

"Well, he would have known. *That* was when I should have hired an outside source. I gotta tell you the truth, at the time, I didn't think too much about it. That was years ago. I was younger, and less confident, and of course, I expected Granddaddy to live forever." Lizzie stopped short, probably realizing she'd been oversharing. "Well, I just wanted to tell you how sorry I am about your friend. And how's your brother doing? This whole thing just keeps getting messier and messier."

"Do you wish you'd never contacted me?"

A moment of silence. "Truthfully, yes, that's what I wish," she said. "Seems like a lot of people have died and they didn't need to. What's changed? What more do I know? Nothing. My grandfather saw a rattlesnake and died. We don't know if anyone else was there for sure. He's still dead. Mariah's dead, and in my head she's not resting in peace anymore, now that I know she died in childbirth. Where's that baby? Is the baby an aunt or uncle of mine? I still don't know. Maybe I'll never know."

"Someone's sure trying to make sure you don't," I said. "Goodbye, Lizzie." And I hung up.

Manfred stopped in, and I was glad to see him, but I wasn't in a mood for talking. He asked me about the backpack.

"It's my sister's," I said. "She left it the day she vanished."

I turned away to answer Tolliver's call. He'd woken up briefly and asked for a pain pill. He drifted back to sleep before he even took it.

When I came back in the living room, Manfred was withdrawing his hand from the backpack. He looked sad. "I'm sorry this happened to you, Harper."

"Well, thanks for the kind thought, Manfred, but it happened to my sister. I was just caught up in the aftermath."

"I'll see you soon. Don't worry if I don't call for a couple of days. I've got a job to do."

"Oh . . . okay, Manfred." I hadn't thought about worrying. He gave me a peck on the cheek when he left, and I was glad to shut the door behind him. I sat and thought about my sister.

It was a long night. I finally fell asleep after midnight.

eighteen

TOLLIVER woke up the next morning feeling much better. He'd slept for twelve hours straight, and when he woke me up he let me know that he was full of energy. We had to be careful, but with me on top, sex was doable. Very doable. An absolute delight, in fact. And I thought the top of his head was going to fly off, he enjoyed it so much. He lay there panting afterward, as if he'd done the work, and I collapsed beside him, laughing in a breathless kind of way.

"Now I feel like myself," he said. "Somehow it makes you feel even less like a man, when you're bedridden and then you can't even stand the physical part of having sex. Reduces you to a kid."

"Let's just get in the car and go," I suggested. "Let's go to the apartment. We could be in St. Louis in a day. You could ride that long, I bet."

"What about staying here to visit more with the girls? What about finding out if my father was connected to the Joyces and Cameron?"

"Maybe you were right. Maybe we need to leave the girls to Iona and Hank. They're stable, in every sense. We travel so much. We'll never be a constant in their lives. And your dad? He's going to hell anyway. If we drop all this, it'll just take him a little longer. We could be free of him."

Tolliver looked thoughtful. "Come here," he said, and I put my head on his good shoulder. He didn't wince, so that was all right. I stroked the part of his chest not covered with a bandage. Looking back on the time between my discovery that I loved him as a man and the time I found out he felt the same and we acted on it, I wondered how I had survived. We were incredibly lucky, and I knew there was a part of me that I found somewhat scary, the part that would do anything to prevent what we had from being jeopardized.

"You know what we ought to do," he said.

"What?"

"We ought to take a day trip."

"Oh, where to?"

"To Texarkana."

I froze. "Are you serious?" I said, raising my head to look him in the eyes.

"Yeah, I am. It's time we went back to just look around and let go."

"Let go."

"Yeah. We've got to realize that we're not going to find Cameron."

"I've got some things to tell you about that."

"Oh?" His voice had an apprehensive edge. If I hadn't liked what he'd said, he was going to dislike what I had to say even more.

"I made some calls yesterday," I said. "And I got some calls. While you were asleep. I've got to tell you about them."

An hour later, Tolliver was saying, "That woman was wrong? All the time they were looking for the wrong thing? She was just *mixed up*?"

"She never said she saw Cameron clearly, only that the backpack was there after she saw a blond girl get into a blue truck," I said. "Who knows? So we're back to square one. In fact . . ." I thought for a second. "In fact, that throws the whole timeline off. She said Cameron had been picked up thirty minutes before I talked to her, and I set out to look for Cameron almost exactly at five o'clock. But now we can be pretty sure Cameron was picked up by someone even earlier."

"She left the school at four, right?"

"Right. That's what—oh, her friend, what's her name—Rebecca. That's what Rebecca said. But she also said that maybe the time wasn't on the nose. They'd worked all last period decorating the gym and kept going after school was out. I'd always thought she stood around in the parking lot talking to one of her friends, but now I'm assuming she went straight home. You were at work at the restaurant. Mark was driving between his job at Taco Bell and his job at Super Save-a-Lot."

"A seven-minute drive," Tolliver said automatically. We'd talked about it so often.

"Your dad was at Renaldo Simpkins's place from around four to six thirty. My mom was passed out, as usual."

We looked at each other. With the timeline changed, Matthew's ass wasn't as covered as we'd thought.

"No matter what I think of him, I don't want to believe it," I said.

"We do need to go to Texarkana."

"Let's call the doctor's office and see what his nurse says."

The nurse said no. The nurse said Tolliver needed to stay in the hotel room. No matter how many precautions we said he'd take, she said no. She was glad that he felt much better, but he would tire as the day went on.

Of course we could simply have ignored her strictures and done what we wanted, but I was against that. I suspected she was right to say no, and though I would have been glad if Tolliver had been up to traveling, in all conscience I didn't want to get some hours' drive away from the hospital and have some kind of emergency. Certainly there were doctors in Texarkana, certainly there were hospitals, but common sense said the hospital and doctor who'd treated him initially would be best.

We sat looking at each other. We had few choices: postpone the drive to Texarkana until Tolliver was better, ask Manfred if he was in the area and could go with me, or ask Mark if he could take a day off work to ride with me. "Here's a novel thought: I could go by myself," I said. Tolliver shook his head vehemently. "I know you can, and I know you'd do fine," he said. "But when it's about Cameron, we both should go. We'll wait today, and tomorrow, if we have to. Then, no matter what, we go."

It was good to have a plan of action, excellent to have Tolliver feel up to forming that plan. Iona called and invited us over to supper at their house, if Tolliver was feeling up to the excursion. He nodded, so I told her we'd be glad to come. I didn't ask if we could bring anything, because I couldn't imagine what we could bring and she always turned me down anyway, as though anything I brought into their house would be suspect. The day was boring, restless, and interminable.

Finally we went down to the car, with Tolliver moving very carefully. I drove to Iona and Hank's house with great care, trying to keep the car away from bumps. That's not easy in Dallas, and I was glad we stuck to city streets instead of getting on the interstate in the early evening traffic.

That area on the east side of Dallas is one big suburb. There are all the stores you can find in any suburban area in the country—Bed Bath & Beyond, Home Depot, Staples, Old Navy, Wal-Mart—and after you see one sequence of them, they start to repeat in another area. On the one hand, if you wanted to buy any item you could think of, unless it was too exotic, you could find it. On the other hand . . . we saw these same stores all across America. We traveled a lot, but unless the climate was radically different, it was hard to tell one part of the urban landscape from another, though a thousand miles lay in between.

Architecture was going the same way as the chain stores. We'd seen Iona and Hank's house from Memphis to Tallahassee, from St. Louis to Seattle.

Tolliver was telling me all this again as I drove, and I was glad it was such a familiar complaint that I only had to say, "That's right," or "True," from time to time.

The girls were full of questions about Tolliver's bandage and what had happened to him. Iona had told them he'd been shot by someone who'd been careless and had a gun accident, so she and Hank could impress our sisters with the need for safety. Hank had a gun, he told us, but he kept it locked up and the key hidden. Since they were trying to be the best parents on earth, he and Iona had instructed the girls from an early age in the gun safety rules. I appreciated that, but to me it would have been more to the point to discuss gun *control.* However, that didn't jibe with Hank's ideas about being a true American, so that idea was not one that made an impression on my aunt and uncle.

After Mariella and Gracie had gotten used to having Tolliver around in his sling, they went off to do their usual things. Mariella had homework, Gracie had a song to learn for chorus, and Iona was finishing up the cooking. Tolliver and Hank went into the family room to watch the news, and I offered to help Iona by taking care of the dishes that had accumulated as she cooked. She smiled and nodded, and I rolled up my sleeves and got to work. This is a job I don't mind. I can think while I do it or talk to a Chore Mate or simply take pleasure in a job well done.

"Matthew was by here today." Iona was stirring a pot on the stove. She'd made chili. "He did call up several days ago, to ask if he could come by. We thought about it. He scared the girls the other day at the skating rink. We thought maybe if they saw him while we were around, they wouldn't be so worried about it. And maybe he wouldn't try to ambush them again, if he knew we'd be reasonable."

This showed good sense on the part of Iona. I found myself nodding at her approvingly, not that she cared whether or not I approved of her. "I'll bet he didn't come just to hang around with the girls and visit with them. What did he want?" Matthew had been a busy bee. I wondered when he found time to work.

"He wanted to take some pictures of the girls. He didn't have any recent ones. We did send him their school pictures, but he said they got taken away in jail. Those men will take anything."

"Matthew is one of those men."

She actually laughed. "Yeah, you're right. Still, if he wants pictures of his daughters, I'm not going to stop him. Though they're our daughters now, and we made sure he knew that."

"Did he talk to them much?" I asked. I was curious.

"No," Iona said. She went to the hall, heard that the girls were playing a video game in their room. She returned to her station at the stove. "That man, I don't understand him. He was blessed with some wonderful children. Tolliver and Mark are both good boys; and he had you and Cameron for stepdaughters, both of you bright and pretty, and no drugs. Then he has these two girls. Mariella's grades are going up. Aside from that one little running-away incident last fall, she's doing good in school. Bless Gracie, she's always a little behind her age group, but she's not a whiner, not a complainer, and she works real hard on her schoolwork. But Matthew don't seem to want to get to know them. He took the pictures, but then he talked to Hank and me. The girls don't know what to make of him."

"I know they don't remember living in Texarkana."

"Not really," Iona said. "Sometimes they mention it, but they never talk about anything specific. Gracie was just a baby, of course, and Mariella was little more than a toddler." She shrugged. "I know there were plenty of times my sister and Matthew weren't there when you needed them."

That was putting it mildly.

"I never said how glad I was you and Hank were willing to take them in," I said, surprising even myself. "It must have been a real shock, going from no kids to two in the blink of an eye."

Iona stopped stirring and turned from the stove to face me. I was drying the dishes and putting them on the counter for Iona to put away in their designated spots. "I appreciate you saying that," she said. "Though I was glad to have them, and taking them into our home was the right thing to do. We prayed about it. That's the answer we come up with. We love these girls like they were our own. I can't believe we're going to have another baby! At my age! Sometimes I feel like Abraham's wife, seventy years old and with child."

Until the meal was ready we talked about Iona's startling pregnancy. We talked about her ob/gyn doctor, special tests she might need as an older first-time mother, and all kinds of pregnancy-related topics. Iona was happier than I'd ever seen her, and anything about her interesting condition was fun for her to talk about. I tried to concentrate on looking happy and asking the right questions, but underneath our conversation, I was worried about Matthew's appearance at the house, about his taking pictures of the girls. He didn't want photos of them for his own pleasure or because he was proud of having two such healthy daughters. Matthew never did anything that simple and straightforward.

Tolliver came to the table first, so he could get into position with his paraphernalia, and then Hank. The girls washed their hands and took their places, and Iona and I carried the food to the table. Iona had made chili and cornbread, and I'd grated cheese to sprinkle on the steaming bowls. We said grace before we ate, and then we enjoyed eating. Iona had none of the characteristics I associate with good cooks—she wasn't passionate; she didn't love fresh ingredients like all the chefs on TV; she'd never traveled much and she was suspicious of foreign cuisine. But her chili was wonderful, her cornbread mouth-watering.

Tolliver and I both had more than one bowlful, and Iona looked gratified at our praise. Mariella and Gracie were full of conversation about school and their friends, and I was glad to hear that both of them seemed to get along well with the other children. Gracie was wearing a green top that matched her eyes, so she looked like a little fairy, though her bold little nose hinted that she might not be a benevolent one. She was a funny little thing. She was really "on" tonight, telling little jokes she'd heard in class, asking Iona if they could have chili dogs the next night if any of the chili was left over. Mariella mentioned Matthew's visit a couple of times, dragging it into the conversation as if it worried her. Each time, Iona or Hank would respond calmly, and I could see Mariella's anxiety abating.

Tolliver and I left soon after we'd eaten, in deference to the girls' evening routine. Our sisters were so excited by a discussion about what to name the baby that the topic of Tolliver and me getting married seemed to have slipped to the backs of their minds, to my relief.

I drove back to the hotel, and Tolliver sat in silence. Now that it was dark, I had to concentrate more on navigating, and we made one false turn before we got back. It was easily corrected, and soon I was helping Tolliver out of the car. I could tell he was tired, but he was moving better.

We were crossing the lobby when he said, "Hank said Dad took pictures of the girls."

"That's what Iona told me. I think they were smart to let the girls see Matthew with them both around, so they could kind of put him in perspective."

"Yeah, that was a smart move," Tolliver said, but not as though he was giving it any thought. "But why would he really want pictures of them?"

"I don't think your dad is the kind of guy who puts pictures of his kids on Facebook, do you? So I can't imagine."

"Oh, I doubt he'd do that," Tolliver said matter-of-factly. "Listen, you took care of the girls when they were little."

"You know I did. Cameron and me. Especially Gracie, she was so frail." The automatic doors swooshed open and we went into the lobby. The desk clerk was eating a cookie. She glanced up at us, then went back to her book.

"Do you remember when Gracie went to the hospital?" Tolliver said.

"Sure I do. I was scared to death. She was maybe three months old, still real little. Her birth weight was low, remember? She was so sick, and she had been running a temperature for four days. We'd been hassling your dad to take her to the clinic or to the emergency room. Mom was so out of it that she couldn't go. No doctor would have let her leave with a baby in her arms. Your dad was really mad at us, but he got a phone call from some friend of his, and I guess the guy was repaying a loan or paying for some dope or something, because all of a sudden Matthew decided he would take Gracie. We barely had time to change her diaper and remind him how to buckle her in the car seat before he drove off. He took her to Wadley."

"How do you know that?"

I unlocked the room door and pushed it open. "What do you mean, how do I know that? He took her to the hospital. He brought her back after a couple of weeks. They'd had her in ICU, so we couldn't see her. He stayed with her. How could it not have been true? When he brought her back Gracie looked so much better, I could hardly believe it was . . ." I froze.

"You couldn't believe it was Gracie, could you?" Tolliver said after a long silence.

I put my hand over my mouth. Tolliver carefully sat down on the edge of the couch.

When I could move, I sat down on the chair and our eyes met.

"No," I said. "I couldn't believe it was Gracie. Her eyes were a hazy blue, but a few weeks after her stay in the hospital, they turned out to be green. So I figured she was older than most babies when their eyes change to their real color. And Matthew said that the doctors told him to put her back on just the bottle, even though she'd started to eat some baby food. . . ."

"You took care of Gracie more than Cameron did."

"Yeah, I did. Cameron was so busy that year, it was her senior year, and I was home more because of the lightning strike."

"Were you still having trouble with the aftereffects?"

"Oh, yeah, you remember, I had trouble for months. Before I learned to cope. I had terrible headaches, and a lot of pain. But I did my best for Gracie and Mariella," I said, knowing I sounded defensive.

"Of course you did. You kept all of us going. But my point is, there might have been things you didn't notice because you were having so many physical problems and you were so distracted by sensing the dead people."

That had certainly been a terrible time in my life. Teenagers are ill equipped to cope with a huge gaping difference between themselves and other teens. "Your point is that I might not have noticed some changes in the baby? You think Matthew left with one baby and came back with another. You're saying the real Gracie is dead."

He nodded. "It was Chip who came to the trailer some," he said. "I'm pretty sure I remember him. Maybe Drex, too, but Chip for sure. He had some drug deals with my dad."

"Oh, my God," I said. "I thought they looked a bit familiar. And if one of them took Dr. Bowden out to the ranch that night, and they wanted to get rid of a baby without killing it . . ."

"They might have called Matthew, who had a real sick baby that wasn't going to make it."

"How could they? How could they imagine that Matthew would switch babies? Why would they want to, anyway?"

"If the baby was the biological child of Rich Joyce and Mariah Parish, then she would be literally worth millions."

I couldn't speak for a minute. "But why not just kill her, and then the millions would stay where they were? With the three Joyce grandchildren?"

"Maybe they didn't want to murder an infant."

"They were willing to let Mariah die when she could've been saved."

"There's a difference between letting someone die and killing someone. And between a grown woman who was pretty unscrupulous and an infant child. More practically, they might not have realized how close to death Mariah was until it was too late."

I shook my head, dazed. "So, if this is true, what do you think Matthew did with the real Gracie, his real daughter? Do you think he deliberately left with her that evening and exposed her or something?"

"I have no idea, and I'm not sure I really want to know . . . though I think we have to try to find out," Tolliver said, and he sounded like an old man. "But I wonder if he ever really intended to take her to the hospital."

"The pictures?"

"He wants pictures of Gracie. He just took some of Mariella to give his story some weight," Tolliver said.

"How did you figure this out?"

"He might have showed up at the skating rink thinking he could take pictures of the girls without us knowing, but we spotted him before he could do it, and the girls were scared of him. He'd already started trying to open communication with Iona and Hank by writing them a letter. When he didn't hear back, he probably thought he could sneak around them. After that didn't work out, he decided to try an open approach, and it worked. Iona and Hank wanted to demystify him so the girls wouldn't be so freaked, so they acted like his visit was normal. They were doing the right thing, but they couldn't imagine what his motives were."

"What will we do?" I had my elbows resting on my knees, and now I buried my face in my hands. "I can't wrap my head around all this. How did Cameron fit into all this? Was it just a coincidence that she went missing then?"

"Maybe we made the whole conspiracy up," Tolliver said. "Maybe we're as bad as those people who think JFK was shot by Martians."

"I wish," I said. "I *wish.*"

"I wonder if Mark knows anything," Tolliver said.

"We could call him."

"Yeah, but Dad's staying there now."

"Maybe he could meet us somewhere."

"We'll call him tomorrow. After we go to Texarkana."

"You sure you're up to that? You're not nearly finished with the antibiotics."

"I think I'm enough better."

"Sure, Dr. Lang."

"Hey, there are other things we need besides being super careful about my shoulder."

"We'll see what the doctor says in the morning," I told him, and he called me bossy. It felt nice, taking care of him. As upset as I was about the suspicion and the uncertainty surrounding Tolliver's dad, I felt a little proud that I had managed so far. We went to bed after some more rounds of fruitless discussion, and I don't think either of us slept very well that night. When Tolliver did fall asleep, he talked out loud; he only does that when he's really upset.

"*Save her,*" he said.

nineteen

INSTEAD of asking a nurse, I talked to Dr. Spradling directly first thing the next morning. To my surprise, he agreed that Tolliver was doing well enough to travel a little, provided he didn't lift anything or exert himself much.

Being able to travel a little made a wonderful change in Tolliver. It was as if he'd been thinking of himself as a sick person because he had to stay still. Now he thought of himself as a well person with temporary problems. I was delighted (and relieved) to see the resolution and decisiveness come back into his face and bearing. But I reminded myself to stay mindful that I had to take care of him.

Since we weren't anchored to the hospital anymore, we checked out of the hotel. We didn't know what would happen during the day or if we'd come back to Garland to spend the night.

It felt so good to drive away from the urban sprawl. We were back on the interstate, together. For an hour we were able to act like we were leaving our problems behind. But the closer we got to Texarkana, the more our questions and uncertainties bore in on us.

We went past the turnoff to Clear Creek, and I said, "We might have to stop here later."

Tolliver nodded. We were pretty close to Texarkana by then, and we weren't feeling chatty.

Texarkana straddles the state line, of course, and about fifty thousand people live there. A shopping area has grown up along the interstate passage through the north part of town, a shopping area with all of the usual suspects. We hadn't lived close to that part of town. We'd lived in the raggedy part. Texarkana is not better or worse than any other southern town. Most of our classmates had come from decent homes, and they'd had decent parents. We'd simply drawn the short end of the stick.

The street where we'd lived was lined with trailers. Their virtue was that they weren't packed together in little parks, at least where we'd been. They each had a little lot. Ours had been planted on its lot with the end toward the road, so you pulled into a rutted driveway and swung around to park in the front yard. Well, it was a yard in that it was a space in front of the trailer, but it never had had any grass, and the azaleas that had once been on either side of the concrete steps had been sickly bushes that were hardly worth the trouble.

Seeing it again was strange. We sat in the car, pulled to the side of the road, and looked at it without talking. A Latino walking by stared at us with a hard face. We no longer looked like we belonged here.

"What do you feel?" Tolliver asked.

"I don't feel any bodies," I said, and the relief made me almost giddy. "I don't know why I was scared I would. I would've known when we lived here, if—anyone—had been buried here."

Tolliver closed his eyes for a moment, feeling his own measure of relief. "Well, that's something," he said. "Where do you think we should look next?"

"I'm not sure why we felt like we had to come here," I said. "Where should we go next? I guess we should go to Renaldo's place. The chances aren't too good that he and Tammy are still there, but we can try."

"Do you remember how to get there?"

That was a good question, and it took me ten minutes longer than I'd assumed it would take to find the ratty little rent house that Renaldo and Tammy had lived in when Cameron had been taken.

I wasn't surprised when someone I didn't know answered the door. She was an African American, about my age, and she had two children under school age. They were both busy with safety scissors and an old Penney's catalog, making some kind of art project. "Just cut out the things you'd want in your house when you build one," the woman reminded them, before turning back to me. "What can I do for you?" she asked.

"I'm Harper Connelly, and I used to live a couple of blocks over," I said. "My stepfather used to have some friends that lived in this house, and I was wondering if you knew where they live now. Renaldo Simpkins and his girlfriend, Tammy?" I hadn't been able to remember Tammy's last name.

Her face changed. "Yeah, I know 'em," she said. "They live in another house, about six streets over. On Malden. They bad people, you know."

I nodded. "I know, but I have to talk to them. They're still together?"

"Yeah, hard to believe anyone would stay with Renaldo. But he had himself an accident, and Tammy, she's taking care of him." The woman glanced back over her shoulder, and I could tell she was anxious to get back to the kids.

"You know their house number?"

"No, but it's on Malden, and it's a block or two west of this house," she said. "It's a brown house with white shutters. Tammy drives a white car."

"Thanks."

She nodded and shut her door.

I relayed all this to Tolliver, who'd remained in the car.

With some difficulty, we tracked down a house we thought was the right one. "Brown" covers a lot of territory. But we suspected a sort of flesh-colored house might fall under the umbrella of brown, and there was a white car in front.

"Tammy," I said when she answered the door. Tammy—whose last name was Murray, I suddenly remembered—had aged more than the eight years since Cameron had been gone. She had been a full-figured woman of mixed race, with wavy reddish hair and a flamboyant style. Now her hair was cropped very short and slicked to her head with some kind of gel. She had tattoos running down her bare arms. She was gaunt.

"Who are you?" she asked with some curiosity. "You know me?"

"I'm Harper," I said. "Matthew Lang's stepdaughter. My brother is in the car." I pointed.

"Come in," she said. "Tell your brother to come, too."

I went back to the car and opened the door for Tolliver. "She wants us to come in," I said quietly. "You think that's all right?"

"Should be," he said, and we walked back to the porch.

"What happened to you, Tolliver?" Tammy said. "You're all banged up."

"I got shot," he said.

This was a place where no one would be surprised by that, and Tammy only said, "Bad luck, man!" before moving aside so we could enter.

The house was tiny, but since there wasn't much furniture, it didn't feel too crowded. The living room was big enough for a couch, where a figure was lying wrapped up in a blanket, and a battered recliner, clearly Tammy's normal station. It was flanked by an old TV tray laden with a remote control, Kleenex, and a package of cigarettes. Everything smelled like cigarette smoke.

We came around the corner of the couch to look at the man lying on it. If I hadn't known this was Renaldo, I would never have guessed it. Renaldo, who was also of mixed race, had always been light skinned. He'd also had a pencil mustache and worn his hair pulled back in a braid. Now his hair was cut very short. At one time, Renaldo had made what passed for good money in our neighborhood, because he'd been a mechanic at a car dealership, but his drug habit had cost him his job.

His eyes were open, but I couldn't tell if Renaldo was registering our presence or not.

"Hey, honey!" Tammy said. "Look who's here. Tolliver and his sister, you remember them? Matthew's kids?"

Renaldo's eyelids flickered, and he murmured, "Sure, I remember."

"I'm sorry to see you in such bad shape," Tolliver said, which was honest if not tactful.

"Can't walk," Renaldo said. I looked around for a wheelchair and glimpsed one leaning against the back door in the kitchen. It almost seemed that since the house was so small, opening up the wheelchair would be a waste of time, but I guess Tammy couldn't lift Renaldo.

"We had a wreck," Tammy said. "About three years ago. We've had some bad luck, sure enough. Here, Harper, take this chair and I'll get a couple from the table in the kitchen."

Tolliver looked frustrated that he couldn't go to get the chairs, but Tammy didn't think anything about doing it herself. She was used to a male that was helpless. I didn't ask any more questions about Renaldo's condition, because I didn't want to know. He looked bad.

"Tammy," Tolliver said after he and our hostess had wedged themselves into the folding chairs, which barely fit in the room, "we need to talk about the day my father was here, the day Cameron was taken."

"Oh, sure, that's all you folks ever want to talk about," she said, and made a face. "We're tired of talking about that, ain't we, Renaldo?"

"I'm not tired of it," he said, in his oddly muffled voice. "That Cameron was a fine girl; losing her was bad."

I felt like I'd bitten a lemon, the idea of someone like Renaldo looking at my sister made me feel so sour. But I tried to keep a pleasant expression on my face. "Can you please tell us again about that day?" I said.

Tammy shrugged. She lit a cigarette, and I tried to hold my breath as long as I could. "It's been a long time," she said. "I can't believe me and Renny been together that long, can you, baby?"

"Good years," he said, with an effort.

"Yeah, we had some good ones," she said tolerantly. "These aren't them, though. Well, that afternoon, your dad called, wanted to do some business with Renny. He told the cops he was going to take some stuff to the recycle with Renny, but that wasn't the truth. We had an overstock on Oxys; your dad had some Ritalin he wanted to swap for it. Your mama, she loved her Oxys."

"My mom loved everything," I said.

"That is the truth, child," Tammy said. "She loved her pills."

"And her alcohol," I said.

"That, too," Tammy said. She looked at me. "But you aren't here about your mother. She's dead and gone."

I shut my mouth.

"So my dad wanted to come over," Tolliver prompted.

"Yes," Tammy said, taking a big drag on her cigarette. I was afraid I was going to start coughing. "He came over about four. Give or take fifteen minutes. It might have been as late as four fifteen, four twenty-five, but it wasn't any later than that, because the TV show I was watching was over at four thirty, and he was at our house by then and in the pool room with Renaldo. They were playing a game. We had a nicer house." She looked around the tiny room. "Bigger. I told the police, I think he was here by a few minutes after four. But I wasn't paying too much attention until my program ended, and they called to me to bring them a beer."

Renaldo laughed, an eerie huh-huh-huh sound. "We drank us some beer," he said. "I won the game. We swapped some pills, made a deal. That was a good time."

"And he stayed here until he got a phone call?"

"Yeah, he had a cell phone, you know, for business," Tammy said.

"That guy who lived next door to you-all, he was calling to tell Matthew to get his ass home, the cops were all over the place."

"Was he surprised?"

"Yeah," Tammy said, somewhat to my surprise. "He thought they were there about the drugs, and he flipped out. But he figured he'd better go home rather than run, because he knew your mama couldn't stand up to being questioned."

"He did?" I was really astonished.

"Oh, yeah," Tammy said. "He had big love for Laurel, you know, girl."

Tolliver and I exchanged glances. If Renaldo and Tammy were right, Matthew hadn't known anything about Cameron's disappearance. Or could he have been acting, to establish an alibi?

"He had a fit," Renaldo mumbled. "He didn't want that girl gone. I visited him at the jail. He told me he was sure she run away."

"Did you believe him?" I leaned forward and looked at Renaldo, which was painful but necessary.

"Yes," Renaldo said clearly. "I believed him."

There wasn't much point staying after that, and we were glad to get out of the reeking little house and away from its hopeless inhabitants.

I could hardly wait for Tolliver to buckle his seat belt. I backed out of the yard without having any idea where we were going. I began to drive back to Texas Boulevard, just to have a direction. "So, what do you think?" I asked.

"I think Tammy is repeating what my dad told her," Tolliver said. "Whether or not he was telling the truth, that's another thing."

"She believed him."

Tolliver made a derisive sound, practically a snort. "Let's see if we can talk to Pete Gresham," he said, and I headed for the police department. There are two police departments in one building on State Line Avenue, the Texas and the Arkansas police. There are two different police chiefs. I don't know how it all works, or who pays for what.

We found Pete Gresham working at his desk. We'd been given permission to go up to his office, and he was poring over a file on his desk, a file he shut when he saw us standing before him.

"You two! Good to see you! I'm sorry the tape didn't pan out," he said, standing and leaning over the desk to shake Tolliver's good hand. "I hear you had a little trouble in Big D."

"Well, the outskirts of Big D," I said. "We were in the neighborhood, and we thought we'd stop by to ask what you knew about the anonymous caller who tipped you off about the woman who looked like Cameron."

"Male, call came in from a pay phone." Pete Gresham, a big man who was a little bigger every time I saw him, shrugged. He still didn't wear glasses, but as Rudy Flemmons had told us, there wasn't a hair on Gresham's head. "Not much to tell."

"Could we hear it?" Tolliver asked. I turned to look at him. That had come out of nowhere.

"Well, I'll have to track the recording down," Pete said. He got up and headed toward the elevator, and I said, "What made you think of that?"

"We might as well," Tolliver said.

But Pete was back too quickly. I know my bureaucracies, and he couldn't have found the recording that quickly. "Sorry, you two," he said. "The guy who stores all that stuff is off today. He'll be in tomorrow. Can I call you and play it over the phone to you?"

"Sure, that'd be fine," I said. I gave him my cell phone number.

"You making a good living finding corpses?" he asked.

"Yeah, we do okay," Tolliver said.

"Hear you stopped a bullet," Pete said. "Whose toes did you step on?"

"Hard to say," Tolliver said, and he smiled. "Matthew's out of jail, by the way."

The detective looked a lot more serious. "I forgot he was due to get out. He turn up in Dallas?"

I nodded.

"Don't let him get you down," Pete said. "He's one of the bad ones. I've known guys like him my whole working life, and as a rule, they don't change none."

"I agree," I said. "And we're doing our best to keep away from him."

"How's those little sisters?" We were walking to the elevator now, and Pete was escorting us.

"They're good. Mariella just turned twelve and Gracie is going on nine." Maybe she was younger. In fact, I was sure she was younger. It was a strange moment to think it, but I realized that Gracie's being classified as lagging behind in her age group might be an incorrect diagnosis. The lag in her development that we'd attributed to her low birth weight and her persistent bad health might actually have been due to her real birth date being three or four months later than we'd believed.

"I can't imagine them that old." Pete shook his head at the passage of time, and I pulled myself back into the here and now to say, "By the way, I talked to Ida the other day."

"Ida? The woman who saw the blue truck? What did Ida have to say?"

When I told him about Ida's conversation with the Meals on Wheels woman, he cursed a blue streak. Then he apologized. "Idiots," he said. "Now I gotta call the woman and then I'll have to go see Ida again. I swear someday I'm not going to get out of that house. She'll say she don't want any visitors, and once I get there, she'll talk and talk until I think I'm going deaf."

I tried to smile, but I couldn't squeeze one out. Tolliver just nodded.

"I see what that does to the timeline, Harper. I promise you, any time I get a lead I chase it down. I want to know what happened to your sister about as much as you do. And I'm sorry your asshole of a father ever got out of jail."

"I am, too," I said, not sure if I could speak for Tolliver or not. "But we don't think he took Cameron."

"I don't either," Pete said, which surprised me quite a bit. "I know what you can do, Harper, and I remember seeing you and Tolliver riding around after you graduated from high school. I know you were looking for her. If you didn't find her, I don't think she's here to be found. If Matthew did it, he'd have had to bury her close, real close, and he didn't have much time. You would've found her."

I nodded. "We tried," I said. "Unless someone took her from the parking lot at the high school and just dumped her bag along the route back to the trailer, which would widen the search area . . ."

"We did think of that," Pete said mildly.

I flushed. "I'm not . . ."

"It's okay. You want to find your sister. I do, too."

"Thanks, Pete," Tolliver said and shook his hand again.

"You get better now, you hear," Pete said and turned to walk back to his cubicle.

"We've wasted a lot of time here today," I said. I was depressed and wondering what to do next.

"I don't know about that," Tolliver said. "We've learned a little. You want to drop by to say hello to the Clevelands?"

I thought about it. My foster parents were good people, and I respected them, but I wasn't in the mood for catch-up conversation. "I guess not," I said. "I guess we ought to head back to Garland."

The cell phone rang. "Hello," I said.

"Harper, this is Lizzie."

She sounded shaky. Though our acquaintance was limited, I'd never heard Lizzie sound less than positive and forceful.

"What's wrong, Lizzie?"

"Oh, gosh, nothing! We were wondering where you were . . . if you could stop by the ranch for a minute."

Stop by the ranch? When for all they knew, we were two hours' drive away in Garland?

"We're in Texarkana right now," I said, thinking furiously but not coming up with anything. "I guess we could come by. What do you need?"

"I just wanted to touch base with you. About poor Victoria, and a couple of other things."

I relayed all this to Tolliver in fewer words. He looked as taken aback as I felt. "Do you feel up to this? I can tell her no," I said.

"We might as well stop by. We're in the area, and they know a lot of people." The Joyces knew a lot of people with disposable income who might want to have some graves read.

I found myself wondering if we'd see Chip again. There was definitely something about the ranch manager/boyfriend that interested me, and it wasn't a physical attraction. At least not in the "I want to jump your bones" sense. But bones had something to do with it. . . .

We didn't talk much as we drove out of Texarkana. I was puzzled and worried by Lizzie's odd request, and Tolliver was thinking about something that worried him, too. I could tell by the way he sat and the tense muscles of his face. We took the exit off the interstate without any further discussion.

We drove by Pioneer Rest Cemetery and turned off onto the long driveway that ran between wide rolling fields. We could see miles in every direction, even with evening drawing in. Finally, we reached the gate to RJ Ranch, and Tolliver insisted on jumping out to open and then close the gate after I drove through.

I noticed that I couldn't see anyone, anywhere. On our previous visit, we'd been able to see people moving around in the distance.

We pulled up in the large paved parking area in front of the big house. We got out of our car and looked around. Everything seemed still. It was a warm day; in fact, it felt like it was spring. But the hush seemed abnormal. I shook my head doubtfully, but after a shrug, Tolliver led the way up the brick-paved path.

The big front door swung open, and Lizzie stood framed by the rectangle. The entrance hall behind her was shadowy. Talk about abnormal; though she was obviously making a huge effort to smile at us, it seemed more like the grin of a skull. Her eyes were as round as quarters and tension screamed in every muscle.

Red alert. Our steps slowed.

"Hey, you-all, come on in." All the natural enthusiasm she'd shown when we'd met here the first time had been replaced by an intense anxiety.

"We shouldn't have said we'd come by, we have an appointment in Dallas," I said. "Lizzie, can we come back tomorrow? We really can't miss this date we have."

I saw the relief on Lizzie's narrow face. "Well, just give me a call tonight," she said. "You-all drive on to Dallas."

"Oh, come in and have a drink," Chip said from behind her.

She twitched, and her attempt at a smile vanished. "Get back in the car," she said, "Get out!"

"You better not," Chip said, his voice calm and level. "You better come on in." We saw that he had revolver in his hand. That clarified our choice.

Chip and Lizzie backed up.

"I'm sorry," she said to me. "I'm sorry. He said he'd shoot Kate if I didn't call you."

"I would have done it, too," Chip said.

"I know you would," I told him. As we eased past Lizzie and stood in the square foyer, waiting for further directions, I understood what had fascinated me about Chip. His bones. His bones were dead. This was a strange connection, and one I'd never experienced before; or if I had, I hadn't understood its nature.

"Where is everyone?" Tolliver asked. His voice was as calm as Chip's.

"I sent everyone on the payroll to the farthest places on the ranch I could think of, and it's Rosita's day off," Chip said. He was smiling again, bright and hard, and I sure would have liked to wipe that look off his face. "It's just me and the family."

Shit.

Chip herded us all down the hall to the gun room. The light was still streaming in all the French doors, and the view was just as beautiful, but now I was in no mood to admire it.

Drex was standing there. He had a gun, too, which was a surprise. Kate was tied to a chair. They'd released Lizzie to lure us in the house. The ropes were loose around another chair.

"Good to see you again, Harper," Drex said. "We had a good time at the Outback, didn't we?"

"It was all right," I said. "It was too bad that Victoria was murdered after that. Kind of ruined my memory of the evening."

He gulped and looked upset, just for a split second. "Yeah, she was a nice woman," he said. "She seemed like a . . . She seemed good at what she did."

"She worked hard for you-all," I said.

"You think they'll ever find out who killed her?" Chip said. He smiled some more.

"Did you shoot Tolliver?" I asked him. There didn't seem to be much point in keeping quiet about it.

"Naw," he said. "That was my buddy Drex, here. Drex ain't good for much, but he can shoot. I told Drex to shoot *you*, but he seemed reluctant." He said the word slowly, as if he'd just learned it. "He didn't want to shoot a woman. Ol' Drex is gallant in his own way. I tried to correct his thinking a few nights later when you were out running, but damn if that cop didn't jump in front of you and take the bullet. I wouldn't have fired if I'd known he was a cop. I thought he looked sort of familiar, and it made me sick when I heard I'd shot a football player."

"Why shoot us at all?"

"Because you knew about Mariah, and you told. Maybe I could

get Lizzie to forget about it if you died, but I knew as long as you lived she'd think about what you said at the cemetery. She'd wonder about her grandfather's death, and she'd ask herself who wanted him dead. Then she'd go looking, if she believed there was a baby. Lizzie would love to have a kid to raise, and she's all about family." He dug the gun into Lizzie's neck, and he kissed her on the mouth. She spat when he drew away, and he laughed.

"Why would I have to be dead?" I was genuinely curious.

"'Cause that's the way my baby is. She pays attention to things when they're right in front of her, but if they're out of sight, they're out of mind."

That seemed like underrating Lizzie, to me. But he knew her better than I ever would. I understood, after a second's thought. Chip knew that failing to prevent me from coming to Texas was his big mistake. If I died, my death would erase that mistake. Of course that couldn't be done. But it would make him feel better.

"Lizzie, I'm sure someone drew your attention to my website," I said. "I'm sure someone pointed you in the right direction, thought it might be interesting to have me here to look at your graveyard."

"Yeah," Lizzie said. The sun was shining onto the terrace at an angle; it was about three thirty in the afternoon. "Yeah, Kate did."

"How'd you come to think of that, Kate?" I asked.

Kate was clearly in a bad state. Her face was white, her breathing panicky. Her hands were tied to the arms of the chair, and I saw her wrists were chafed raw. It took her a moment to understand the question.

"Drex," she said, her voice jerky. "Drex told me that he'd met you once."

Chip's head whipped around like he was a snake about to strike. "Drex, thanks to you, we've lost everything," he said in a deadly voice. "What were you thinking?"

"It come on the TV when we were watching the news," Drex whispered. "About her being in North Carolina, finding those boys' bodies. I told Kate I'd gone to her trailer when she was living in Texarkana, 'cause I knew her stepfather. I'd met her."

"And you told Lizzie," I said to Kate.

"She's always looking for something new," Kate said. "That's the name of the game, here. Find things for Lizzie, keep her happy."

Lizzie looked absolutely astounded. If we lived through this day, she would have a lot of mental rearranging to do.

"So it's a TV newscaster that brought me down." Chip laughed, and it was an awful sound.

"How much of a snake handler are you, Chip?" I asked.

"Oh, now, that's Drex's strong point," he said, grinning at the man standing beside him.

"Jesus, no!" Lizzie said, shocked out of her senses. "Drex? Chip, are you saying that *Drex* threw a rattler at Granddaddy?"

"That's what I'm sayin', darlin'," Chip said. His grip on Lizzie's shoulder never wavered.

"Have you gone nuts, man?" Drexell said, and his face looked different now. He didn't look as bewildered and befuddled as he had. He didn't look as weak as he had. He looked craftier and harder. "Why are you telling my sisters lies?"

"Because we're not going to get away with it," Chip said. "You hadn't gotten that yet, I see." Drexell looked blank. "There're too many loose ends, fool. We should have killed the doctor. Yes, you asshole, sometime within the past few years we should have moseyed on over to Dallas and taken care of that old idiot. And we knew Matthew was getting out of jail sooner or later. We should have been waiting outside the gate for him with a gun."

Now there was a sentiment I could agree with.

"You say we're not going to get away with it," Drex said. "So why are you doing this hostage thing? I thought you were playing a deeper game. I thought you had a plan. You're just crazy."

"Yes, I am, and I'll tell you why," Chip said. He let go of Lizzie's shoulder, and she swung around to face him, taking a step backward, closer to the wall covered with guns. "I had me an appointment with a much better doctor than Bowden last week, and you know what he told me? I'm eaten up with cancer. At thirty-two! And I don't give a fuck what happens when I'm not on the earth anymore. I don't have long enough to live for you-all to do anything to me. Since I'm not getting away with anything, I sure as hell don't want ol' Drex to."

His eyes were mean beyond belief when he said this.

"You're going to die?" said Lizzie. "Well, *good*. I wish Drex had cancer, too. I want you both to die." She seemed to have shaken off her fear, and I wished I could do the same. I looked at Tolliver, and I thought we would not make it through this. Chip would take us all out, because we were going to live and he wasn't.

With one incredibly fast motion, Lizzie grabbed a rifle off the wall, the one right by one of the doors. It was pointed at Chip in a split second. "Go on and shoot yourself, since you're going to die anyway!" She meant it, too, and she was ready with that rifle. "Save me the trouble!"

"I'm not going by myself," said her lover, and he shot Drexell Joyce in the chest.

Katie shrieked and went over backward in her chair, covered with the mist of her brother's blood, and as we all looked at the falling dead man, the screaming woman, Chip put the gun barrel in his mouth and fired at the same moment Lizzie did.

twenty

I was so tired after the sheriff's department finished with us that it was hard to focus when I got behind the wheel to drive back to Dallas. In fact, we never did make it to Garland. When I realized there was no real reason why we should, I pulled off at the next exit and got a room. We were just about out in the middle of nowhere, except it was nowhere with an interstate and a motel. It wasn't a very good motel, but we could be pretty sure that no one was going to shoot us through the window.

I was still confused about several things, but both the shooters were dead.

Tolliver took his medicine, and we crawled into the bed. The sheets felt cold and almost damp, and I got back out of bed to turn the heater up. It made the curtains billow in an unpleasant way. I've run into that before, and I keep a big clip in my overnight pack for just such a situation. It came in handy tonight. As I got between the sheets, I realized that Tolliver was already asleep.

When I woke, the sun was up outside. Tolliver was in the bathroom, trying to take a sponge bath, and he was grumbling to himself about it.

"What are you talking about in there?" I asked, sitting and swinging my legs out from under the covers.

"I want to shower," he said. "I want to shower more than anything."

"I'm sorry," I said, and I was. "But we can't get the shoulder wet for a few more days."

"Tonight we'll try taping a garbage bag or a grocery sack over it," he said. "If we tape it good, I can shower and be out before the tape starts to give."

"We'll try," I said. "What should we do today?"

He didn't answer.

"Tolliver?"

Silence.

I got up and went into the bathroom. "Hey, you, what's with the silent treatment?"

"Today," he said, "we have to go talk to my dad."

"We have to," I said, letting only a hint of a question seep into the words.

"We have to," he said, absolutely positive.

"And then?"

"We're going to ride off into the sunset," he said. "We're going to go back to St. Louis and be by ourselves for a while."

"Oh, that sounds good. I wish we could skip the part about your dad and go right into the 'be by ourselves.'"

"I thought you'd be straining to get at him." He'd started working on his stubble, and he paused, one cheek still gleaming with shaving gel.

I'd thought so, too. "There's a lot I almost don't want to know," I said. "I never imagined I'd feel like this. I've waited so long."

He put his good arm around me and held me close. "I thought about leaving Texas today," he said. "I thought about it. But we can't."

"No," I said.

I called Dr. Spradling's nurse that morning and told her, as I'd been instructed, that Tolliver wasn't running a temperature, wasn't bleeding, and his wound didn't look red. She reminded me to make sure he took his medicine, and that was that. Despite the shocks of the previous day, Tolliver looked better than he had since the night he was shot, and I was sure he was going to be fine.

The drive into Dallas was easy, with only a few traffic snarls. We had to find Mark's house, which we'd visited only once before. Mark was a solitary man, and I wondered how he and Matthew were getting along together.

To my surprise, Mark's car was parked in the little driveway. His home was smaller than Iona's, which made it mighty small indeed. I automatically noted the buzz around the neighborhood, and it was faint. No dead people here.

There was a narrow raised strip of concrete running from the driveway to the front door. There were cobwebs on the lighting fixtures on either side of the door, and the landscaping was nonexistent. It looked like a house that the owner didn't care about.

Mark answered the door. "Hey, what you two doing over here in my neck of the woods?" he said. "You come to see Dad?"

"Yes, we have," Tolliver said. "He's here?"

"Yeah. Dad," Mark called. "Tolliver and Harper are here." He moved back so we could step inside. He was wearing sweatpants and an old T-shirt. Clearly, he wasn't going in to work today. He caught me looking. "Sorry," he said, "it's my day off. I didn't dress for company."

"We didn't give you any warning," I said. The living room was almost as basic as Renaldo's: a big leather couch and matching chair, a big-screen TV, and a coffee table. No lamps for reading. No books. One picture, a framed one of the five of us kids, taken at the trailer. I had forgotten there was one of all of us.

"Who took that?" I asked, surprised.

"Some friend of your mom's," Mark said. "Dad packed it away with the other stuff when he went to jail. He just got it out when he got the stuff out of storage."

I stood looking at the picture, tears in my eyes. Tolliver and Mark were standing side by side. Mark wasn't smiling. Tolliver's lips were turned up slightly, but his eyes were grim. Cameron was by Mark, and she had her arm around him, and she was holding Mariella's hand. Mariella was smiling; like most very little kids, she'd loved to have her picture made. I was holding Gracie, and she was so little! Which Gracie was it? Gracie after the hospital.

"This was taken not long before," I said.

"Not long before what?"

"You know," I said, astonished. "Not long before Cameron was gone."

He shrugged, as if I might have meant something else.

We were still standing when Matthew came in. He was wearing jeans and a flannel shirt. "I've got to get to work in an hour, but it's great to see you," he said to Tolliver, then turned his face so his smile could include me.

Thanks, but no.

"We went to see the Joyces yesterday," I said. "Chip and Drex were talking about you."

I wasn't imagining the alarm that flashed across Matthew's face then. "Oh, what did they have to say? That's that rich family, right? On the ranch?"

"You know who they are," Tolliver said. "You know they came by the trailer."

Mark looked from his brother to his father. "Those rich guys?" he said. "They're who you and Harper went to work for last week?"

"We've had conversations with quite a few people recently," I said. "Including Ida, remember her?"

"The old woman who saw your sister getting into a blue truck," Matthew said.

"Except she didn't," I said. "Turns out it wasn't Cameron."

The surprise on their faces seemed more or less genuine. That is, they were surprised about *something*.

"I saw you at the doctor's office," I said to Matthew.

He was surprised again. "I went to see a doctor a couple of days ago," he said cautiously, "about this cough I've had since I got out of—"

"Oh, shut up," I said. "We know you took Mariah's baby. What we don't know is what happened to the real Gracie."

There was a long moment of silence; there seemed to be no air in the cramped living room.

"That's crazy talk, Tol," Mark said. "Who's this Mariah?"

"Dad knows, Mark," Tolliver said. "Tell us all, Dad, who is the little girl living with Hank and Iona?"

"That little girl," Matthew said, "is the daughter of Mariah Parish and Chip Moseley."

This was so not what I'd expected. "Not Rich Joyce and Mariah," I said, just to be sure I understood.

"Chip told me old Mr. Joyce never had sex with Mariah," Matthew said. "Chip said the baby was his."

Mark was looking from speaker to speaker, and he really didn't seem to know what we were talking about.

"Chip had been buying drugs from me," Matthew said. "He and Drex liked to come to our part of town to party. Chip was always smart and hard. He'd been raised in foster homes, and he was determined to make a place for himself with the rich people. So he started work for Rich Joyce, started out low, worked his butt off until Rich really depended on him. After his divorce, he gradually got Lizzie interested in him. He knew Mariah; she was in the foster home with him. Chip helped her get the job with the Peadens, and she learned a lot while she was there. Chip made sure Rich got to know the Peadens well enough that he was able to introduce him to Mariah. Then when old Mr. Peaden died, it was natural for Mariah to ask Rich if he had a job for her. He'd had the stroke, and he knew his family wanted him to have someone. It tickled him to have someone as young and pretty as Mariah around, even if he didn't plan on making any moves on her. She knew his heart was weak. She knew he was fond of her. She just hoped he'd leave her some money. She liked the old man."

"So what happened?" I asked.

"She didn't plan on getting pregnant, but when she did, she put off doing anything about it until it was too late. She wore loose clothes and overalls and such because she didn't want the old man to know she was somebody else's bedmate. And she was afraid he'd find out if she had an abortion. She was tough, but she wasn't tough enough to do that. Chip went nuts when he found out. She was maybe eight months along by then. He came over to Texarkana to get some dope; he wanted to be numb for a while, not think about it. While he was at my place, Drex called on his cell to say that he was all alone in the house with Mariah, and something had gone wrong. Mariah had had the baby all by herself, but she wouldn't stop bleeding. And by the time he'd cut the cord and wrapped up the baby—he'd helped deliver calves and foals—she was near dead. Chip bolted out and the next I heard from him was when he called me about taking the kid off his hands."

"Chip didn't want her at all."

"No," said Matthew. "He didn't."

"And you offered to help him out, maybe thinking that someday you might get some money out of the Joyce girls by saying that the baby was their grandfather's."

"I know it was pretty low," Matthew said. His deep-set eyes looked shadowed. "I know that. But you know how I was then. It sounded like a good moneymaking scheme, one I could leave on the back burner, in case we ever needed it."

"And your own baby was about to die because you hadn't taken her to a doctor," I said. "Or was she already dead when Chip called?"

"That's where you got the different baby!" Mark said. I'd never seen so much emotion on his face. "Dad, why didn't you tell me?"

Now it was Matthew's turn to look confused. "You knew it wasn't really Gracie?" he said to his son. "I never worried about you! You were hardly ever around. How'd you know?"

And all of a sudden, everything clicked into place.

"I know how," I said. "Cameron told him. She didn't know right away, any more than the rest of us did. It took her a while to figure it out. But when she did her senior biology project, she did it on eye color and genetics. You and my mom couldn't have had a green-eyed child."

Mark collapsed onto the couch. His legs simply gave out from under him. "Dad, she was going to call the police," he said. "She was going to tell them you'd kidnapped a kid to take Gracie's place, because Gracie had died."

"It was you, Mark," I said, feeling that my voice was coming from somewhere very far away. "It was you. You picked her up when she was on her way back from school. You told her—what did you tell her?"

"I told her that you'd had an accident," he said. "I was on my motorbike that day, so I told her to leave the backpack by the road. She didn't ask any questions. She got on. I went toward the hospital, but I pulled off at an empty gas station because I told her something was wrong with my bike. I told her to go around back to see if there was an air pump. I went after her."

"How did you do it?" I said, very quietly.

He looked up at me with an expression I hope I never see again. He was ashamed, he was horrified, and he was pleased. "I choked her to death," he said. "I have big hands, and she was so small. It didn't take long. I had to leave her there, because I couldn't get her back on the bike. I went later, with Dad's truck. I wanted to leave her there, but I was afraid you'd find her, you freak."

My head swam and I sat abruptly on the armchair. Tolliver hit

Mark with everything he had, and Mark collapsed sideways, bleeding from the mouth. Matthew was standing exactly where he'd been, his mouth literally hanging open.

"I did it for you, Dad," Mark mumbled. He spat out blood and a tooth. "Dad, I did it for you."

"And then they arrested me anyway," Matthew said, as if that was the important part of the story.

"Where is she, Mark?"

"You and your family," he said. "You've been nothing but trouble. First the baby, then Cameron going to call the police on Dad, and now you getting Tolliver to marry you."

"Where is my sister, Mark?" I wanted to bury her, finally. I wanted to know where her bones were. I wanted to recognize her one last time. Somewhere over in Texarkana, she waited for me. I just wanted a location so I could get in the car and start driving. I could call Pete Gresham and ask him to meet me there.

"I'm not going to tell you," he said. "You can't have me arrested unless you find her, and I'm not going to tell you. My dad won't say a word, and my brother won't, either. Our word against yours."

"*Where is my sister?*"

Matthew was still staring at Mark as if he'd never seen him before.

"Of course I'll tell the police," Tolliver said. "Why wouldn't I, Mark?"

"We're family, Tol. If you tell them about Cameron, then we'll have to tell them about Gracie, and she won't belong to anybody but Chip. Iona and Hank would have to give her up. You can imagine what Chip will do with her."

"Chip's dead, Mark. He killed himself yesterday."

Mark looked blank for a minute. Then he said, "So then she'll go to foster care, like Harper had to."

"You're trying to blackmail me into keeping quiet about my sister's death by threatening my other sister? Mark, you are lower than a snake's belly," I said. "I can't imagine you being related to Tolliver."

"That's the deal," Mark said, and his mouth set in a mulish way.

There was a knock at the door. Talk about bad timing.

I was the only one who could move, apparently, so I got up and went to the door. It was a relief to be facing away from Mark and Matthew.

I was so numb I wasn't even startled to see Manfred. "This is a very bad time," I said, but I waited for him to tell me why he was there.

"He's got a rental shed under another name," Manfred said. "He brought her body with him. I know where it is."

We all froze in place. Finally I said, "Oh, thank God." Tears were running down my cheeks.

We called the police. I thought it took them hours to get there, though only a few minutes passed. It was really hard to explain what had happened.

We'd taken Mark's plastic key from his wallet before we climbed into Manfred's car. Tolliver was sitting in the backseat. He'd explained to the patrol car officers that his brother had just confessed to murdering his stepsister, and he was sure his dad would want to stay to be with his son, and then we were out the door. We got into the storage compound by using the key, and when the gate rolled away, we drove in, leaving it open behind us. There was a police car on its way, but we weren't going to wait any longer.

"I knew it was him, after I touched the backpack," Manfred said, trying to suppress the pride in his voice. "So I followed him."

"That's what you've been doing the past couple of days."

"He came here twice in that time," Manfred said.

I found that amazing. Did Mark feel so guilty that he had to keep revisiting Cameron's body? Or was he like a squirrel storing something choice for the winter, so afraid someone would steal it that he had to keep checking?

I had never known Mark at all. And if I felt that way, how must his brother feel? I looked back at Tolliver, but I couldn't read his face.

Manfred stopped in front of the garage-style unit numbered 26 and used the key again.

The room wasn't half full. There were things I vaguely recognized as being from the trailer, and I wondered why anyone would save such things. Evidently, Mark had thought Matthew would want them someday. I looked at the clutter, closed my eyes, and began searching.

The buzzing came from a large blanket chest at the back of the unit. There was a box of magazines on top of it, and some pots and pans. I knocked all of them off. I put my hands on the lid. I couldn't open it. I reached inside with my lightning sense and . . .

I found my sister.

twenty-one

THE legal mess surrounding Gracie—the girl I'd always thought was my sister Gracie—may take some time to unravel. With both her natural parents dead, it's not like her custody was in doubt. After all, Iona and Hank had legally adopted both girls. To them, it was irrelevant that one of the girls wasn't exactly who they'd thought she was. Iona and Hank, after a few minutes of shocked surprise, made up their minds they'd keep Gracie, no matter what. After all, Iona told me, when God had told her to take on the raising of those girls, he hadn't specified what their parentage was. If Gracie had really been the daughter of Rich Joyce, the complications would have been tremendous, and it was really just as well for Gracie that she wasn't. At least, that's what I thought.

Matthew went back to jail, though not for long enough. He hadn't murdered his own baby; not that anyone could prove. The real Gracie's tiny skeleton had vanished from the place where he said he'd buried her, in a public park off the interstate.

His story was that he'd set off to take Gracie to the hospital, but she'd died in the car on the way. He'd buried her and lied to us all about the ICU and the rest because he'd been afraid that my mom would go crazy if she knew Gracie was dead. (Since my mother had already been crazy for years by that time, I didn't believe him.) He's stayed away for a few days to give credence to his story that Gracie was in the hospital in ICU. When Chip called him, Matthew had been more than glad to take a baby whose dubious background he thought might come in handy someday; and of course, producing a healthy girl baby would also keep him from being accused of negligence. We'd expected to get Gracie back from the hospital. Only Cameron suspected that Matthew had sunk low enough to substitute another child.

Cameron's throat was crushed; there was enough left in the trunk to determine her cause of death. Mark confessed that she had shown him the genetic chart she'd made that proved my brown-eyed mother and her brown-eyed husband couldn't have a green-eyed daughter. Cameron hadn't known whose baby "Gracie" was, but since she had started with the certainty the child wasn't the same baby, Cameron's realization had explained several puzzling things about Gracie's different behavior since she'd come back "from the hospital." After Mark killed Cameron, he'd taken her body to the freezer of the restaurant where he worked and put her in a box at the back of the shelf in the meat locker for a couple of days. Then he'd rented the storage unit in Dallas and driven over there with her in the blanket chest, at the height of the hubbub over her disappearance. There she'd stayed, and he'd tossed in the items from the trailer when he'd moved himself to Dallas. He'd watched over her bones ever since.

Poor Cameron. She'd trusted the wrong person. Mark was the oldest, and steady; it was natural she would turn to him. She'd underestimated his devotion to his father. But she'd been sharp enough to put together all the puzzling things about the green-eyed baby living in our trailer.

I had noticed some puzzling changes, too. After all, I'd taken daily care of Gracie. But it had literally never occurred to me that the baby I was tending to wasn't my sister. I can only attribute that to the stress and strain caused by the lightning strike, and the fact that I couldn't imagine that Matthew would do such a thing, even as low as he got. I do remember marveling at how much Gracie's health had improved. It seems incredible now; I attributed it all to modern medicine.

Mark confessed—what choice did he have, after all. He's doing time now, hard time. I don't think I could stand to ever see him again.

Manfred got a load of free publicity, which I fed with as much fuel as I could. He got the offer of an appearance on one of those ghost-hunting shows, and he looked great on camera. He gets marriage proposals every week.

We never found out who the woman at the Texarkana mall had been. We didn't recognize the voice on the police tape, either. At least from now on, we can ignore any Cameron "sightings."

Tolliver and I went back to St. Louis and got his shoulder checked out by a doctor there, who found all was well. We were glad to see our apartment. We turned down a job offer or two so we could stay home for a while.

We got married.

The girls might be disappointed because they didn't get to wear pretty dresses and pose in pictures, but we got married all by ourselves in front of a judge. I still call myself Harper Connelly, and Tolliver doesn't seem to mind.

When Cameron's remains were released, I brought them up to St. Louis to bury. We bought her a nice headstone. Oddly enough, that didn't make me feel as wonderful as I thought it would. I visited her every day for a while, until I realized that for me, she'd be forever frozen in the moment of her death. I could not move on until I quit going to the grave. Still, at last I know what happened to her.

We'll hit the road again, soon. After all, we have to make some money.

And they're all out there waiting for me. All they want is to be found.